Crime for the Books

Crime for the Books

A JANE DOE BOOK CLUB MYSTERY

Kate Young

CROOKED LANE

NEW YORK

Copyright © 2022 by Kate Young

Published in the United States by Crooked Lane Books, an imprint of The Quick Brown Fox & Company LLC.

Crooked Lane Books and its logo are trademarks of The Quick Brown Fox & Company LLC.

Library of Congress Catalog-in-Publication data available upon request.

ISBN (hardcover): 978-1-63910-108-5
ISBN (ebook): 978-1-63910-109-2

Cover design by Mary Ann Lasher

Printed in the United States.

www.crookedlanebooks.com

Crooked Lane Books
34 West 27th St., 10th Floor
New York, NY 10001

First Edition: October 2022

10 9 8 7 6 5 4 3 2 1

For my son, Matthew, our resident comedian. You're one for the books.

Chapter One

The clouds looked ominous as I walked our client out of the office and locked the door. An inconspicuous glance at my watch informed me of the late hour. I needed to get to the library ASAP. I turned with a smile, extending my hand. The older woman's brow wrinkled with the stress of her situation, and a tad of guilt overtook me. "Relax. We have everything in hand, and I assure you, you have absolutely nothing to worry about. The case is straightforward. The will is solid."

Elaine took my hand and gave me a slight smile. "Thank you. Your grandmother nearly twisted my arm when we were at the beauty parlor last month. She insisted you would be able to make sense of this mess and put my mind at ease. And she was right. You've been a godsend. Not that I would go around touting that Daisy Moody saved me." The older woman chuckled. "It'd go straight to her head."

I grinned. "Wise. Gran's ego is large enough. And I know how convincing she can be when she puts her mind to something. She means well, and in this instance, I am glad she pushed you my way."

The woman shook her head in a bemused fashion. "Me too. And I know how Daisy is. I was only teasing. She has a heart of gold." She glanced at her watch. "I appreciate you waiting for me to get this check to you. I know I'm old-fashioned. But I still like to use my checks and hand-deliver them when feasible."

"I understand, and we're glad to accommodate whatever method of payment our clients feel comfortable with." I'd been a little surprised when she insisted on the paper transaction. We'd not had one client pay by check in all the years I'd worked for my uncle. Personally, I didn't even own any checks. Never seen the need for them.

"I do appreciate it." She took a step off the curb just as an old gray Mustang came roaring down the street.

"Elaine!" I reached out and grabbed her arm, jerking her back onto the sidewalk seconds before the car nearly hit her.

"Maniac!" I shouted at the driver, who flew over the train tracks like a bat out of hell. Several other pedestrians jumped out of the way. A man threw his hands in the air and shouted as the woman next to him began snapping pictures of the car with her phone. Good.

"Are you okay?"

Elaine looked a little dazed as she patted her damp forehead. Then she let out a little nervous chuckle. "Yes. Wow. My life flashed before my eyes."

Her hand went to her chest and rested on her heart, which was probably pounding and definitely causing me some worry.

"I thought gridlock in the city was bad on my way here. But at least I didn't nearly get mowed down by some lunatic." She took a deep breath, and another little giggle escaped her lips.

Her reaction reminded me of my friend Melanie. She always laughed when something frightened her too.

"Wowee! It's nuts like that who make me grateful for my move to Sweet Mountain back in the eighties. I thought back then that God only knew how bald I'd be now from yanking my hair out during the Atlanta traffic jams. But I might be bald yet." She cast a glance in the direction the car had gone. Her face was flushed, and the whites of her eyes were showing. "Sheesh."

"I'll report them, and I think several others will too." I motioned to where a little crowd had congregated in the center of the square. I took her hand and squeezed it. "Are you sure you're okay to drive?"

"Yes, yes. I'm fine." Thunder rolled. Elaine glanced up, and her hand went to her newly permed brown hair as if her hands would protect her curls. "Looks like another front is coming through today. I was hoping that last downpour an hour ago was going to be it."

Elaine dug through her bag, retrieving her umbrella. Her hand shook a little.

When she noticed me watching, her face flushed. I glanced up at the angry-looking green sky to avoid causing her any embarrassment. The scent of rain hung in the air, and the humidity seemed to thicken around us. It felt more like spring than fall.

"The weather has been crazy lately," I said.

"Indeed. It's been years since we've had severe weather this late in the year." The older woman leaned forward and surprised me with an impromptu hug. It felt a little awkward with her large patent leather bag and umbrella between us. "You've been a godsend, young lady. Truly."

"Oh, well, I'm glad." I gave her a little pat on the back before she retreated to where she'd stood a moment ago. "We appreciate your trust in us, and I can assure you, your cousin doesn't have a chance at mounting another attempt at a case."

"That's good to hear." She seemed to be calming, and I could tell talking to me was helping her. I could be a little late to my club meeting.

"Daisy's insistence isn't the only reason I came to you." She tucked her umbrella under her arm. "Calvin's reputation—and yours too, of course—for stellar work has traveled far and wide." She briefly motioned to our sign above the door, *Cousins Investigative Services Inc*, displayed in a glossy bold gray blue and outlined in white.

Far and wide sounded like a bit of a stretch to me, but it's always nice to know people think well of the job you're doing. Reputation could make or break a business like ours.

"That is kind of you to say. This case is all but closed, but if anything comes up that needs my attention, you give me a call, and I'll take care of it. Or if you feel threatened in any way, don't hesitate—call the police immediately." I touched her arm. "I can't stress this enough."

She shook her head. "Thank you, and I will, but I'm sure, since they served Patricia the paperwork, this whole nightmare is over." Her shoulders rose and fell with the deep breath she took. "On a positive note, we are all so excited about the Halloween party this weekend."

Elaine's smile made it to her gray eyes then. She pulled out the folded-up issue of the *Sweet Mountain Gazette* that had been sticking out of her purse and chuckled as she turned to the ear-marked section.

"We all had a good laugh from this." She pointed to the page of the newspaper advertising our party—a fun little write-up that I'd called in a favor to have printed.

The announcement read: *A murder is announced: A murder will take place on Friday, October 15th, at Magnolia Manor bed and breakfast at 6.30 p.m. Come for a night of fifties-themed sleuthing fun and join the Jane Doe Book Club in discovering whodunnit.*

"What a clever party idea. I read a lot of Agatha Christie in my thirties. She sure can weave a tale."

"Yes, ma'am. And the credit all goes to the Queen of Mystery. After all, she came up with it. I simply borrowed it for an evening." I smiled. The Jane Does had all agreed it would be a nice touch to keep with the book's era. "I can't wait to don my new frock and have a ripping good time," I said in my best British accent, which was terrible.

Elaine's smile widened. "You're too much." She gave me a little tap on the shoulder with the paper before putting it back in her bag. "The B and B is completely booked, and the phone still hasn't stopped ringing. We've been sending business to the Holiday Inn & Suites up the road, and I hear they're almost at capacity. Isn't that something?"

She was being modest. Her bed-and-breakfast never had any issues booking up. You usually had to schedule your stay months in advance. The manor was constantly being reserved for weddings and anniversary parties. We'd only managed to secure the date because of a last-minute cancellation. Elaine's kindness hadn't gone unnoticed.

"We are so grateful for the use of your beautiful property. It will be a night to remember. I simply can't wait."

"I'm glad to accommodate. It was meant to be." A drizzle began to fall from the sky, and we both opened our umbrellas. "I better run. I'm sorry to have kept you so late."

"Not a problem," I assured her. "And drive safely."

We waved our good-byes before I dashed across the street toward my car.

"Lyla!" Someone called just as I tossed my bag onto the passenger's seat. Not seeing anyone and believing I'd imagined it, I slid into the car.

As I leaned over and dug through my bag for a comb, my passenger door opened, and my little gran slid onto the seat. "I've been hollering and hollering at you from down the road a piece." She sounded out of breath.

"Sorry, I didn't hear or see you." I hugged her and pulled my bag onto my lap.

"Yeah, well, you and Elaine were gabbing." She forgave me and pinched my cheek.

I rubbed the spot she'd created. "I thought you were getting dropped off at the library."

We were going to be so late. But it couldn't be helped. Earlier, I'd texted my best friend, Melanie, who would be leading tonight's book club discussion, with news of my tardiness.

Gran shook her head. Her once reddish-gold hair was now snow white and had currently lost its body thanks to the rain. I'd inherited the red-gold hair gene. "Sally Anne and I were having an early dinner at the Market Deli. And Elaine mentioned she'd be stopping by here after she met with her lawyer in Atlanta. I decided to meet up with you and catch a ride."

I started the car. "You should have called me. I would have picked you up."

"I needed the exercise. Poor Elaine looked tired when I saw her yesterday. How was she?"

"Okay." Elaine had seemed tired today as well. The case had taken a toll on her.

"Bless her heart; she's still having moments of going back and forth on whether she should just give that second cousin of hers something. Can you believe that?"

Elaine hadn't mentioned that to me. After all the trouble her cousin had caused her, it was surprising. I wasn't in the judging business, but it seemed counterproductive at this late stage of the case.

"That's her choice. The business is hers solely. She can do what she wishes with it." I stowed my purse behind my seat.

"Yeah, well, if that second cousin of hers would stop showing her worst side, then she might have a better chance at a reconciliation. It's a mess. It's a good thing Elaine came to you when she did. I told her my little Lyla will straighten everything out."

"Thanks for the vote of confidence."

Gran had always been my biggest fan. I smiled at her, and she pinched my cheek again.

"Ouch." I pushed her hand away as I pulled out of the parking lot. "What's with all the pinching lately?"

She shrugged. "Sally Anne pinches her grandkids. She said all good southern grandmothers do that. I thought I'd try it."

"Well, stop. Sally Anne's words aren't gospel."

"Okay. It didn't feel right to me either." She pointed toward the orange leaves as the trees blew violently around the downtown square. "Look at that wind."

Workers on ladders were abandoning their task of stringing lights around tree bases and across storefront awnings

7

throughout our sleepy little town. In a few days, the city would host our annual Octoberfest Pub Crawl. I hoped we had better weather for it. My friends and I looked forward to the crawl every year. I pulled up to the stop sign. A horn blew the second I came to a complete stop. I glanced in my rearview mirror to see the gray Mustang behind me.

"Oh my God! I think that's the jerk who nearly ran Elaine over a few minutes ago."

"What?" Gran craned her neck to see behind us. "They almost ran y'all over?"

The driver flashed their lights at me and laid on the horn. *Maniac!* What was his problem?

"Hold your dang horses!" Gran shook her bony fist at the driver.

I'd started to move forward when the driver accelerated. The tires squealed as the car maneuvered into oncoming traffic, nearly sideswiping a minivan. I slammed on my breaks. The minivan swerved into my lane but managed to straighten out.

Gran swore a blue streak and leaned over to slam her hand on my horn.

"We should tail him! If I had one of those big pickup trucks, he'd be sorry. I would be just like that fella in the *Unhinged* movie your daddy was watching the other day." Gran's eyes flashed hot. "Nobody gets away with nearly killing my granddaughter."

"I will be reporting them for this as well as the earlier incident. Probably stupid kids."

"Yep." She nodded. "I bet you're right. Kids like that are the ones that make me still a proponent of spankings. I know what folks say about that nowadays, but some kids, that's all they understand. Looks like their parents were light on the disciplinary action."

"Let's put it out of our minds. We're going to the club meeting. Better late than never." I slowed my breathing and forced a smile as my mind went a million directions. Who was the driver? And why had I seen them twice in one day driving recklessly?

Chapter Two

The rain was coming down in buckets when I parked my car in front of the Sweet Mountain Library, where my book club, the Jane Does, was meeting. Since we were already late, we decided that giving it a few more minutes to see if the rain let up would be okay.

Gran went back to her concerns regarding her friend Elaine as she applied orange-red lipstick to her lips. "So where are we exactly on Elaine's case? I mean, specifics. And before you say it's all confidential or some nonsense, Elaine's going to tell me herself when we meet up for dinner later this week."

"There's really nothing more to tell." I glanced up at the sunroof. The rain pelted the glass.

"You got the lawyer to drop the case, didn't ya?"

"Yes. That's all settled. I'm just running down a small personal matter for Elaine now."

Gran leaned closer to the visor mirror and wiped the lipstick off her teeth. "These family disputes can take a toll on people. Not all families can be like ours."

I gave her a sideways glance.

"What? We're normal."

"Uh-huh."

"Normal-ish, then."

"Okay, I'll give you normal . . . ish." I smirked.

She slashed her hand in the air, dismissing me. "Anyway, all I'm saying is that wacko woman has some nerve. Did you know"—she leaned closer to me—"Elaine hasn't seen hide nor hair of her in fifteen years, and then when she finally gets word of old Mrs. Peterson passing, she comes a-running with her hand out shouting foul play."

"Yes. You know good and well that I'm aware of that." I leaned over and gave her a swift kiss on the cheek. "Now, don't get riled up. It's all sorted now." Gran tended to rehash things and get herself all worked up even well after the fact. I reached behind the seat and grabbed my purse.

"I just care about my friend. Most folks aren't as tough as we are, sugar." She patted me on the shoulder. "I always knew you'd be a great private investigator."

"Who needs a cheering section when you have Daisy Moody, grandmother extraordinaire." I winked at her, and she beamed.

I'd been working for my uncle as a receptionist/PI for almost three years now. My uncle had needed a receptionist/secretary after Harriet Wiseman took maternity leave to have baby number three. I'd leaped at the opportunity. I'd come a long way since that first day on the job and was now a trusted part of my uncle Calvin's team. Something I'd had my heart set on for many years—to be an asset instead of a trainee.

The job had been a natural fit for me. True crime and unsolved cases got my blood pumping. And that was one of the reasons I enjoyed my book club so much. We had a great group of fellow mystery-loving members who understood the need for closing a case, even if most of them were fictional.

Since our club had recently merged with another book club in the area, we had almost a dozen consistent members and about a dozen or so who showed up when they could make it—or when we were reading a book they especially enjoyed.

Our core group of founding Jane Does hosted and scheduled the meetings. Some months, if we had a special speaker—like a mystery writer or a Georgia Bureau of Investigation investigator—or were watching a popular docuseries, we had close to twenty or more in attendance. Utilizing one of the libraries' conference rooms had become a necessity.

When we'd hosted a retired special investigator from Atlanta, who'd discussed the ins and outs of investigations involving John and Jane Does, we'd been nameless, oscillating between a couple of ideas. True crime stories had always intrigued the club. Because of our deep interest in such cases, it only seemed natural to our founding members that the club should be called The Jane Does.

And hosting special guests had become infinitely more accessible when I started dating Special Agent Brad Jones. We'd met two years ago while working together on a Jane Doe case. My first case as a PI in training had ignited something in me that solidified my desire to work in the field professionally.

A clap of thunder vibrated through the car.

"Wow, it's really whipping up out there." Gran rolled her lipstick down and put it back in her purse.

The banner outside the large three-story brick facility located a few blocks from the town square flapped violently. A few stray limbs blew past my car. It wasn't tornado season, but our weather hadn't been taking typical patterns this year.

"I better check my weather app."

"You don't need an app to see what's right in front of you. Are those sirens?" Gran rolled down her window, and a giant gust blew rain inside.

"Gran!" I held up my hand, ineffectively blocking the spray.

She quickly rolled her window back up. "Sorry, sugar. It's going to be a doozy of a storm. Hope it doesn't run folks off from the club meeting." She dabbed at her damp face with spare napkins I'd kept in my glove compartment. Gran sporadically attended our club meetings. She enjoyed the social aspect of the club. Gran never read the club pick until after the meetings. She enjoyed the wine, coffee, and snacks while pestering everyone with questions. Gran's a real card, and my club loved her colorful personality.

I laughed and held out my hand for a napkin and wiped the water from my screen. My screen saver of Brad and me at the local brewery appeared. I smiled, admiring my man. He was close to forty, with thick black hair cut close to his scalp, a sharp nose, and eyes a little closer together than average. He wasn't what you'd call traditionally handsome, but I found him immensely appealing.

Gran gave me a mischievous grin and wagged her brows. "If I were a few years younger, I'd give you a run for your money with that one."

I chuckled and tapped my weather app. "I don't doubt it."

A stream of people rushed from the library doors, racing for their cars. Several I recognized as regular attendees. There went what was left of the club meeting.

I grabbed my umbrella and ran around to get Gran, and she and I huddled under my umbrella and ran across the parking lot. The rain pelted us from both sides as the wind swirled around us. We took shelter under the awning just as Mel came out the front door.

"I was so worried." Mel hugged Gran and me as a few more people dashed past us. "Y'all just missed Amelia. She left about five minutes ago. Some family stuff came up. Her sister, I think."

I nodded, recalling Amelia mentioning to me something about a sister and how they weren't close. Amelia Klein was one of our core members. "I hope she makes it home okay."

"I told her to text me the second she pulled into the driveway."

"That's good of you, little Mel." Gran touched a strand of Mel's blond hair. "You're looking good. Even with this frizzy mop atop your head."

Mel's hand went to her hair, and she made a face. "Thanks, Gran. The bottom fell out when Amelia left, and I forgot my umbrella. Not all of us can rock the messy hair thing, like you." Mel grinned and hiked her purse up higher on her shoulder and glanced toward the parking lot where she'd parked.

Alerts blared over our cell phones with a tornado warning just as the local sirens sounded.

"Terrific," I grumbled. "Guess we better get inside."

"Yeah, I guess so. Well, we were aiming for an exciting meeting this month." Mel pulled open the door and fussed with the frizzy hair stuck to her forehead and the back of her neck.

"Yeah, and this is an exhilarating day." Gran followed Melanie while I held the door.

Chapter Three

The library, built with a mixture of stone and brick to keep with the style of our town square, had a lot of large glass windows. We would need to be far away from those lovely additions.

We rushed inside and heard the scrambling in our usual meeting room. Courtney Hampton—or I guessed it was Daniels now, since she'd married our chief of police—looked like she was directing traffic. Courtney hadn't mentioned whether she'd be changing her name, but I assumed she would, being the traditional type. Courtney had taken the job as library manager last year, and now she stood, looking positively frustrated as her blond hair escaped her messy bun. She pursed her lips when she saw me. I wasn't sure exactly why she didn't like me, but she sure didn't.

"Everyone, quickly yet calmly, make your way inside conference room A, please." Courtney's arm pointed toward our usual room.

Mel, Gran, and I walked with purpose toward the meeting room. Thankfully, there weren't many windows in that space.

The few people who remained sat on the floor in the corner of the room containing no glass windows. Rosa Landry, another one of our core members, waved us over.

I went and took a seat next to her on the floor. "Wow, it's coming down out there. Not the way I envisioned this night going."

Rosa shifted on the floor, sitting crisscross style. "It's a fast-moving storm. It'll be here and gone in less than half an hour. The heavy stuff is directly over us. The storms you worry most about are the ones that hang around for too long."

"You okay?" I asked her when I noticed how exhausted she looked.

"Yeah," she half laughed. "I guess I got that raccoon eye thing going on. I've worked way too many graveyard shifts lately. But we've all got to take our turn."

"You're a trooper." I nudged her with my shoulder and said hello to a few members who weren't busy on their phones with family. Several were talking to their kids, attempting to calm them down.

"Here." Mel thrust a cup of coffee into my hand as she took a seat next to me a minute later. "Courtney is in fine form. She about bit my head off when I went to the refreshment table. But we're soaked to the bone here."

I took it gratefully. I glanced back to where Courtney was fussing at several other brave souls in need of a generous dose of caffeine.

Gran pulled one of the chairs from against the wall, and I handed Mel my coffee and got up to move the chair for her. She sat down with her coffee as I settled back on the floor.

Courtney opened her mouth, and Gran raised her finger. "Nope! Don't order me around, young lady. I'm in my eighties, and I'm not sittin' on the floor. If the tornado gets me, I'm good with it."

Courtney physically deflated and shook her head.

"Besides, I don't mind living dangerously," Gran continued. "Lyla and I nearly were killed by some crazy driver in a gray Mustang on the way over."

Eyes went wide, and Gran smiled.

"They didn't nearly kill us." I cut my eyes playfully toward Gran, who grinned like a Cheshire cat, before I explained to Rosa what happened.

"License plate?" She had her phone out.

I shook my head and took another sip from the cup. "It was raining too hard. But someone else might've. It's something you should look into, for sure." I held her gaze, and she nodded, understanding.

The lights flickered a few times, and the sirens blared. Sounds of alarm among the group were audible.

"Oh my God. I shouldn't even be here today. But that's what I get for being a good employee and trying to get things in order before going on my honeymoon. Now I might die before I ever get a chance to see another country," Courtney said as she settled on the floor.

Wow. Melanie and I held back snickers as we sipped our coffees. The woman was a tad on the dramatic side. Tornadoes were part of our lives here. They could be deadly, yes, but every time we had an alarm didn't mean we were going to be hit by one.

Her hysteria excited several folks, and they started rising, stressing that they needed to leave and get home.

"No." I shook my head. "This is a fast-moving storm. I think we should all stay put for now."

Courtney threw up her hands. "Well, if Lyla Moody thinks we should stay, I guess we all better."

"Ouch," Melanie said as she sniggered loudly into her cup. "She sure likes you."

Gran nudged me with her knee, and I waved my hand. I would not be engaging in any arguments this evening. Courtney was allowed not to like me.

Courtney whispered to the woman next to her, and they both started to rise.

Rosa stood, her cop voice steady and authoritative when she spoke. "No. We all need to remain inside." She then relayed the storm data. People still stirred, faces drawn with concern. Several were furiously texting on their phones. Courtney's coworker consoled her as she settled back on the floor.

I turned away from the blubbering Courtney and scrounged up a smile for those seated next to the wall. "How amazing was Agatha Christie's book *A Murder Is Announced*?"

"Incredible!" Mel said from my left. "We were just all raving about it earlier. Right?"

Heads began to nod.

"I just love that we've decided the month of October is exclusively Agatha Christie novels. It doesn't get any creepier than the old-school classics. The characters are portrayed raw and desperate instead of gruesome, like in horror novels."

Tammy, one of our newer members, piped up from the far end of the corner. "I've read almost every novel Christie has written. The notoriety her name carries is warranted." Tammy had belonged to the other club that merged with ours.

"I completely agree." Rosa ran a hand through her dark hair. "Like I told the club earlier, the boldness it took to put the ad in the paper riveted me. For the killer to prophetically proclaim their premeditated murder without fear of getting caught takes guts."

"Yes." Tammy's head bobbed up and down. "I read that novel years ago for a high school assignment. It was way better this time around. When the lights went out—"

Sharp intakes of breath were audible as the lights flickered again. A few giggles went up, followed by several sighs of relief when the lights didn't go out.

"Anyway," Tammy continued with a smirk, "it's a compelling read. Even better the second time around. I caught things I'd missed the first time. I think tailoring the Halloween party around this novel is magnificent. And making it fifties themed is the icing on the cake. I put the advertisement up on my refrigerator."

"I got mine right here." Gran dug through her bag and waved it around. "It's going to be a jim-dandy of a party!"

I informed everyone of what Elaine had told me about the bookings and how excited she seemed.

"That goes along with what Joel told me," Tammy said, speaking of another club member who had left early. "He said the Holiday Inn had never been booked solid for as long as he worked there."

"I'm not surprised." Melanie's watch pinged, and she glanced down at it. "It's all anyone talks about when they come in the shop."

Melanie owned Smart Cookie, located right next door to my office at Cousins. We were neighbors both in business and at home. Her townhouse backed directly up to mine.

"Amelia?" I asked, referencing Melanie's watch notification.

Mel nodded with a smile. "She's home safe and sound."

Melanie, Rosa, and I all let out a little sigh of relief. We were a tight-knit group.

"Well, I think it's truly clever of you girls." Gran smiled.

Ten minutes later, the conversation had livened up, and the sirens halted. People began to rise and check their phones. As everyone else calmly filed out, Courtney dramatically stormed out instead, but not before she informed Rosa that Quinn would hear of her rudeness. Rosa rolled her eyes after the woman left, and she, Mel, and I cleaned up.

Gran waved at me from the doorway. "I'm gone too, sugar."

I paused with my hands full of empty Smart Cookie boxes. "Wait, I'm your ride."

"Nope. My honey just texted me. He's outside."

Gran had been seeing a widower from the senior center for three months now. I wasn't sure which one, because she didn't keep them around all that long. When I asked her about her dates, she told me life was too short to be bored to death. When death came knocking, she was going out with a bang. I couldn't argue with her logic, though I did worry about her.

My parents did too. My grandmother lived with them. She had moved in with us when I was thirteen after my grandfather suffered a heart attack. She'd been a coconspirator in all my endeavors and remained one of my best friends. Mother always said she deserved a prize for allowing Daddy's mom to move in with them. I always thought Gran was the prize. She certainly added a missing element with her presence.

"Tell him he better be careful on that bike of his." I dropped the boxes in the trash.

"A biker?" Rosa's eyes went wide.

"Yeah, he's got a sweet red three-wheeler with purple-and-black flames down the side."

Rosa hooted, clapping her hands. "Go, granny!"

Melanie grinned.

I shot my friends a look that I hoped they understood: *Don't encourage her.*

"Rock on!" Gran flashed the universal sign.

I shook my head, mumbling, "Oh Lord."

Gran turned to me. "You know who you sound like, Lyla?"

"Oh, I know!" Mel raised her hand, enjoying this way too much.

"Don't." I held up my hand in a stop motion before striding over to Gran. I bent down and gave her a giant hug, being careful of the sharp corners. I forced the image of an accident with my bony little gran crushed on the road from my mind and took a deep breath. "Have fun, but be careful."

"Sure, I'll be careful. Night, girls!" Gran released me and gave a finger wave to Rosa and Mel. "See y'all at the party." She reached up and pinched my cheek. "Tell your folks not to wait up."

I knew she had done it to annoy me. "Oh no, you're telling them that, and—"

She winked at me. "Night, Frances."

At the mention of my mother, my friends roared with laughter.

Chapter Four

My phone blared with my Mother's ringtone while I searched for the perfect shade of lipstick. "Hel—"

"Lyla Jane, where is your grandmother?" my mother said without preamble. "Your father is wearing out the rug with his pacing."

I smoothed out my dress and checked my reflection in the mirror, pleased with my transformation. I cleaned up quite nicely. "I have no idea where Gran is. I haven't seen her since she left the book club meeting the other night. She's probably out buying last-minute touches for her costume. Our party is tonight." Gran had always been the last-minute type. A trait I hadn't inherited.

I applied a daring red to my lips. "Have you tried her cell phone?"

"Of course I've tried her phone. Multiple times. She is too old to be going out and behaving like a rebellious teenager." Mother tended to be more on the old-fashioned side, but recently, she had started to come around to a more modern way of thinking.

Still, as much as she'd evolved, Gran staying out late did not sit well in that household.

"I'll track her cell phone." I opened my laptop and began my search.

"Thank you, dear. I apologize for my derogatory tone. It's just your father and I worry about her, and she came home on a motorcycle the other night *in the rain*."

"Yes, I know, and I understand. But you can't expect Gran to give up her independence." Just then, Gran's cell popped up on the screen heading down Main Street. "She's on her way home. You can tell Daddy to stop with the pacing. ETA less than five minutes."

Mother let out a sigh and relayed the message to my father. "Your father says thank-you."

"Not a problem. I'll catch you later. The Jane Does have to set up early for the party."

Mother cleared her throat. "I read your announcement in the paper. I understand it's a party, but did you have to make it sound so dark and menacing? I've been getting calls for days." Her tone held a tinge of disapproval—just the thing to refocus my attention. Strategic thinking on her part. I almost laughed. Bless her heart, she tried to understand me.

"It's an Agatha Christie–themed party." I chuckled. "It's supposed to be dark and menacing." I secured my brooch to my dress. "Our community page is abuzz with excited people who do get it." Our club had an online Jane Doe Community Page where we did most of our advertising. The paper ad had been for effect. "And as Halloween parties go, it's quite glamorous. You should see my costume. It's a lovely vintage piece. I'll look like I walked right out of a fifties fashion magazine." I glanced down at my lovely dress.

"Well, that does sound nice." Mother's tone brightened. The Moody women were fashionistas to the core. "You'll have to send me a picture. Oh, your grandmother is finally here. Speak to you later."

"Night." I'd started to hang up when I overheard Gran's chatter, and when Mother didn't disconnect the call, I knew my grandmother would be asking to talk to me. It's how it usually went when Mother and I were on the phone.

"I couldn't hear the phone ringing with my helmet on," Gran said, not speaking to me, but I could tell by the volume increase that she'd commandeered the phone. "Y'all need to get out more. Have some fun and quit worrying about me. James, you seem to forget that I'm your parent and not the other way around." Gran sneezed and then said to me, sounding congested, "Hey, sugar pie. I just wanted a quick word with you. I saw Rosa at the record store downtown a few hours ago. I'm a little worried about her because she was crying and yelling at someone."

"What? Who was she upset with?" I gripped my beaded handbag.

"I don't know. She was on the phone, and something had her all worked up. When I went over to her, she hung up fast and tried to act like nothing was wrong."

Gran blew her nose. Loudly. "I only caught bits and pieces of the conversation on my way over to her. She got all red-faced when she told the person to back off or they'd pay. I wonder if she has a stalker or something. You might want to call her." A coughing fit overtook her.

"Are you ill?"

"I might be coming down with a cold."

"Oh, take some of Mother's organic elderberry syrup. That stuff works wonders."

"Yeah, I will."

"Why would you mention a stalker?" My stomach clenched.

Gran sneezed again. "She kept looking around as if someone might be following her. And when Rosa left, she dropped her keys when she went to unlock her cruiser. I know she's a cop and all, but we single ladies have to stick together. I hear you, Frances."

Gran didn't sound well. "I hate to say this, but you should stay home tonight. Get to bed and drink lots of fluids."

"Yeah. I will. I think I might take it easy for a few days. Have lots of fun for me! Night."

"Night." When Gran didn't argue with me about not attending the party, I knew she must be feeling rough. I'd miss her there but consoled myself with the knowledge that the family doctor would take care of her. Even if my daddy, Dr. James Moody, was technically a psychiatrist, he still felt the need to look everyone in the family over when they were ill.

I pondered what Gran had said about my friend as I locked up my townhouse. Rosa would hate to think anyone might feel sorry for her or pity her on any level. It was a pet peeve of hers. Besides, Gran sometimes got things mixed up. I'd speak to Rosa at the party and get a feel for what was going on. Everything was probably fine. I joined Mel in the car.

Magnolia Manor, located at the end of Magnolia Lane, was brightly lit. When I parked my car in the small lot located a short walk from the B and B, the sun had just set behind the mountains, and even in the dusky light, the outdoor string lights sparkled brightly.

"Wow," Melanie breathed as she closed the passenger's side door.

I smiled. "Yeah, it looks better than I imagined."

We strolled down the street in our 1950s boat neck vintage rockabilly cocktail party dresses that we'd picked up on Amazon, tailored after *The Marvelous Mrs. Maisel*, one of Mel's and my favorite shows. I wore black and Mel a gorgeous Tiffany blue. When Mel had initially suggested making the party an era theme straight out of the Queen of Mystery's novel, I'd pictured us doing exactly what we were now—arriving together, dressing together, and chatting with excitement like schoolgirls. And we'd had such fun fashioning our hair and getting our makeup just right to complete the look. It had reminded us of going to prom a hundred years ago. Except our dates would be joining us later this evening. Thankfully without one of those awful wrist corsages.

I glanced around and spotted Amelia's car. Ever the early bird. Then froze where I stood.

"What is it?" Mel glanced back at me from a few steps ahead.

"That car!" I marched over to where a gray Mustang was parked next to Amelia's tan sedan.

I cupped my hands at the passenger's side window and peered inside the empty car. A paper sat on the seat, and the highlighted advertisement glared back at me.

"Is this the car that nearly ran over Elaine the other day?" Mel asked from behind me.

"Could be. But I'm not positive." I went around and snapped a few pictures of the car. There was a cardboard square where the plate should be. Someone had written *Tag Applied For* in a black sharpie. Huh.

Mel began walking in place, rubbing her hands together. "Come on. It's starting to get chilly."

I took a couple more pics of the car and followed Mel. I wouldn't let this spoil the night. If this was the same car and the driver was somewhere on the property, I had no way of knowing who they were. Other than that they were a rude, obnoxious driver, I had nothing to go on. It was a little early for guests, not that we'd turn anyone away. Another explanation could be that they worked for the bed-and-breakfast. Which would mean they had nearly run their boss over the other day. Or—and I hated to consider the possibility—it could belong to Patricia Donaldson, Elaine's second cousin. That prospect made me nervous. She hadn't exhibited any violent tendencies during the investigation, but crazy things sometimes happened when a large sum of money was involved. Not that Patricia had ever had a stake in the property or the business, though she disagreed. It would be easy to deduce whether the car belonged to her if she was on the premises. I'd speak with Elaine.

I took off my professional hat for now and smiled as I spotted the bright moon sitting above the old, renovated manor behind a stately iron fence lined with red azaleas and neatly trimmed boxwoods. The sounds of soft jazz carried across the cool fall air as we entered through the iron gate. Lanterns hung from the limbs of large oak trees.

The illuminated winding pathway led to the elegant three-story Victorian mansion offering airy rooms with fireplaces, a large lounge, two oversized porches, and a courtyard. The rooms were lavishly decorated with tapestries, tasseled silk lampshades, billowing fabrics, and floral patterns that produced a riotous sense of opulence. The manor's twenty-four bedrooms and suites were sumptuous hideaways where people came from all over to enjoy luxurious accommodations and sensational cuisine.

Large potted mums and heirloom pumpkins strategically placed on both sides of the pathway and the scent of something spicy made the journey breathtaking.

This place was picture-perfect.

"I can't believe how lovely the manor is." Mel grinned over at me and squeezed my arm. "You forget that we have such a gem right here in Sweet Mountain."

I was in awe. "You really do. Wow."

Looking right at home, Elaine stood out on the large front porch as if she were waiting there to greet us. And she *was* home, having lived on the property for the last twenty years. The place had once belonged to one of Sweet Mountain's founding families. When the last living member of the line passed away, he'd willed it to the town, and it went up for sale. The Peterson family swooped in and bought it, turning it into the beautiful bed-and-breakfast it was today. The late Thelma Elaine Peterson had willed her business to her granddaughter, who was also her namesake. Our friend Elaine Morgan was now legally the sole owner.

She didn't appear upset in any way. A promising sign; maybe I'd been off base with my theory that the car belonged to her cousin. Perhaps Patricia'd finally come to a place of acceptance. It hadn't taken much digging to put together a file on this second cousin of Elaine's who'd kicked up a fuss about the will. The woman had no claim to the property, and once I'd sent my file over to the attorney considering taking the case, the situation seemed to resolve. Patricia made one more lackluster attempt, which went nowhere.

"Don't you ladies look beautiful." Elaine sighed, taking us in with a smile. "Now, those were the styles I adored. Fashion made sense back then."

"Thank you, and I agree. The designs were lovely. This era suits me." Melanie mounted the steps before I did to hug and greet our host.

"It'll come back in style. My grandmother always used to say that there is nothing new under the sun." Elaine crossed her hands in front of her. "Amelia is already inside setting up, and Chef John has some amazing tapas prepared, if you'd like to sample them."

"I'm sure they're wonderful. The chef never disappoints," I said as a bit of a chill ran through me. Not wearing a coat had been a mistake. My mother had hired Chef John for several of her more significant charity functions. Everyone always raved.

Melanie went inside, and Elaine placed her hand on my arm before I crossed the threshold, halting me. "I just wanted to thank you again for all you've done. For the life of me, I'll never know what I could have done to deserve such dreadful treatment from an extended member of my family. She's been the thorn in my side for months now. The last two days have been the peace I so desperately needed."

I covered her hand with mine and smiled. "It was our pleasure, truly. With the cease-and-desist letter, she shouldn't be a problem moving forward. You haven't had any other communications with your cousin, have you?"

She shook her head. "No. It's been nice and quiet."

"Good." I smiled and then waved my hands around, motioning to the manor. "And we should be thanking you for the price break you gave us on renting out your gorgeous B and B."

What a delightful surprise we'd had when I settled the bill this morning.

The older woman waved my gratitude away. "Parties like this liven up this town."

True. Our sleepy little town hopped tonight. We were practically bursting at the seams, accommodations-wise. Plus we were bringing attention to literary and classic works that needed more recognition. In my opinion, anyway.

"I always enjoy showing the place to locals who don't usually frequent the establishment. I find it amusing that we get more out-of-town business than any other—except for weddings, that is." I thought back to Quinn and Courtney's lovely wedding on the lush green lawn. The fall foliage had been the perfect backdrop for their beautiful affair. And they were a gorgeous couple. I was glad Quinn had found someone who made him happy. He and I had gone out a lifetime ago. And though it hadn't worked out between us, I'd always wanted the best for him.

"I suppose when people think of vacation spots, they envision travel." In the lobby, plush furnishings and an ornate painted ceiling greeted me. Every decorative piece selected had a luxurious feel, and an evening spent inside these walls felt worth the hefty price tag.

"Yes, I believe you're right." Someone called for Elaine, and we parted, she going left, I going down the hall and to the right and into the ballroom. My breath caught in my throat. The room was stunning—a trellised ceiling over a cloudy blue trompe l'oeil sky, hand-painted gold wallpaper gracing the walls. I marveled at the large windows. The French doors opened out onto a lush garden with a columned veranda overlooking the gorgeous foothills of the North Georgia Mountains. Not that we could see the view tonight, but it was still lovely to know what lay beyond the wall. The fire that crackled in the fireplace at the end of the room gave off a cozy vibe. There were no words to adequately describe the ambience.

"I feel like I'm on a movie set!" Amelia beamed as she unboxed donated copies of *A Murder Is Announced*, placing them in one of the premade gift bags on the mahogany table positioned at the sidewall.

"Or an old southern plantation." Melanie began tying a gold bow onto each bag.

"It's like a dream," I agreed as I greeted Amelia with a kiss on the cheek. "You look gorgeous. The emerald-green dress is stunning."

"Thank you. The makeup isn't too much, is it? I went a little heavy on the eyeshadow." Amelia fluttered her über-long eyelashes. "I read that was typical for the era."

"No. It's perfectly applied. God, I'd kill for your lashes, and that flawless skin."

"I know, don't you hate her?" Melanie smirked.

"My skin is a blessing, but the lashes, well, I can't take credit for." Amelia whispered theatrically, "They're extensions."

We all laughed, and I said, "I'll think about buying some extensions, but I'm more jealous of your skin anyway." The sparkle she'd added to her eyelids complemented her copper-colored complexion. Maybe the fifties makeup should come back.

"This place is unbelievable." Rosa came into the room with a gold-framed print of Agatha Christie and placed it in the center of the table. We all nodded in agreement. Elaine would be pleased with the publicity she'd receive from us. Not that she needed it.

The four of us stood back to admire the table. I glanced over at Rosa, who looked positively radiant, but I noticed she avoided making direct eye contact with me. "Rosa, you have a sec?" I said in a low tone.

"Sure." Rosa lifted her head and smiled. The smile did not make it to her lovely eyes.

Gran *hadn't* misconstrued what she'd seen.

"Hello, Jane Does." A male voice came from behind us.

We turned and saw a tall, lanky man holding a professional camera rig.

"Let's talk later." Rosa squeezed my arm. "Hello! We'd love to get a shot of the four of us before the guests arrive."

"Sure. No problem. I love shooting here. How about in front of the fireplace?" The photographer smiled encouragingly.

"Perfect." Rosa beamed.

The four of us lined up. The photographer moved us around a bit and then snapped away. I had a feeling the picture would be frame worthy.

Chapter Five

G uests were arriving, and we all went into hostess mode. A gaggle of oohing and aahing women dressed to the nines came inside the room, and the night to remember began.

We mingled, and everyone enjoyed tapas and champagne. I glanced around to see all my friends and their dates, feeling a little blue because Brad wasn't here with me. He'd texted, of course, to say he'd be running late. He was working on a new Jane Doe case, and they had gotten a lead. Couldn't be helped. Still, I was disappointed that he might miss the main event. We'd worked so hard on it, and I wanted him here to experience it all with me.

"Excuse me." A woman tapped me on the shoulder, and I turned. "You're one of the Jane Does. I see you're wearing a brooch."

"Oh, yes." I'd forgotten for a moment that the four of us were wearing matching crystal flower brooches for the guests to identify us as the hostesses.

"I was wondering if there was any sparkling water. I couldn't find a server." The woman frowned apologetically and put a hand on her stomach. "I'm so sorry to bother you with this. I've just had a little too much champagne."

I glanced around and was surprised I didn't see any servers on the floor. Huh. "It isn't a bother. I'll go find out." I waved to Amelia, who was laughing with her dashing Ethan, signaling to her we would be starting soon before gliding down the hallway toward the kitchen, stopping along the way to chat with other club members here and there.

The overcrowding in the ballroom had warmed me up, and I realized I wouldn't mind a little water myself. A thunderous clap sounded overhead, and I hoped we weren't in for more severe weather.

As I came to the kitchen area, which was roped off with a sign that read *Staff Only*, I heard a woman bellow, "I don't care what that stupid lawyer or you say! Nanny Thelma swore to me I'd be a partner in this business. That'd I get half! You took advantage in the late stages of her disease."

I recognized Elaine's shaky voice say, "Put the gun down, Patricia."

My God. I searched for my phone like it was an absent limb. Then for my watch, with the same result. Always accustomed to having a device with me, I felt naked. My watch was at home; it didn't complement this outfit. And my phone was in my checked bag. I'd planned to get it later before the big event. *Ugh.*

I'd gone two steps deciding I'd just have to go in alone when I spotted a cowering staff member in the corner right outside the kitchen. *Thank God!*

Quietly I moved over to her and whispered, "Go get Rosa Landry. She's a cop." I gave a brief description and feared I wasn't getting through. The young woman's brown eyes looked vacant. "Go!" I whispered, and she went.

I stepped over the rope and went into the kitchen. Slowly. Elaine had her hands raised and her back against the counter. Patricia Donaldson looked nothing like I'd pictured. She was much younger than Elaine, and they did not resemble each other. She stood about my height, a tall, hefty woman who didn't appear to know how to handle a gun properly. Her hands shook and her finger placement was all wrong, terrifying me.

"You knew you could manipulate her when she was diagnosed with Alzheimer's disease," Patricia said through clenched teeth. The rest of the staff stood huddled together, off to the side with pale faces and wide eyes.

"Hey," I said with my hands raised. "Let's calm down in here."

"Lyla, careful." Elaine's eyes were petrified.

Patricia whirled toward me. "You! You're the one who sent those lies to my lawyer. Lyla Moody, the woman who destroyed my case. Destroyed my life!"

Having her direct her vehemence toward me would draw her attention away from Elaine and allow Rosa time to get here. "Why don't you put the gun down, and we'll discuss this civilly. Perhaps we can come to some understanding."

"There's nothing left to discuss. Someone has to pay!" Spittle left the woman's lips, and I flinched as she shook the gun. I hated being weaponless. I'd locked my weapon up at home.

"Your life will be over if you don't rethink this. Put the gun down." I swallowed. "Please. Please tell me what I can do to make this right. I'm sure we can work something out. I see it all the time in my line of work."

Patricia chewed on her bottom lip as she considered my words.

Chef John edged backward toward the butcher block island. His hand slowly went to where his chef's knife lay, and our eyes locked. I gave my head an infinitesimal shake, which I hoped was imperceptible to everyone else. When he allowed his hand to drop by his side, I let out a tiny sigh of relief.

"Lyla's right. I'm sorry you're so upset. What can I do to make this right?" Elaine's pale face looked gaunt.

Patricia shook her head. Her hair flew wildly around her face. "Nothing now! My life is over, and it's all your fault." She oscillated her aim between Elaine and me. "Over! You'll be sorry, Elaine Morgan!" Her lips pulled back, and she bared her teeth venomously as she backed slowly toward the rear exit. "I'll ruin you just like you ruined me." She stormed out the door.

Chills spread like a virus after her ominous declaration. But as the seconds ticked on, relief swept through the room.

"Everyone okay?" I surveyed the space.

"That woman should be locked up," Chef John said.

"I agree. And she will be. Rosa should be here, and she'll call it in. I have no idea what's taking her so long." I cast a glance toward the doorway. I supposed her late arrival might be a blessing. The threat of police action might have sent Patricia over the edge. "Elaine, are you all right?" I glanced over at Elaine, who gave a nod of agreement. I turned toward the staff and asked again, "Everyone else okay?"

Nods went all around just as Rosa came into the kitchen, the staffer in tow. Rosa's face looked flushed, but I didn't have time to figure out why. I briefly relayed what had taken place. She'd have to run to arrest an armed woman.

"Everyone, remain here. I'll need to speak with each of you."
And she went in search of the perpetrator. We'd all have to give
her statements after she apprehended Patricia.

"My God. I thought this was over." Elaine finally spoke. Her
face crumpled, and she deflated onto a chair.

"She'll have to appear before a judge now if she doesn't plea
out. Either way, it'll go on her record. We'll get a restraining
order to make sure she can't come within a thousand feet of you
or your property. I'm kicking myself for not doing that sooner."

Elaine shook her head, her shoulders slumped. "Even I didn't
believe she'd go this far."

"She's desperate. Desperate people are dangerous." I should
have known that. Still learning. I would probably always be
learning.

"Perhaps I should've been more receptive to her desire to
work here."

I put my hand on her shoulder as she scrubbed her face with
her hands. "You had every right to fight for what's rightfully
yours. And she doesn't seem stable enough to work anywhere at
present."

Chapter Six

When Rosa came back into the kitchen, Elaine had calmed. Rosa hadn't been able to find Patricia, but she'd put a call in and reported the incident. There would be officers on the premises in less than half an hour, which gave Elaine the peace of mind to encourage us to continue with the night's festivities. Rosa agreed, since ending the event would only make the guests scatter, which might impede the search.

Surprisingly, other than the staff, Rosa, and me, no one was the wiser about the domestic dispute that had transpired. A couple of the kitchen staff had gone home, and I could tell Elaine was upset that her team had felt threatened. She mentioned that several employees probably wouldn't return to work. She said she understood, of course. No one wanted to work in an environment they felt was unsafe. Once Patricia paid for her crime, they'd all feel better. I hoped. Thankfully, Elaine's head chef had a different reaction. He was livid about Patricia's audacity.

When Rosa agreed we could continue the party—she believed the police presence around the property would deter any other lashing out—I decided to throw myself back into the festivities after a mad dash to the lady's room.

We were all in the ballroom fifteen minutes later, ready for the big event. Shaken but otherwise fine, I focused on my tasks. We'd put far too much work into all of this, and I wouldn't let my club or the other guests down. When I'd retrieved my phone, I breathed easier, as if it were a security blanket or something. I'd ponder that later.

I glanced around as my club discreetly took their places. Mel and I exchanged a slight grin, and excitement overtook me when I caught the glint in her eyes.

A loud clap of thunder sounded overhead, and the rain began to pour, pounding against the large windows. I no longer minded the threat of the storm; it would add to the drama. There was movement at the double French doors. *Too early!* I sent the text to signal the appropriate contacts quickly. Ethan was probably getting rained on and was eager to begin.

The seconds ticked on. Timing was everything. I cast a glance around the room, searching for my fellow Jane Does. The space was too crowded to spot everyone.

The lights flickered three times, and everything went dark.

Phew, just in the nick of time.

Shrieks went up from the crowd, along with a few nervous giggles. One of which I recognized came from Mel. Her boyfriend, Wyatt, let out a deep belly laugh. Mel giggled along with him, but I caught a shushing noise as well. I shook my head. They were doing their best.

The double doors leading out to the veranda swung open, and as if planned, lightning lit up the sky, and the shadows of the mountains came into view a second before a blinding light shone into the room.

Amelia gripped my arm, and I moved aside a little, making room for what was to come next. I could tell it was her by her perfume. "Sorry," I whispered, feeling bad I'd gotten caught up in the drama, and moved toward the doors.

"Stick 'em up!" Ethan panned the crowd with the light.

"That's Amelia's husband!" Someone close to the doors hooted with laughter.

Excitement erupted from the crowd as the sound of three loud gunshots echoed through the room. A cacophony of glee-ridden guests filled the space. When a fourth shot fired, one I hadn't expected, my shriek joined the rest, surprising me.

When a hand gripped my ankle, I jumped and got myself back into character. I must've been standing too close. A gurgling sound came from the floor. Wow, Wyatt must be improvising and putting all he had into his act.

I moved two paces to my left, apologizing when I bumped into someone.

But when I had to jerk my foot from his grasp, something inside me clenched.

The doors slammed shut, and the lights flickered back on. I opened my mouth in mock horror and got ready to play my part. I began to let out the scream I'd practiced, but it died in my throat. Patricia Donaldson, not Wyatt, lay on the floor at my feet. Red bloomed in the center of her blue blouse.

Chapter Seven

I dropped to my knees beside the woman. "Call an ambulance!" I glanced around wildly, seeking out someone I knew. Amelia already had her phone to her ear.

Wyatt, who'd been close beside the woman, cracked open his lids a sliver, and they went round like saucers as he shouted, "Is she . . . ? Oh my God!" He scrambled away from the bleeding woman.

Her eyes were wide and full of panic. My trembling hands went to the wound on her chest, and I pressed hard. "Hang on, Patricia. Hang on."

Laughter erupted, followed by roars of applause.

Comments were flying. "It looks so real."

"Do you think they used real blood?"

"Wow! We should totally make this a yearly tradition."

"I'm definitely joining the Jane Does."

The double doors swung back open by the force of the wind as it howled. Rain blew inside the room, wetting my face and arms. The shock of the temperature change caused my breath to catch. And then, for the second time this week, October tornado sirens blared.

"Everyone, move away from the doors and calmly make your way into the hallway." Elaine sounded so soothing as she ordered her staff to secure the French doors banging against the walls. My back was to her as she called my name. "Lyla, please get out of character. A tornado warning is a serious situation, and we need everyone to stay safe."

I wanted to tell her it wasn't an act. To plead for help. But Patricia's panic-stricken eyes locked on mine, holding me there. Her lips were moving, and I leaned closer. "I'm sorry," the woman whispered in a barely audible voice. Seconds later, her eyes went vacant. Mere seconds it had taken.

A scream tore through the room. Blood rushed in my ears, loud and whooshing. I heard muffled shouts; no, orders barked. The floor rumbled beneath me. People were running. Shoving. More screams. A few people bumped into me, yet I couldn't take my eyes off the woman. Numbness flooded my body when I realized the screams were coming from me.

"Lyla," said a deep male voice softly against my ear.

I blinked several times as I turned toward the voice, struggling to focus, and Brad's face filled my scope of vision.

"Where did you come from?" I mumbled.

He smiled soothingly. "I arrived a few minutes ago."

"You did?" I tried to stand, but my legs wouldn't cooperate.

"Yes." Brad nodded slowly. "I had to park way down the street. Come with me. The medical personnel need to do their job."

My heart sank. "She's already gone," I heard myself whisper.

He lifted me by my arms, and I struggled to rise, not having command of my limbs.

Paramedics flooded the room. I barely registered walking down the hallway filled with onlookers, their faces drawn in panic as I passed by, then arrived in the kitchen and positioned myself on a chair. I stared down at my hands. My palms were red, the insides of my fingers stained. My knees were shaking, violently knocking together, and I noticed my dress too had been marred with Patricia's blood. I shuddered; my teeth violently chattered together.

The house rattled, and I nearly leaped from my skin.

Brad's large hands landed on my shoulders. "Thunder. The worst has passed us. The sirens have stopped already. Here." Brad placed a glass of water on the table in front of me. I stared at it, glancing from my hands back to the glass.

A paramedic knelt in front of me. He flashed a light in my eyes and checked me over. "She's in shock. There's a lot of that going around." He stood, and Amelia, Ethan, Melanie, and Wyatt filed into the room. Rosa began questioning everyone, trying to understand how our fun murder mystery had turned into an actual crime.

"As I told you, Rosa, thrice now," I heard Ethan say, sounding agitated. "I used the starter pistol loaded with blanks. You're the one that gave it to me."

"Don't cop an attitude." Rosa's voice had an edge as sharp as a razor.

"Your tone is uncalled for, Rosa. Ethan didn't shoot that woman with a starter pistol," Amelia said, her arm protectively laced through her husband's.

I glanced up at the bright lights in the kitchen. They seemed to buzz like a sparkler on the Fourth of July. I could hear Wyatt and Melanie both giving their statements as well. Melanie kept giggling and apologizing. Bless her heart.

People came and went like ants, rushing past the door. I struggled to get my thoughts together. I had to pull myself back from no-man's-land.

I shook my head and tried not to focus on my stained hands, quelling the tears that threatened to fall. Like a loop, my mind kept replaying the events over and over. I'd seen only Ethan at the door. No one else. How had this happened? When had Patricia entered the room? And why? She'd said she was sorry. Why?

It took a few moments for me to feel like myself again. After a couple of silent deep breaths, I felt calmer, and suddenly, my hands relaxed. That's when Ethan's words struck a chord in me, and I sat up straighter and forced my knees to still. "There were four shots!"

"What?" Rosa turned to me.

"Yes. There were the three Ethan fired, as we planned, but then there was another one."

"I thought that was a lightning crack," Melanie said.

"Me too." Wyatt ran a hand through his messy blond mop-like hair.

I could tell from Rosa's expression that she'd identified the noise as gunfire as well. I met her gaze and held it.

"She said something to me before she . . ." I picked up my glass, proud when my hands didn't shake, and took a sip before I whispered hoarsely, "She said, 'I'm sorry.'"

Rosa leaned closer to me. "Are you sure those were her exact words?"

The visual of Patricia's lips moving played back through my mind like a bad rerun.

I nodded emphatically. "Those were the woman's last words."

Another officer had come into the room. He looked about middle-age and was balding and paunchy. I'd never met him before.

He was watching me, and he waited for me to finish speaking before interjecting, "Crime scene is secure. Forensics is held up in a traffic jam, but they're on their way. The medical examiner just left with the body. We're searching for the firearm. The ME couldn't conclusively confirm our suspicions, but if this crime turns out to be self-inflicted, it could have gotten kicked around during the stampede. We're searching."

Self-inflicted.

"An accurate description." I tried to focus on keeping it together as I put the glass down. "A stampede." I was sure I'd have bruises to prove it. My shoulder ached, as did my left thigh. They could've trampled me.

"One of the witnesses said she saw the victim arguing with an officer in the parking lot before the shooting."

Heads whipped toward the officer.

"She's mistaken. I know because it was only me and Hansen at the time, and he was in the parking lot, and I canvassed the area and didn't see her. We were on alert."

"I'll want to speak with the witness myself," Rosa said.

"Of course."

The officer and Rosa turned back to me and stared at my stained hands. I'd left a red handprint on the glass.

Melanie let out one of her hysterical giggles, all high-pitched and manic sounding, and all eyes went to her.

"Jeez, Mel." Wyatt cut his eyes in her direction.

"I'm sorry." Melanie pinched her lips together, and I cast a sympathetic glance her way. She reacted to stress and trauma differently than most. She couldn't help it. Her body's response to brewing emotions always came out in the form of giggles. "I just can't believe a woman was shot right in the middle of everything. It could have been any one of us on the ground bleeding out."

The weight of our friend's words was palpable.

Chapter Eight

Rosa cleared the room of all the witnesses except Brad and me, instructing everyone to remain on the premises. The room had been too crowded for direct or deep questioning. Though it had surprised me that she'd kept us all together in the first place. As I understood it, the procedure was to question each person individually, so their statements weren't influenced by another's. I supposed that, in the absence of a large force, she'd done the best she could.

Brad spoke up when the room cleared. "Like I told you when I first arrived, it was chaos. People were running to their cars, but—"

What a disaster. How was Rosa going to track down everyone who'd already left? That would take a lot of manpower.

"Let's take a step backward. You arrived exactly when?" Rosa had her pen poised over her notepad.

"About fifteen minutes before I came inside. I got a call about a case."

Rosa scribbled on the pad. "Did you see the victim before entering the ballroom?"

"No. But as I walked up the street past the parking lot, I may have seen an officer questioning a civilian by a gray Ford Mustang."

"May have?"

"I'm just putting it out there. Leveling with you that I was distracted and didn't pay close enough attention to say I'm one hundred percent sure. The woman was flying off the handle at the officer. Or the person I perceived as an officer."

"Elucidate," Rosa said.

Brad looked abashed. "The person or officer's back was to me. By the attire, I assumed." He kept his tone even and direct. "I couldn't clearly identify anyone in the dimly lit lot. I thought the officer was writing up a citation or perhaps giving a verbal warning. As I said, it was an assumption."

I sat up straighter and turned in my chair to face Brad. His gray shirt had a stain on the front of it. It must have happened when he helped me up. I glanced up to focus on his face. "The civilian, was it Patricia?"

"I don't know." Brad met my gaze; something sad swam within the dark depths of his intelligent dark-brown eyes. "I'd received a text about a situation at . . . work. I had to get somewhere more private to take the call. Then all hell broke loose. People were scattering, and the rain was coming down in sheets by then."

I covered his hand with my own where it rested on my shoulder. "It's okay."

As I turned back around, Rosa was furiously rubbing the back of her neck.

"Okay." Rosa glanced over at the officer. "Question every officer again."

I readjusted my position on the chair to read his badge. *Daniels.* Huh. The corners of his mouth tightened. It was only the briefest of movements, but I caught it. "Of course. But I assure you that I didn't question anyone, nor did I write any tickets, and with us all on the hunt for the perp at the time, I highly doubt Hansen would have stopped to write a citation. But if this is true—and I'll find out—the perp would be on her way to a holding cell instead of the morgue."

Rosa's eyes flashed hot, and the officer averted his gaze and said, "I'll ask around again. We need to know for certain if a dispute transpired with one of our own."

"Check the security footage. I was distracted with the text," Brad interjected, sounding frustrated with the situation. "I can't believe you don't have someone on that already."

"The security system was disabled," the officer said, and he and Brad locked gazes.

"What?" My fingers went to my lips as I tried to read what nonverbal communication passed between the men.

Silence stretched in the room. What in God's name was happening here?

"Elaine said the security system goes off-line a lot during storms. Sometimes the system deactivates after it comes back online," Rosa informed us. "There's something I'm missing. I can feel it. Lyla, let's go through this again."

I complied, beginning with the altercation between Patricia and Elaine. I let out a labored exhale when I finished with the dead woman on the floor. I had no idea where Elaine was or if she was okay. The possibility that this was a suicide weighed heavily on me, given Patricia's last words, and guilt that perhaps I'd played a part in her decision to end her life had me spiraling. I worried Elaine would be wrestling with the same guilt tenfold. Especially since, technically speaking, they were family. Fatigue settled in, and I had a difficult time rehashing the events entirely. I'd done the best I could, though I was sure I'd missed some things.

When Rosa asked me to go over the details right before Patricia fled again, frustration overtook me. "You're wasting time having me go over and over this. I told you what happened. Elaine told you. The staff corroborated my account. You need to determine if the storm disabled the security system or if it happened earlier. And find out whom that Mustang belongs to." My tone came out harsh and accusatory.

Officer Daniels cleared his throat.

I closed my eyes and rubbed my forehead. "I'm sorry. I know you need this from me. I'm sure you're following investigative protocol, and I'm trying."

Rosa put her hand briefly on my shoulder and gave it a quick squeeze. "It's okay. Take your time."

I thought back and focused as I glanced around the kitchen, visualizing the events. Chef John reaching for the knife. Elaine, pale and sweaty. The deceased shouting, *I'll ruin you just like you ruined me.* I relayed the vivid memory to Rosa.

"What?" Rosa furrowed her brow. "That wasn't in your original statement."

It had been. I was sure of it. "Yes, I told you that's what Patricia said before she stormed from the kitchen." I met Rosa's gaze. Her eyes were darting from side to side as if she were searching for the recollection in her memory.

She glanced down at her pad and flipped a page. "Right. You did."

I let out a little sigh. I worried for Rosa. Not that I wanted to call her out on coming across as scatterbrained. The trait wasn't like her, but this was a big case, and *she* was in charge. I'd stick to relaying the events. "And then, with her last breath, she apologized." Lending credence to the self-inflicted theory.

Brad stood behind me with his hand on my shoulder. His way of offering me support, I supposed. I appreciated the gesture, but I didn't glance back at him this time. With all these warring emotions, I worried it would weaken me somehow. And perhaps cause me to break down completely.

"I know we've been at this a while, and it's difficult, but I'm going to ask for just a little more. I need to understand the case you handled against the deceased, for the record." The expression on Rosa's face further told me the uncomfortable predicament she was in. She stated the standard spiel she'd learned at the academy, forgetting I understood.

With all crimes, it's standard procedure to speak to the witnesses right away. The first forty-eight hours are crucial to any investigation. People tend to forget valuable pieces of information as time passes, and with all the voices to be taken into account in this crime, mine would be critical to record. I'd been in the kitchen when the threat occurred. I'd handled the legal dispute between the cousins. And Patricia had passed from this life into the next in front of me. All the procedural facts made sense in my head, but the shock made things difficult to process. I had to get myself together.

"Chief Quinn will want everything by the book." The officer at Rosa's side felt the need to mention their absent police chief. I studied him more closely. Was he related to our chief of police? He was tall like Quinn, but other than that, they looked nothing alike. Quinn had dark hair—well, more salt-and-pepper these days. And his eyes were cool blue. This guy was fair skinned and freckled, with a scruffy brown beard that matched what hair he had left.

Not being able to make the connection visually, I asked.

"Yes, ma'am. I'm his cousin, Officer Harry Daniels."

Quinn hadn't mentioned anything to me about his cousin joining the force, and neither had Rosa. Not that they had to run all the new hires by me; it simply seemed curious.

Harry's radio went off with a domestic dispute call, and he stepped out of the room to radio in. A lot of domestics going on this evening. I'd once heard that during a full moon, crime increased. I'd never considered it a fact before. I had no idea how the small force would be able to manage tonight.

After another sip of water, I noticed my hands again. All of a sudden, I had to get them clean. I got up and hurried over to the sink and began scrubbing.

"Sergeant Landry," Brad said. "I'm here and can help."

Brad patted Rosa on the shoulder. It hadn't escaped me that he'd offered her the respect of addressing her formally. I gave him a small smile as I dried my hands.

"Thanks. I appreciate it, and we could use you."

"Anything you need." Brad pulled his shield from his pocket and clipped it to his belt. "I'll go help take the rest of the statements. Get the contact info from everyone still here. I assume we have the guest list."

"Yes. Officer Daniels can forward it to you," Rosa said.

"I'll make sure the witnesses understand we may need to call them to come in and speak with us further."

Rosa and Brad shared a perfunctory head nod before he left the room.

Once we were alone, Rosa pulled out a chair and sat down. She rested her head in her hands.

I sat down next to her and gave her a few minutes to collect herself.

She lifted her head. "God, this is a shit show. The crime scene is contaminated. Tracking down everyone that came in and out will be a nightmare."

If this was a suicide, why did she need to track everyone down?

"You're leaning toward suicide, right? The coroner must have given you some inkling if he believed that to be the case. Christopher usually is quick to give an initial assumption, though he doesn't commit until after the autopsy." I'd worked with him before. Never in person but on the phone, and we had a decent rapport.

"It'd be simpler for sure. Christopher said he couldn't rule it out."

Simpler. I understood Rosa's meaning, and an uneasiness swam in my stomach.

"You said you handled the background of the case against Ms. Morgan." She'd gotten right back on track, and I focused on her question.

I nodded. "Yes. It was cut-and-dry. Pat—" I cleared my throat. "Patricia hadn't a case, not really. The case was never officially filed with the court. Nor did she manage to come up with substantial evidence to contest Elaine's grandmother's will. I only stepped in to help Elaine stop Patricia from harassing her and sent a few documents to Patricia's lawyer. She didn't have a history of serious mental illness or self-harm—that was recorded, anyway. I had no idea she'd do something like this." I touched Rosa's arm. "Unless . . ."

"Sergeant." Quinn's cousin came back into the room, and she stood to converse with the man.

"Forensics is here and working on prints. You're right about the crime scene; it's tainted. But we'll do our best. We're also checking for gunpowder residue on the victim." Disapproval of Rosa's methods was written all over Harry's face.

"I still contend that we should reach out to the chief," Harry said. "He'd want to be in the loop."

Rosa shook her head, her face flushed. I turned away to give them the pretense of privacy.

"No. The chief left me in charge. We are not going to disturb him while he's on his honeymoon. Understood?" Rosa must have proven herself to Quinn over the last year. When he'd announced his engagement, I'd wondered who'd he choose to take the reins while he was away. Rosa made sense to me. She had experience, and not just from working in law enforcement. Originally from Baton Rouge, Rosa had moved here after her Afghanistan tour and had worked as the Sweet Mountain Police Department's desk sergeant for a while and then become active in the field. She'd gone all-in on day one and hadn't wavered a moment since. She'd seen her share of macabre scenes.

Unlike me, who quaked to my core. I'd never in my life seen anyone slip away in front of me. Sure, I'd seen crime scene photos and been on the scene after the fact, but tonight stood in a category all its own.

Harry frowned until he caught the irritation that rolled off Rosa, as I had. "Yes, Sergeant."

The officer's head bowed forward in acceptance, the stiffness in his defiant posture undeniable as he turned to leave the room. Challenging a superior's authority would benefit no one and could potentially hurt the case.

"Hold up." Rosa raised a hand. "Special Agent Jones offered his help; go find him. He's worked cases like these. Let him take the lead. With three officers, this will take all night." She sounded as tired as I felt.

Chapter Nine

The core Jane Does minus Rosa sat in the outside courtyard of Nobles Coffee Company the following day. The rain had moved out finally as a cool front blew through. The temperature hovered in the low seventies, the crispness of the air seasonally perfect—usually a happy time. Yet, after last night, the pumpkin and gingerbread scones sat untouched on the plates. The crowds were light, especially for a Saturday morning—something the three of us were grateful for under the circumstances. Mel, Amelia, and I all shivered as a brisk gust of wind rustled the fallen leaves around us.

I'd had an uncomfortable conversation with Brad late last night. He'd had some concerns regarding the statements he'd taken the night before.

"I saw the body, Lyla," Brad had said. "The theory of suicide doesn't sit well with me. It didn't for Officer Daniels either. He may not be as experienced as some, but he has his doubts. He doesn't want to cross Rosa. He has concerns about her prowess in heading up the investigation."

Brad had assured me that Daniels respected Rosa and believed her to be a good cop—his issue was just that he thought she might be too close to this one, and he doubted she'd ever headed up an investigation of this type. And inexperience usually meant a botched investigation.

When he brought up Harry Daniels again, I'd asked, "You don't think his problem is that Rosa is a woman?" He'd not known how to answer that question. Which annoyed me, and I plowed forward. "If you have concerns," I'd told him. "Then Rosa probably does too. She may not be as experienced as you are in law enforcement, but you forget, she spent time in Afghanistan. She's seen her fair share of death and murder."

I'd reminded Brad that he hadn't witnessed the domestic dispute where Patricia all but told us her plans to ruin Elaine. However, I hadn't told him about my conversation with Rosa after they left the kitchen. She'd thought the theory of suicide had fit the scene. Or maybe she'd said she hoped. No, she'd said it certainly would make closing the case simpler.

Not that she'd been callous about the woman's death. I also hadn't told Brad I'd noticed a stinging sensation from a deep scratch on my ankle in the shower. What I'd thought had been a playful gesture by Wyatt had been Patricia clinging to life by her fingernails. The recollection was horrific and so heart-wrenching that I'd sat on the floor of the shower and sobbed.

I'd felt much better after the emotional release. The tears had cleared my head, and my focus improved.

I'd just finished sharing my worries about Quinn's cousin with my friends. I wanted to talk to them about Brad but couldn't bring myself to discuss it out loud. Something had felt off between us this morning. Our relationship felt tenuous—a first for us.

And I was glad I hadn't brought it up, because Mel had decided to hang on to my mention of Brad leaving for the city a few sentences prior. "Brad left for Atlanta?"

I nodded and pulled my denim jacket closed, adjusting my scarf in the process.

"Even after your traumatic ordeal?" Mel looked appalled.

Not pleased with her tone, I narrowed my eyes. "It's fine. Brad has work, Mel."

"Okay." Mel raised her hands in a posture of defense. "I'm just looking out for you."

"What's that supposed to mean?" A wave of panic flooded me, but I managed to quell it. *Why? Everything is fine.*

"That he's your boyfriend, and he should be with you during this trying time."

"He sat up with me last night. You know our relationship is different from other people's. Our jobs require more of us." My tone edged on hysterical. Mel's and Amelia's eyes were wide.

Why am I so defensive?

"Lay off, Mel. She's been through a lot. We all have." Amelia squeezed my hand.

"You're right. I'm sorry. I just want to make sure Brad is good to you is all," Melanie took a sip from her paper cup.

Amelia gave me a sympathetic smile. Or was it a pitying one? I was probably being paranoid. Last night had rattled us all. Yet, as I replayed last night with Brad in my head, I recalled he'd been the perfect boyfriend. He'd sat up with me, and we'd talked through the ordeal. He'd rubbed my back and spoken soothingly. Then I recalled how his phone had never stopped pinging. He'd apologized but hadn't muted it—a case, he'd said. I shook my head. Even my thoughts sounded suspicious.

I forced myself to settle. "I tried Rosa on my way over, but it went straight to voice mail. I thought she could use a friend. I can't shake the notion that she's doesn't have the support of her officers."

"I spoke to her briefly. She said she was going to try and catch a few winks." Melanie adjusted her hair, smoothing the strands that attempted to take flight with the breeze. "And I wouldn't worry about Harry or those other officers. Rosa can handle them."

I wasn't concerned about Rosa's ability to handle the situation. I simply didn't think it was fair or professional for Harry or any officer to challenge her. Especially in the middle of an investigation. Harry would have Quinn's ear. Or at least as a relative, I believed he would. Family roots in our neck of the woods ran deep. Not that I would voice any of that now. Mel was in a mood. I simply had to trust that Quinn would rely on his better judgment and confidence in Rosa. He wouldn't have left her in charge otherwise.

Amelia's chocolate-brown eyes were bloodshot, and I asked how she was holding up.

"I couldn't sleep last night. The image of the poor woman appeared every time I closed my eyes. And I didn't even get an up-close-and-personal view, as you did." She reached out and gave my hand another squeeze. "I can't imagine how you're dealing with all of this. You practically held that poor woman's hand as she slipped from this world."

"I'm fine." I smiled, and I hoped the smile made it to my eyes. It would be more convincing if it did. I'd had my hands on Patricia's chest when her heart took its final beat. The moment had been defining for me. Going forward, every Jane Doe case I investigated would remind me of how fragile life was. Each Jane Doe case mattered. As determined as I'd always been to close those cases, I'd be doubly so now.

"Are they certain it wasn't a suicide? Did Brad say?" Amelia looked worried. She took a sip from her cup and leaned in.

Mel and I mirrored her movement, getting as close as possible over the table.

"I don't think anyone can be certain while the investigation is ongoing. But I can't get Patricia's words out of my head. She said she'd ruin Elaine. And then when she uttered those words on her dying breath . . ."

We all three shivered. A couple of groups of laughing people came into the courtyard, carrying drinks and food.

"Could it have been an accident? Maybe in the dark, someone's gun went off?" Amelia's brows drew together.

I kept my tone low. "I highly doubt that, or I can't see a way that would have happened."

"I still can't get the thought out of my mind that it could have been any one of us. Someone fired a gun, in the dark, blindly." Melanie fiddled with her cup.

My phone rang, and I dug into my purse to retrieve it. The face that came up on my screen belonged to Piper Sanchez, our famous town reporter—well, famous for Sweet Mountain. I answered it. "Hey, Piper." I took a nibble from the scone and washed it down with a sip from my cup.

"Hey, can we meet? Now or as close to now as you can manage." The urgency in her tone made me sit up straighter.

Mel mouthed, "What is it?"

I held up a finger. "Sure. I can meet you at my office. I'm just down the street at Nobles with Melanie and Amelia."

"Perfect. Listen, Lyla, this needs to be kept between the two of us. Remember our pact."

"Okay," I said slowly. Piper and I had come to an agreement of sorts. As a reporter, when she had information that could aid me in an investigation, she slid it my way, and when I could help her, I'd anonymously give her quotes or push her in the right directions. Piper had loved the idea of two powerful women running this town behind the scenes, and I did as well. I recalled the moment we'd pinkie sworn, like junior high schoolers, to seal our agreement. I'd hold up my end.

"See you in ten." She disconnected the call.

I slid my phone back into my bag and smiled at my friends.

"You better tell Piper to be respectful. I get that she wants the inside scoop"—Mel unhooked her purse off the back of the chair and rose—"but Elaine doesn't need any bad press."

"I don't think she'll spin it negatively toward Elaine." I finished my coffee and realized that might not be the truth. "Well, I won't be sharing details about Patricia's threats. It could impede the investigation."

Perhaps I could control the narrative on some level. Paint a different picture than some of the news I'd read on my feed this morning. The headlines that read *Halloween Party Turned Deadly* and *A Shooting at Magnolia Manor Leaves One Dead* were what had kicked off my dawn discussion with Brad.

Amelia leaned in and raised her brows. "Weren't there quite a few people in the kitchen with you? Any one of them could talk. And they'd have all the dirt on Elaine. It isn't out of bounds to think Piper could paint Elaine as a money-hungry relative who wouldn't offer help to an unstable woman."

"Did you speak to the press? To Piper?" Melanie asked.

Amelia smoothed a couple of silver strands behind her ear. "No. I wouldn't have the inside scoop, Mel. Her staff would."

Mel slowly sat back down, her voice hushed as she said, "You can't possibly believe Elaine is partly responsible? Patricia made her own choices."

Amelia's eyes lit with an indignant fire. "I didn't say I believe she was responsible. But I can't help but sympathize with the poor deceased woman. Patricia was undeniably desperate. Who knows what she was dealing with in her personal life?"

"And how is any of that Elaine's problem?" Mel's face flushed. It didn't surprise me that Mel would be partial to Elaine. We all thought fondly of the woman, but Melanie's grandmother, the woman who'd raised her, had been best friends with Elaine for decades.

Amelia huffed. "Isn't that a productive and loving stance? How is a struggling person anyone's problem? It's common decency, Mel. At the very least, Elaine could have seen how desperate her cousin was and offered to get her some professional help."

"Let's not turn on each other," I said calmly, hoping to lower the tone of discussion. I didn't want us at each other's throats. Tragedy had that effect on some. "We don't know for certain Patricia wasn't under a doctor's care."

"Well, I doubt it. Health care in this country is a joke. She clearly didn't feel she had the financial security she needed," Amelia whisper-railed. "And that in itself is reprehensible."

"Here you go again with your political views on the health care crisis." Melanie looked as though she was about to burst a blood vessel.

People were beginning to stare in our direction.

Melanie hiked her bag up on her shoulder as she rose. "I'm done with this conversation. I'm meeting Wyatt. We're going hiking. He needed to get out after what he dealt with last night." She zipped up her hoodie. "He's doing fine, in case either of you wondered."

"I called and checked on both of you last night." I sighed and rose too. There would be no placating Mel now.

"I know you did. Thanks." She let out a huge sigh and closed her eyes. "I'm sorry, Amelia. I just—I can't today."

Amelia rose too and held her hands up. "I'm sorry too. We'll talk later."

"Yeah, okay. Love you." Mel gave her a small smile.

"Love you too." Amelia returned it just as Mel turned and left, though her brow stayed tensed.

Something more was definitely going on with Amelia. Not that what had happened last night wasn't enough, but I could sense something more profound, more personal, warring inside her. We tried to stay away from politics for the most part. There were times when it was unavoidable, but we did our best. Our friendship had begun based on our love of books and true crime, but it had evolved over the years to something more like family. "Okay, hon, what's really going on?"

"I'm sorry." Her eyes filled with tears. "I didn't mean to attack Mel like that. I could see she was stressed out."

I looped my arm through hers. "And Mel didn't mean to come at you either. You know her. She'll simmer down. She just needs time. I'll walk you to your car, and you need to unburden." That's what we called getting everything off our chests— clearing the air so we could breathe freely again. It was one of the bonds of our core group. The trust we shared wound us tightly together. We could get through anything if we were honest, cleared the air, and didn't allow anything to fester.

"My sister and I have never been on the best of terms, you know," she said as we crossed the street.

"Is she the family issue from the other day?" The wind whipped up, and we huddled closer together. Amelia had explained to us early on that she and her family weren't close. Her sister constantly struggled with addiction, and the relationship had always been a toxic one. Amelia had felt forced to close the door on that part of her life for her mental health.

"Yes." Amelia opened her car door and tossed her purse inside. "When I separated myself from that side of my family all those years ago, I swore I'd never reopen it. My sister and I haven't really spoken for more than five minutes in the last five or so years. When she called me last week, I didn't even answer. I thought she was using again. She calls a lot when she's high, raving. I thought about changing my number, but something inside me told me not to."

I gave her a minute. I recalled how difficult it had been for Amelia to confide in us about her past. After her mother died, she and her sister had been in and out of foster care. And judging from her stories, the homes weren't the best. Despite her challenging beginnings, Amelia had done well with her life. Her sister hadn't. Their father's frequent incarcerations had left them with significant baggage.

She wrapped her arms around herself and stared up at the sky as if hoping she'd find courage there. A few beats later, she said, "I have a niece that I was unaware of, and she's ill." Her voice hitched. "She has a blood disorder. My sister hasn't any insurance, of course, and the prognosis isn't good if she doesn't receive a specialist's care."

My heart dropped, and my fingers went involuntarily to my throat. "Amelia . . ."

"Yeah. It gets worse. My sister has a court date for possession with intent to sell, and she's going in for a long sentence this time. She wants Ethan and me to adopt Sasha."

"I don't know what to say." I rubbed my friend's arm.

"We have the means, and Sasha is only two years old. Young enough . . ." Her voice trailed off. Amelia had done well for herself in real estate. It was a seller's market, and she consistently brought in offers above the asking price. Bidding wars weren't uncommon either. She'd told us about all the money they'd been able to stash away. I knew she'd be thinking of delving into the nest egg she'd worked hard to earn.

I reached out and pulled her into a hug. "You've been dealing with all this on your own. I'm so sorry. Please tell me what I can do." No wonder she was livid about the healthcare industry. It had hit home with her and become personal.

Amelia gripped the back of my jacket. "You're such a great friend. I just wasn't ready to talk. There's a treatment. It's expensive, and we have to work through all the nuances in our insurance plan regarding preexisting conditions, but Ethan thinks they'll cover part of it." Her voice hitched, "When I saw her on a FaceTime call with her foster mother, she looked so much like my sister and me when we were little—lost and scared. I loved her instantly. I just don't want to let the child down. She deserves a chance."

I held her tighter. "You couldn't. That little girl couldn't ask for better parents."

She nodded against my shoulder. "We leave in the morning for Maryland. I'm not sure how long we'll be gone, and there's so much to be done."

"You leave me a key to your house. I'm sure you'll need lots of stuff for a toddler. I'll organize something, and we'll get everything you need."

"She'll be so scared at first. I don't know how she'll react to me, since my sister and I look so much alike."

I held her arms and stared her straight in the face. She needed to see how serious I was, see that I loved her and had meant every word I'd said. "It's going to be fine. You're not alone. We'll love this little girl so much. You've got us. Always. Melanie would be mortified with herself if she knew. She'll jump in with both feet to help. And you know how my mother loves to fundraise." Frances Moody enjoyed volunteer work like no one else on the planet. Since marrying my father, she'd dedicated her life to helping those less fortunate and decided not to work outside the home. "If it's money you need for Sasha's treatment, we'll raise every single penny. If it's family you need, you have it."

She nodded, and we were both doing a little sniffling. I dug through my bag and handed her a tissue.

"I don't know what I'd do without you." She wiped her nose and fisted the tissue as she smiled.

"We're your family. It's what we do."

She nodded again, dabbing at her pouring eyes. "Thank you."

"You'll call me day or night if you're struggling, right? And you'll keep me posted?"

"Yes. Yes." She hugged me again, and we both bawled like babies.

Chapter Ten

"Miss Moody!"

I turned, adjusted my sunglasses, and scanned the street. Sweet Mountain's newest officer stood on the other side of the road, waving toward me. He motioned for me to stay put, then he held up his hand in a stop motion at the crosswalk, halting several cars as he trotted across the street.

"Harry, isn't it?" I squinted my eyes to pretend I'd struggled to come up with his name.

"Uh, yes." The officer gave me a lopsided smile and scratched his bearded chin. His eyes were hazel, I noticed. "Could I have a minute of your time?" He motioned to the bench under the maple tree.

I glanced at my watch.

"Won't take long."

"I'm supposed to be meeting someone." I looked down the street toward the office. "I don't see her, so yes, I can spare a few minutes. My office is just down the street, if you'd like to accompany me."

"That'll work." He smiled. "You know, we've met before."

"Have we?"

"Yes. Years ago when you and Quinn were an item. It was at the Daniels family reunion."

I glanced over at him and tried to place him.

"I had a lot more hair then." He rubbed the top of his head. "And none on my face."

"Ah, that must be why I can't recall us meeting. I'm surprised I didn't see you at the wedding."

He smiled, his round face flushing slightly. "I was there, and I saw you. Guess I have one of those forgettable faces."

"I wouldn't say that." I kept walking. "Where do you live, Harry?"

"Here, in Sweet Mountain. I moved here from the Carrollton area when the job opening came available in Quinn's precinct. I still can't get over how much you haven't changed."

Wow, this was beginning to become uncomfortable.

"Quinn did nothing but talk about you back then. I thought for sure you were the one."

"We're better as friends. He's found the one now." I smiled. Quinn and I had had a complicated relationship for a while, and I was glad we were finally in a good place. Courtney and I would never be best friends, but I'd be kind and treat her as I wanted others to treat me. That was the way we were raised around here—not that everyone followed the rule. Besides, Quinn and I had to work together, and having his wife hate me would not make the job any easier.

A couple intercepted us on the way. The older man with wiry gray hair extended his hand. "Morning, Harry."

"Good to see you, Mr. Carver." Harry shook hands with the man, who was smiling broadly.

"Who's this lovely lady?" The older gentleman eyed me with interest.

"This is Lyla Moody."

Mr. Carver tapped the brim of his ball cap. "Nice to meet ya."

"Same to you." My office was steps away, and I wanted to flee. I had no interest in standing around while Harry engaged in casual chitchat or listening to him stroll down memory lane. If he believed this display would create a connection between us—by demonstrating that he was a man in touch with a town I loved—he'd sorely misjudged me and my understanding of law enforcement procedures.

"Tell your old man I'll be looking for him at the next fishing tournament," Mr. Carver said to Harry. "I got me a sweet new PENN Spinfisher at the Bass Pro Shop."

Harry whistled. "Bet that set you back a pretty penny."

The man adjusted his ball cap, exposing more hair. "Wasn't too bad. Gotta watch those sales."

"Nice to meet you. I have an appointment." The second it would no longer be perceived as rude, I had my keys out and strolled with purpose toward the office.

"Sorry about that," Harry said at my back as I unlocked the door.

I flipped on the lights, and we entered.

He pulled a little pad from his front pocket and flipped a few pages before pulling the cap off his pen with his mouth. "My dad and I always participated in the One Fish Wonder tournament at Lake Allatoona every year. Have since I was a boy."

I nodded, my politeness threatening to wane, not sure why he would be sharing any of that with me.

"You ever attend the tournament?"

I gave my head a shake, put my purse on the desk, and perched on the edge.

"No, I didn't think so. I don't recall ever seeing you there. Quinn and his dad go too."

"Uh-huh." I scratched my arm. "Fishing isn't my thing. When I go out on a boat, I usually sunbathe." I cleared my throat. "What is it you really want to ask me? I know you didn't hold me up to talk about the past or your love of fishing."

He studied me. "Just thought you'd like to know we have history, however small. I care about this town too."

"Noted."

He cleared his throat. "I want to go over a couple of points in your statement from yesterday."

"All right." I folded my arms.

"Did you happen to witness any conflict between the deceased and Elaine?"

"Other than the conflict I told y'all about?" I raised my brows.

He bared his teeth in what I imagined was supposed to resemble a smile. "Yes, other than that. A couple of the witnesses overheard a heated argument at the bed-and-breakfast a few days before the incident."

"I wasn't aware of it." I wondered why Elaine hadn't mentioned it to me when we'd arrived at the manor.

He nodded and scribbled something on his notepad. "Odd she didn't contact you, since you were investigating the potential civil suit. When the lights came on and you discovered the victim on the floor, you said you tried to stop the bleeding."

I swallowed as goose bumps traveled up my flesh. Harry had seen my hands. Taken specific notice of them last night. Who wouldn't? "Yes. I tried applying pressure until the ambulance arrived."

He nodded. "Did you see a gun near the body?"

"No." I cleared my throat. "Has a gun been found?"

The seriousness in his eyes deepened. "I'm not at liberty to discuss that."

"I figured. Just thought I'd ask." I considered how they must be turning Elaine's lovely establishment upside down. I also wondered how long the business would be forced into closure and if the hardship would affect Elaine financially. Whatever the cause of death, Patricia's threat to ruin Elaine had come to pass, even if only in a small way.

"Before the party, did you have any personal dealings with the deceased?"

I shook my head. "Not directly. Cousins Investigative Services handled the background of the case she hoped to mount against Elaine. We had no personal contact with Patricia during the investigation, which was cut-and-dry. She had no case. I think she just wanted to kick up a fuss for the sake of it. I hadn't realized how far she'd go."

"Was Elaine angry about the ordeal?" He scribbled on the pad in a fashion that told me the pen had run out of ink.

I leaned back and took a pen from my holder, then held it out to him. "*Upset* is a more accurate description. Patricia's behavior was defamatory. She came by Elaine's house a few times, ranting about the unfairness of the will. She trashed her to several people in town. We did file a cease-and-desist order, and I believed it brought the desired result until last night. She went quiet."

"That you were aware of?"

"Yes, to my knowledge at the time. Now it seems to have merely added fuel to the flames. I suppose I should have taken the nasty grams she sent Elaine more seriously."

"Nasty grams?" He raised his nearly translucent-looking brows.

"Oh, sorry." I smiled, shaking my head. "It's how Elaine referred to the hateful emails and phone messages Patricia kept leaving and sending her. We kept them all." I turned around and extracted the flash drive from my drawer and handed them over. "I told Rosa I'd be giving them to her this afternoon. I suppose you saved me the trip."

He put the drive into his pocket. "Thanks. Elaine didn't fear for her safety?"

"At first, then she seemed pleased with the result of the cease-and-desist. I followed up several times to make sure."

"Did the deceased threaten anyone else at the party?"

I shook my head, feeling unnerved that he kept referring to Patricia as the deceased. "She aimed all her venom at Elaine."

He closed his notebook and put it back into his front pocket with the pen. "Thanks for taking a minute. And for the flash drive." He started for the door.

"Oh, did you know if y'all had any luck with the Mustang? Find out whom it belonged to or if a citation was filed?"

He shook his head. "The car seems to have vanished."

"Vanished? How?"

He slightly raised his shoulders.

"Don't you find that odd?"

He stared right at me. "Yes, I do. I find a lot of things odd about this case." He saluted me with the pen. "I hope you have a good weekend."

"I'll try." I rose from the edge of the desk.

With his hand on the door, he turned back toward me. "Oh, one more thing."

Something about the movement seemed rehearsed. Something Harry had learned at the academy? On the force, maybe? Allow the interviewee to relax and then, wham—hit them with the real question. Amateur.

"Sergeant Landry was in attendance during the entire ordeal, correct?"

Wham. "Yes," I replied cautiously.

He tapped his fingers casually on the door and cocked his head to one side. "She was in the ballroom when the lights went out?"

"Sure."

He squinted. "You saw the sergeant?"

The situation felt very sticky. What was the man driving at? If I said yes, would Rosa say otherwise? Had she already? My suspicions about him rang loud and clear. "Well, I suppose I couldn't absolutely say where she was the entire time. In the house, I mean. She had a part to play in the staged murder. In the packed ballroom, there was so much going on. But she had to be there even if I didn't see her the entire time." I sighed. "To play her part."

"Which was?"

"I beg your pardon?" I tucked a strand of hair behind my ear.

"Her part in the staged murder. What was it?"

Hmm. Rosa would have told him all of this. "She set off the screams from her phone after Ethan fired the starter pistol. Her phone connected via Bluetooth to the B and B's sound system. She'd have to have been in the room to time the screams appropriately. Honestly, Harry, you should just speak with your sergeant."

He pointed his finger at me and smiled. "I'll do that. But it does beg the question: If the Bluetooth sound system was functional, why wasn't the security system?"

He had me there. I had no idea.

"Hello!" Piper Sanchez said from the doorway just as he'd turned to leave. He flushed as she hit him with a one-hundred-watt slow smile.

Piper had that effect on men. She was average height but way above average in figure, face, and hair. She had large brown eyes rimmed with those superlong lashes, gorgeous olive skin, and a head of thick dark curls I'd have killed to have. Her sharp wit was the icing on the cake. Piper was a force. She'd made lead reporter at *Sweet Mountain Gazette* last year and wrote freelance for several larger outfits. I'd even seen her on the news a couple of times. Great things were ahead of her, and she would let nothing hold her back. I admired that.

Piper laughed and placed her hand on the officer's arm. "I'm so sorry. I didn't mean to nearly run you over."

"No, I'm sorry. I should have been watching where I was going."

"Well, since you're here, you've saved me a trip. I know you're swamped with this investigation, but if you could spare a minute for me, I'd be so grateful."

Harry's shoulders went back, and his spine went ramrod straight. "Of course."

"Be back in a sec, Lyla."

Piper and Harry stood just outside the door, their heads close. When Harry glanced back and saw me watching, he took her arm, and they moved out of sight.

Curiosity overtook me, and I walked over and leaned against the exposed brick wall to peer out the window. Was Harry going to become Piper's new inside guy at the police department? From the look on his face, all flushed and eyes sharp and eager looking, she'd had no trouble working him for intel. Quinn would not like this.

"Bye," Piper put all the slow southern drawl she could muster into her voice as she waggled her fingers in the direction, I assumed, Harry had gone.

Piper let the act drop when she came through the door. "God. He isn't too bright, is he?" She embraced me and gave me a quick kiss on the cheek. "You're late."

"You're the one who's late. And what's going on?"

She glanced around. "This is the first time I've been here since the renovation. It's nice."

I followed her gaze as she took in the fifteen-hundred-square-foot functional space. We had exposed brick walls with sandstone-colored columns. The ceiling we'd painted black to hide the exposed ductwork and beams. The hardwood floors were new but looked old and distressed and fit perfectly. You wouldn't know they weren't the original hardwood. I made sure the space remained completely fêng shui. I'd hung up some abstract art for color and added a couple of large floor plants and a small fountain to bring in life.

"Thanks." I went and took a seat in the sitting area near the new coffee bar we had installed last month.

"You doing okay after seeing that woman die like that? It seems not many recognized that her death wasn't part of the game."

I nodded my head slowly. "Yeah, I'm good. I wish the ambulance had arrived in time to save her. A tragedy on so many levels."

"Yeah, definitely." She moved her head from side to side, her bottom lip caught between her teeth. Something had Piper spooked. And she didn't scare easily.

"Sit. Talk to me." I placed my arm on the back of the leather settee and tried to appear relaxed. "I know you don't need me for an inside scoop on what happened at the party. I checked my news feed this morning and saw yours trending. Everyone has the story, or some version of it, anyway."

"No." Piper smoothed out her pencil skirt—which didn't need it—and vacillated further, adjusting and readjusting her belt before taking the seat opposite me. "Where's Calvin, any-way? My pop mentioned he hadn't seen him at the diner lately."

"He's out of town until the end of next month."

"Ah, out on one of his secret missions, is he?" She raised her brows.

Calvin was ex–Navy Seal, and Piper had been on him for months trying to convince him to give her some intel on what he did for his Seal buddies. She'd had no luck, of course. Even I didn't know what went on while Calvin was out of pocket. Often, he didn't even call while on one of his missions, which he referred to as "helping an old friend out with a bit of a problem."

"Enough stalling. You're making me nervous with all this prattling." The way she dithered caused my anxieties to ratchet up. I raised my palms. "Why was it so important to meet this morning?"

She leaned forward, crossed her legs, and folded her hands together and laced them over her knee. She released her hands and sat back, then relaced them over her knee, leaning forward once more. She inhaled deeply. "Okay, listen. You remember that cute little ad you had me write up as a favor?"

I nodded slowly. The irony that my advertisement had been prescient made us both shiver.

"Well." Piper fidgeted. "Someone reached out to me about another one. I refused, of course. But . . ." She dug through her bag, opened her iPad, and handed it to me. I read the entry on the *Gazette*'s announcements page. It was down at the bottom in small font.

A Murder Is Announced: Jane Does, your host for the evening, is informing everyone that a murder will take place on Friday, October 22nd, at Oak Mill Cemetery, 15 N Erwin Street. Come for a night of swinging All Hallows' Eve fun!

Chapter Eleven

I glanced up from the screen. "Is this a joke? Is someone using our book club to rip off our Halloween party idea? And wait a minute, I thought you refused to print the advertisement."

"I did refuse." Her shoulders elaborately rose, then fell. "But after I refused the woman via email, she called the *Gazette*. One of the administrators set it up, thinking it was like your party, and just happened to mention it to me this morning."

I studied her. "Okay. But your staff wrote this before what transpired last night, correct?"

She nodded.

"As in bad taste as this is, it's nothing to get you worked up over. You think we should be reading more into this?"

"It doesn't feel right."

I ruminated, a deep, sinking dread forming in my gut. "Did you run down who paid for the ad? This woman who contacted you?" I handed her the iPad back, deeply curious as to who would throw the party and if they'd had something to do with Patricia's demise. I had to consider the possibility that the crime might be a homicide.

Piper nodded. "That's where it gets creepy. There is an online event set up on Facebook for the party, and many people have marked themselves as going. The event shows the Jane Doe Book Club as hosting the event." She tapped on her iPad screen and handed it back.

"I'm confused." I sat forward, taking the iPad, and clicking on the event listing. "Who would have the audacity to pull a stunt like this? We can at least place a retraction in the *Gazette*, and I can contact the organizer of the Facebook group."

"I wouldn't count on them being cooperative." Piper frowned.

The group wasn't private, and I could see comments. More than fifty people were going, and some of them were on my friends list.

I read the headline of the event. It read the same as the one in the paper but added:

This party will top our last. Don't miss out.

"The audacity!" I shook my head and continued to read some comments.

Oh! Can't wait!

A Halloween Keg party at a cemetery? Count me in!

Maybe someone else will die? Exciting!

"My God." I kept scrolling, shaking my head.

*You insensitive jerks! Someone **actually** died at your last party. I'm deleting every one of you that is on my friend's list.*

I rubbed my forehead. "Thanks for the heads-up. We'll need to post something on our Jane Doe community page and contact everyone we know personally and"—I sighed—"attempt to reach out to those we don't. I'll prevent anyone from getting caught up in this mess if I can."

"You're as suspect about this dubious behavior as I am." Piper studied me.

I raised my brows. "Did you think I wouldn't be?"

Her head cocked to one side. "I wondered. And you might want to see if your friend Rosa is concerned."

"Why? She has her hands full with this case. I can take care of damage control. And if I see evidence that validates our concerns, I'll speak with her. I don't want to muddy the waters of her current investigation."

"Lyla." She stared at me as if I'd lost my mind. "Rosa Landry's name was under the Jane Does on the advertisement invoice." She took the iPad from me and pulled up a pdf. At the bottom of the page was Rosa's signature. Or what appeared as Rosa's digital signature.

"This can't be." My stomach twisted into knots. "I can tell you with one hundred percent certainty the person behind this uncouth action isn't Rosa. We're obviously dealing with some form of identity theft or impersonation."

"To what end?"

"I don't know yet. But someone is trying to stir things up, or"—I contemplated Rosa's work situation—"or someone has a vendetta against Rosa."

"Or someone is using what happened to Patricia as a jumping-off point. The Facebook listing went up last night, after the murder."

"Murder?"

"Harry is leaning in that direction. You got to admit, it's fishy."

I tapped my foot against the floor. "Yes. But you weren't there. The ballroom was pitch-black. The shooting was at close range. I never even saw Patricia in the room before the lights went out."

"Can you be positive she wasn't there? What about the witness who claimed she fought with an officer beforehand? Can we even be sure that didn't take place?"

She'd done her homework. "We can't be sure of anything. I suppose it's possible someone walked her into the room at gunpoint and then waited for the appropriate moment to pull the trigger. God, I wish the security system had been online."

"What?" Piper's eyes bulged.

"That's off the record." I supposed she hadn't gotten all the specifics from her sources. I could have kicked myself. Not that I didn't trust Piper; I did. But there was an order to these things, and we both had different roles to play. "I mean it."

"Fine." She grumbled, and I let out a little sigh.

"You're right, Rosa needs to know about this."

Piper pursed her lips. "Okay, here's the thing. Perhaps you shouldn't be completely open with our Sergeant Landry. I did a little digging before I came here."

"Digging into Rosa?" I shifted on the seat. "Come on, Piper. Don't be ridiculous. She isn't behind this. Any of it."

She stared at me. "She's not as squeaky clean as you might think. After her tour in Afghanistan, her life got a little messy. I reached out to her because I agree with you. She needs to know about all this. And she said in no uncertain terms to stay the f-bomb out of her life."

"Are you serious?" I gaped.

Piper nodded. "And in my experience, when someone reacts that way, they have something to hide. Something they are terrified might ruin them."

"Rosa is entitled to her privacy. I know she had some struggles, and maybe she battles with PTSD. Who wouldn't after living through all that?"

"But you're stunned by her reaction. I can see it."

I shook my head. "I am surprised. This case must be weighing on her. Perhaps she feels a tremendous amount of pressure because it took place at a party we were hosting. I know I would. Especially with Quinn being out of pocket; you know when he gets back, he'll scrutinize her every move. Not to mention Harry trying to undermine her at every turn." I motioned toward the door to reference his visit.

"I might buy that, but when I asked her point-blank about the ad, she said you handled it, and she didn't have time for the"—she used finger quotes—"likes of me."

Hmm. "Rosa has her hands full," I said firmly.

"Say she isn't involved. Fine. But what if this"—she held up her iPad—"turns out to be something?"

I sighed heavily and massaged my temples. "What name was on the credit card used as payment? I can track them down."

Piper huffed and leaned back against the chair. "Like I can't? If that were possible. The payment was made with a prepaid Visa card."

"See, it's probably a juvenile prank."

She ran her fingers through her curls. "I know, I know. And normally I'd agree with you, but the threat feels heinous."

I chewed on my bottom lip. I could almost see Piper's thoughts running away with her. And mine were doing the same. Somewhere out there, a possible predator could be attempting a copycat crime. One we could cut off before they strike.

"When you tried to track down the email, the phone number they used, you came up with nothing but ghosts?"

Piper nodded.

"It's brazen to use a local police sergeant's name and attempt to blame the Jane Does." I didn't want to consider Piper's insinuation about Rosa.

She dropped her hands, her gaze sharpening. "Okay, whatever. Clearly if something happens in this town that has a link to someone you care about, you put blinders on." She shook her head and put her iPad back in her bag. "I'm disappointed. When we decided to work together last year, we made a pact to be honest and forthright with one another, no matter what. We deal with serious situations. Life-and-death sometimes. And if you can no longer hold up your end"—she shook her head—"perhaps this—"

"Wait a minute." I scooted to the edge of my seat and searched her face. "You just dropped a bomb about my friend, and you expect me to simply jump to the same conclusions because of a hunch you have? That isn't fair."

I studied her, suspecting she'd kept something from me. Not something our usual professional agreement allowed. I felt my eyes widen as realization struck. "My God. Harry told you something, didn't he? Something more than suspicions."

Her lips thinned, her usual aplomb with information nonexistent, and that sealed it.

I deflated, sitting back against the settee. Brad's opinion that the condition of the body didn't quite match the initial forensic assessment came back to mind. Her fears were warranted.

She raised her brows. "I see we're on the same page, and I had to tell Harry about the ad to be on the safe side. If Rosa isn't taking this seriously, someone else should. I wanted to see where your head is."

"Okay. Thanks. And since we're sharing . . ." I told her about the gray Ford Mustang, about being nearly mowed down and about a witness claiming they saw an argument between Patricia and the officer beside the car. It would be helpful if we could find out who owned the vehicle. For some reason, I believed the car could be linked.

"Got it." Piper made a note.

Our gazes locked. We were indeed on the same page, sentence, and word now. Not that I suspected Rosa. Piper didn't know her the way I did.

"The trust we've built as well as your friendship, I'd hate to lose." She picked up her bag and stood. We'd both understood when we engaged in this partnership that we'd never speak again if it ever was severed. Our jobs were too integral to who we were for a breach of trust not to destroy everything.

"Harry has concerns about Rosa overseeing the investigation. I wonder why?"

"Yeah, me too." I rose as well.

Her lips thinned. "Maybe someone should call Quinn."

Chapter Twelve

Magnolia Manor didn't have the same glamorous shine it'd had a week ago. There were no cars in the parking or overflow lot, and the grounds weren't bustling with excited travelers enjoying the scenery. Elaine wasn't on the front porch in a teak rocker with a cup of coffee. She'd sip her dark brew while she waited for her paper to be delivered—a scene from days gone by. Guests always mentioned her ritual in their reviews on Yelp. I'd read tons of them before we booked the party.

Now the darkness of crime encompassed the grounds. Patricia might not have intended to end her own life when she spewed threats, but this, I felt sure, was what she'd meant when she vowed to ruin her distant cousin, her greed and hatred eating up everything in its path like wildfire.

When Elaine had called last night and asked me to come by, I'd not hesitated. After my conversation with Piper, I needed to walk the crime scene myself.

The door creaked open ominously. Had it always creaked? The hallway bore the markers of forensic processing. I couldn't even imagine the amount of fingerprints and DNA found in this place. I had no idea how the police could process it cleanly with all the contamination. I pulled a couple of blue shoe coverings from the box forensics had left on the front desk. I had my own gloves and had already donned them.

"Lyla! You here?" I heard my gran calling.

"Gran? What are you doing here?"

"I had lunch with Elaine. Where are you?"

"Back here in the ballroom." Yellow crime scene tape blocked off the room. I ducked under it and scanned the space, not even sure what I was looking for yet.

"Thank you for coming." Elaine stood next to Gran outside the doorway.

When they started to duck under the tape as I had done, I held out a hand in a stopping motion. "No. Please stay in the hallway."

The pair of them nodded, looking anxious. Elaine said, "The reason I wanted you to come by isn't to go over the crime scene. I mean, I'm glad for you to, but I need your help again." She glanced back at my gran.

"Help with?" I watched the contemporaries' silent exchange. Eyebrows rose and lowered. Mouths contorted oddly in a rather comical display.

I continued slowly walking the room's perimeter while they sorted out whatever they wanted to tell me. I'd eventually find out everything anyway. Gran wasn't known for her ability to keep a secret.

"With Rosa. I think she is blaming me for Patricia's death," Elaine blurted.

"Why would you think that?" I stared down at the outline and bloodstain where Patricia had died.

"It's the way she looks at me. She's questioned and request-
ioned me about my whereabouts when Patricia did that horrible
thing to herself. She never looks like she believes me. I told her
I wasn't even in the room when it happened. She blames me! I
know she does."

"You aren't to blame. Please don't take that guilt upon yourself. Rosa is simply thorough. It's not uncommon to requestion
witnesses." I squatted down by the outline. "Have they found
the gun?" I didn't expect her to know everything that went on
here, but I still had to ask.

"No. Perhaps it's best if the police don't." Elaine sounded
distraught, and I glanced back to see Gran consoling her friend.
"Maybe this will all just go away if they don't. And I can't stay
at the hotel another night. All the looks and questions about
Patricia are unraveling my nerves."

"Hush, now." Gran hugged her friend. "Lyla is going to sort
this out."

"I'm sure we can find you another place to stay until they
wrap this all up."

"See." Gran patted Elaine's back. "I told you Lyla will solve
everything."

The confidence Gran had in me was astounding. I didn't
tell Elaine that we needed to locate the weapon. She wasn't
in any state to handle the news. It shouldn't be difficult to
find the gun if Patricia had used it that night. That probably
wasn't the first tip the cops had to go on. I could believe the
stampeding people had kicked the gun around the room; I
could not wrap my head around the possibility that the police
hadn't found the weapon, even with the number of people in
the room.

"Has their investigation kept them in this room?"

"Mostly. But cops have been all over the property looking for the gun. My bushes and walkways are in terrible shape."

"Huh." I rose and sighed, moving around the room. I futilely checked the corners and under the credenza, never expecting to find the gun. The police were looking to see if the perp, in a panic, had dropped the murder weapon in a bush as he fled the scene. They were operating under the assumption that this was a murder case. And that was why Rosa and Harry were handling the case the way they were. Their plan struck me as an intelligent one. If the guests believed the cause of death was a suicide, they'd be unguarded, speaking freely about what they recalled. But then, why wouldn't Rosa hear Piper out?

I slowly spun in a circle. What was I missing?

The party should have been fun. A murder mystery to be solved, with everyone going home unharmed and with a memory that would last a lifetime. We'd succeeded in the memory part.

I drove Gran and Elaine to my parents' new home. That was the easy part of helping Elaine. The house erected on twenty acres of land right outside of town would be far enough away to give her some seclusion and close enough for her to speak with the police when necessary. The land had once belonged to my father's great-uncle, who'd been a cattle farmer. My father had inherited the land years ago but had never done a thing with it. Last year they'd renovated the old two-story farmhouse to make it more modern and added more than a thousand extra square feet. It was a glorious modern farmhouse-style plantation with fruit trees and a long driveway lined with beautiful red maples.

Near dusk, Mother and I sat on the front porch, sipping a glass of wine. Her long elegant fingers wrapped around the glass. "Poor Elaine. I'm not sure how she's going to keep her business after something like this. She might as well sell the place. If anyone will buy it."

My mother looked just as at home in this setting as she had in my childhood home. I'd grown up on a street of pre–Civil War plantation-style houses. The structures were designed to handle Georgia's hot, humid weather, with large, deep front porches that boasted comfortable rocking chairs and whirling ceiling fans. I'd adored that street and the memories I had made there. But this place . . . I sighed as I took a deep sip from my glass. It felt like home too. And more to my taste.

"It was kind of you to offer her your guest room. Even though it's not ten minutes from the town square, being out here feels like a different place. It'll be good for her to have a respite."

Mother's big green eyes took me in. "I was glad to help. You aren't wearing yourself out, are you, dear? You've got big dark circles under your eyes. I wish Calvin would hire more help. He can't expect you to run the entire operation while he galivants around."

"He's hardly galivanting. It's work." I smiled into my glass. I didn't want to encourage my mother's worry. The changes that had occurred in our relationship were miraculous. She respected my work now and thought I was good at it. Not that she fully approved, but I couldn't expect everything. We were closer today than we ever had been.

My mother and Uncle Calvin had a tragic past. Something relating to their childhood. She'd hardly spoken about it before last year, when a tragedy had shined a great big spotlight on their past. She'd been seeing a therapist once a week for over a year now. And even though she'd once been adamantly against such measures, she'd gone in with an open mind. Odd, since my father was a psychiatrist. I commended her progress. Mother had even used her past to form a charity for women in need. She'd used her tragedy to inspire and help those desperately struggling to start new lives. Used it to save lives.

"I've got some concealer that would help with those."

She started to rise, and I put my hand on her arm. "Let's just sit here for a while. It's so lovely."

Mother settled back and smiled. "I arranged for a fund to be created for Amelia's niece. I could help with a shower, if that would be of use. Your plate is full."

I started to protest and insist I could manage to arrange the shower but decided against it. Mother wanted to help me. To feel she was doing something. It had come out in one of our sessions. "Thank you. It would help me a lot. We can tag-team the shower."

"Tag-team." A slow smile spread across her lips. "I like that."

Chapter Thirteen

Surprisingly, life settled into a mundane routine over the next few days. The Mustang had vanished, which meant it more than likely belonged to an attendee from out of town. We still hadn't had any luck finding the organizer of the Facebook party. The organizer had a bogus account. Go figure. And that had me concerned. I'd posted on our group page to alert our members and notified Facebook.

I went to work and ran by and checked on my parents, Gran, and Elaine, who had made herself at home with my folks. And wonderfully, I believed my mother enjoyed having her around to entertain Gran. Mother found Gran to be a little much at times. My gran had a boisterous personality—something I adored. Nothing had broken regarding Patricia's death. Not publicly, at least, and the town needed closure, Elaine especially. The police had released her property, but she'd decided to keep it closed for a while longer. The constant news reports were hurting her business anyway. She'd told me about all the cancellations during my last visit.

What plagued me, and I had a hard time dealing with, was the idea that someone had shot the woman while we were all laughing and enjoying ourselves. While we believed the shouts and protests were part of the staged death, Patricia had fought for her life. The thought gave me a sick feeling in the pit of my stomach.

Rosa was worrying me as well. She'd been distant on our last phone call, and I'd gone to her several times with my worries regarding the false Jane Doe party listing. Rosa had explained that work had her busy and told me not to worry. She was adamant that the listing was nothing more than a stupid prank. Her tone told me she wanted to drop the subject. For some reason, I couldn't get what Gran had told me about Rosa out of my head. Whatever had upset my friend that night might be contributing to her stress. Clearly, personal issues were going on in her life that she didn't want to discuss with me. She'd made that crystal clear when I'd asked her point-blank about it.

"God, Lyla!" she'd yelled. "Can a person have any privacy in this town?"

Then she'd said she had to go without letting me explain, which I'd found particularly bothersome. And after that, I'd begun to reconsider the secrets Rosa harbored. I'd even gone as far as to have Piper forward me what she'd found. I'd done an initial search on Rosa as well, telling myself better safe than sorry. Rosa would have done the same in my situation. I hadn't found anything other than a former complaint against her from a soldier who'd dealt with anger issues after a tour, but most of the specifics were redacted from the report. It would take some serious digging to find out more.

Once the case was closed and life had calmed down, we'd have a long conversation and sort things out. I'd explain my position, and Rosa would understand. While she didn't see a potential connection between Patricia's death and the ad or the person impersonating her, I would rule nothing out. I still hadn't given up on the Mustang, and she had. I'd asked Brad to see if he could pull records of Mustang sales in the area in the last four weeks. I had to know for sure it hadn't belonged to a local.

It was Tuesday night, and Brad and I were drinking at our favorite local bar spot downtown. We usually had dinner on date night, but Brad had texted at the last minute informing me he'd be late and we'd just meet for a drink. I'd swallowed my annoyance and uneasiness when he'd turned down my idea of coming straight to my house and having takeout. I'd been battling with the recent changes in him as well. A couple of months ago, our relationship had seemed perfect, but now it gave me a sense of instability—something I detested.

When Brad had arrived, he'd been all smiles, and I'd almost convinced myself everything was fine. Now, though, he stared at me over the rim of his beer glass. His expression was an unsteadying one. One I couldn't quite identify. The nerves kicked up again.

"You never sent me the car records. Did you have trouble getting your buddy to pull them?" I took a sip from my wineglass.

"No. I went through them. There were only three cars around the similar year model that would match sales, and they have been ruled out."

"Oh. Why didn't you send the records to me? A second set of eyes could be useful." I couldn't keep the annoyance from setting in.

"Because I'm telling you, they weren't a match. A statewide search would be better, but without good cause, I can't ask that favor." He took another sip from his glass.

"You didn't think it would be prudent to have the eyewitness take a look? Just to be safe." I was the one who'd had an up-close-and-personal view of the car.

He leaned back in his chair. "Fine. I'll see that you get the records."

"Thank you." I sighed.

His brows drew together. "You seem rattled. More than I anticipated. Not taking anything away from the brutality of the crime, but we've investigated a lot of ugly murders."

"I think I'm appropriately rattled." I leaned forward. "Did you say murder?" I glanced around to make sure no one had overheard me. Given the noise level, no one paid any attention to us. "Did you hear something from Harry? You mentioned he'd kept in touch with you the other day. Are they making the official ruling?" I'd been surprised when Brad had told me Harry was eager to pick his brain about working on cold cases. Harry hadn't struck me as the ambitious ladder-climbing type.

He nodded. "Harry has been pushing the coroner. They expect it any day now."

"I wonder why Rosa didn't say something when we spoke yesterday." Probably because she'd been miffed with me for questioning her.

He shrugged ambiguously. "Maybe you're too close to this one."

Piper's point that I might struggle with blinders came rushing back and made me even more cautious in my speculations. And right now, Brad seemed like he was withholding from me too. I'd wanted to call my uncle and run everything by him. He'd been my boss and mentor way before I'd had Brad to mull cases over with.

But not being able to contact Uncle Calvin forced me to dig deeper and find my inner strength, which I found positive. I began to wonder if, when Patricia's death was ruled a homicide, Rosa would arrive at the same theory Piper and I had—that someone could be playing a sick game with us. In that scenario, we would need to find out what made Patricia a target.

I stared at Brad, who was looking handsome in his tan slacks and flat bronze button-down shirt, and didn't recognize him. "Did you literally just make that statement?"

He didn't waver. Didn't blink. "I did. And you didn't answer my question."

I held his gaze. "What question?"

"Why do you think this woman's murder has shaken you?" He wiped his mouth and leaned back against the chair. He wasn't calloused; I could read that if nothing else. Death was something he and I saw a lot of in our line of work. Some cases struck deeper than others. Jane Does were those cases for me. Cousins Investigative Services worked alongside the GBI on some of the Jane Does cases Brad worked up Interstate 85. There were nearly thirty open cases to date. And the number seemed to keep growing. The bodies were discovered in the rural areas off the interstate far north of Atlanta. That area had been dubbed the dumping grounds. And most of the murders were gruesome.

"Okay, you got me. I guess this one feels more personal somehow. Seeing the light leave someone's eyes makes a mark on you. At least it has with me. I need to know what happened to the woman and why."

"Even if she made your client's life a living hell?"

"What kind of question is that? Yes, even then. Elaine didn't hate the woman, and she simply wanted what was rightfully hers." I studied Brad, pondering. The brackets around his mouth, the intensity of his dark eyes, the lack of the usual warmth they held for me. "What's going on, Brad?"

He raised his brows, his expression blank. "I'm not sure I know what you mean."

I felt my brows pull together. "Yes you do."

He glanced around for the waitress and held up his empty glass.

Why was he evading? "Just tell me."

He made a grumbling noise and said, "I've caught a case."

He always had a new case, or so it seemed to me. And I wasn't buying that as the excuse. New cases invigorated him. Gave him purpose, he'd once told me.

"That's it?"

"That's it." He met my gaze and held it.

Okay, maybe I was off base. "Anything you want to share?"

"Can't." The waitress deposited another beer on the table. He thanked her and took a sip. "This one is . . . different. I'm on an active investigation. Not one of my usual cold cases."

That sounded interesting and poked holes in my original assumption of the situation. But why would they take Brad off cold cases if he hadn't requested it? Or had he been looking for a change? Wouldn't he have felt comfortable discussing that with me? Had he lost the zeal for the Jane Doe cases? My heart sank a little as I realized this could be the end of our working relationship.

"Okay," I said slowly, deciding not to push. Brad would discuss it with me when he could. Though this would be the first case he'd ever caught that he hadn't shared with me—that I knew of, at least.

"I take it you and Rosa are on the outs." He steered us back to our normal territory, and suddenly I felt grateful.

I kept my voice low. So low Brad had to lean in to hear me over the soft music playing in the background. "Not on the outs per se. But she's acting strangely. I'm not sure if it's from the pressure of being the acting chief, the undermining from Harry's misgivings, or something else altogether." I rubbed my finger down the condensation on the glass. "If it's the latter, well, then we may have bigger problems."

"How do you mean?" Brad folded his big hands on the table.

I told him about the announcement in the *Gazette* and the online presence the author of the announcement had. "I wasn't able to get the group closed online but made it publicly clear that the group didn't belong to our club and personally contacted the people on my friends list."

Brad seemed to ponder my words, then shook his head. "Small towns. It's probably a prank. And it wouldn't even raise eyebrows if this case—which should be well under way—was being run efficiently."

I frowned. "What are you saying? That Rosa is to blame?"

"Take your pick who's to blame. The inexperienced officers, a medical examiner who is stretched between two counties, and an acting chief who is clearly out of her depth." He waved a hand toward me. "Then you have the investigator thinking she knows better than the police."

I blinked at him, stunned for a few seconds. I didn't recognize this man across the table from me. "That isn't fair." My voice cracked, and I hated myself for it. "I don't think I know better. I'm just trying to be thorough. Piper's just doing her job and alerted Harry to be on the safe side," I said, a tad hurt and a great deal miffed. He didn't dismiss my instincts often. Or insult me ever.

"I'm sorry." His expression softened, and he placed both elbows on the table and placed his fingers on his forehead. "The stuff I've seen over the last week has been unimaginable."

I placed my hand on his arm. "You can talk to me."

He dropped his hands and pulled back. "See, I don't want to. And why would you want me to?" He didn't wait for me to answer. "That's what I loved about Sweet Mountain." He gave me a sad smile. "None of that BS makes its way here. I need a place where I can put that part of my life away. Just for a little while."

Our eyes were locked. My heart pounded. I could see how desperately Brad needed to escape whatever case he'd caught. How tired he was of discussing such matters. But there was so much more there.

His phone chirped. He dug it out of his pocket, and his eyes lit with their usual sharp glint. "Jones here. Give me a minute." Brad slid to his feet. "Listen, I know you're worried and have good instincts. But life is too short to go chasing dead ends. Until you know otherwise, I'd put it out of your mind and really consider what it is you want with your life." He made an imperious gesture with his hand. "I've got to take this." He put the phone back to his ear. "Yeah, I'm here." He mouthed, "Sorry."

My mind reeled. *Figure out what I want for my life?* What an unusual thing for him to say; it was so unlike Brad. He knew and understood what I wanted for my life. Or so I'd thought.

Put it out of my mind. He knew it wasn't that simple. And it wasn't a response I would ever give him if he were in a similar situation. Brad weaved through the crowded bar toward the exit.

I could hardly see him from where I perched at one of the small high tables in the back of the bar.

Sighing, I decided not to dwell on his lack of attention, chalking it up to his grueling schedule and cases. Clearly, he had more pressing matters than his girlfriend and her woes. And from his expression when he'd alluded to how horrific the case he was working was, I'd give him some leeway. When he got back, though, we'd have to talk this out. He'd seriously confused me.

I finished my wine and glanced around the dining room. Locals were enjoying their night out, all smiles and lots of laughter. I tried not to be envious. A couple to my left caught my attention. She had both hands to her mouth as she stared down at her date. He was on his knees before her with a small velvet box in his hand. My heart rate sped up as the woman began nodding her head emphatically. It was a scene right out of a romance novel I'd read years ago—well, except for the location. Then man scooped her up in his arms and spun her around. The entire bar cheered as he shouted, "She said yes!"

I sighed and glanced back in the direction Brad had gone. My mother used to tell me how different life would be if I'd chosen another path. Was that what Brad had meant? That not only had I gone into investigations, but I'd also chosen a man who'd spent his life doing the same? And even he got tired of dinner conversations being about criminals and murder. We could discuss other things, of course. Sports, the weather, town gossip, whatever—I could do that. But as to my path, this was the only one I knew how to walk, and the only one I desired to. And most of the time, we were blissfully happy.

Our jobs kept us busy. Brad had his work, and I had mine. We worked together often. Lately, though, it seemed, we'd had less and less time together, which gave my earlier assumption more weight. And Cousins hadn't taken a Jane Doe case in three months. I thought back to Mel's comment about Brad leaving the morning after Patricia's death and Piper's about blinders. Had this relationship run its course and I'd not seen it? Was that what he was trying to tell me? Tears stung my eyes, and I fought to keep them at bay.

Tammy, our server and a member of our book club, came around with a bottle of champagne and two glasses. "The happy couple is treating everyone to a glass. You want?"

"No thanks." I simply wasn't in a celebratory sort of mood.

She nodded and went back to the bar. I was surprised when she came right back with my favorite drink, a pear martini. "Oh, I almost forgot with all the excitement. The drink"—Tammy dug into her black apron pocket—"is from the man at the end of the bar there." She pointed to the farthest end of the bar, close to the door.

I cast a glance toward the bar and couldn't tell whom she was referencing. I sat back.

"He asked me to give this to you." She handed me a folded slip of paper. "I know you're with Brad, and I told him you weren't available. He insisted anyway. He's smokin' hot."

"Which one is he again?" I leaned back and craned my head in the direction she motioned and saw a man standing with his glass raised. I couldn't discern much about him except his enormous size. His stature was much larger than that of most of the men in the room. "You go for him," I said when I saw her flush as she stared at the man.

A couple of local guys called, "Tammy, we need another pitcher here, sweetheart."

"I think I might." She winked at me. "Gotta scoot."

Not being able to resist my favorite cocktail, I took a sip of the martini. Tammy had to have guided his drink choice. I smiled when I glanced back and noticed the man still staring. Whether I was interested or not didn't take away the rush of pleasure from knowing someone found me attractive. Especially after the conversation I'd just had with Brad. I opened the little folded paper and expected to find his number or a tired pickup line.

Instead, I read:

He's a cheater. You deserve better.

I gaped, anxiety drying out my mouth as I slid off the stool and went looking for the man, but I could no longer locate him through the throngs of people.

My phone pinged three times in succession.

I pulled it from my bag and felt like I'd been sucker punched right in the gut as I read the texts.

Sorry.

I had to run.

Call you later.

Chapter Fourteen

I stood outside the bar, brooding and glancing down at my phone, while I waited on Mel to pick me up. How could Brad do this to me? Not even come back in to say he had to leave? Seriously? *A text!* A freaking text!

"You look like you're ready to murder someone. Not me, I hope."

I glanced at the man on the periphery of my attention. He'd been standing there for a minute or so, not speaking. For which I'd been grateful.

I took a step farther away while I vacillated on whether to engage. I supposed the man had been waiting for me to notice him and become impatient. He was a huge man, standing at least four to five inches above my five-foot-night frame. His biceps stretched the limits of the gray button-down shirt he wore. He had curly dark-blond hair pulled back in a tiny ponytail.

He cleared his throat. "I hope I didn't put you off by my note. I—"

He's the one! Mortification nearly overwhelmed me, but I got a handle on my insecurities, turned toward him, and stared him straight in his chiseled-looking face. "Who are you?"

"Just a guy in a bar who can relate."

"I haven't the foggiest idea as to what you're referring to. Leave me alone." Having no desire to discuss my private life with an opportunistic male, I turned my back on him.

"Hey, listen, I didn't mean any harm. It just rubs me the wrong way to see someone mistreating a woman. I overheard your man talking on the phone and glancing back at you. Some people haven't any scruples." He took a step closer toward me, and when I didn't budge, he gave me a small smile. "I sent the drink over not as an attempt to pick you up, just a hello from one dejected person to another."

My heart began to ache within my chest. I forced myself not to focus on it. I blinked a few times and kept my expression blank. Anger radiated through my body. "My boyfriend had a work thing. It's no big deal. And this is none of your business."

Why am I explaining myself to this stranger?

"Sorry, I didn't mean to intrude. If I've overstepped, I apologize." The wind kicked up, and I caught the scent of his cologne. It was rich, warm, and spicy.

I cleared my throat and realized that I must look unhinged, judging by the glances of those passing by. "I didn't mean to sound so hateful. I'm not normally like this. I apologize. Have a nice night, and thanks for the drink."

I turned and had started to stalk away when I realized I hadn't any place to go. My car wasn't in the lot. Melanie hadn't arrived yet. I decided to move down the sidewalk and took the vacated seat on the bench.

"Hey, you have nothing to apologize for," the man called after me, and I felt my shoulders slump forward as he took a seat next to me on the bench. I didn't have the energy to ask him to leave. I hoped I wouldn't regret that later. Or the fact that I might be using his attraction to me as a confidence booster.

"Let's start over." He extended his hand. "I'm Dean," he said, his voice warm as melted butter on a hot biscuit. His tone was devoid of a Georgia accent. It still sounded southern but more low-country. South Carolina, maybe.

I took his hand. "Hi. I'm Lyla."

His eyes lit up with the hope a man gets when he thinks he has a shot.

I expelled a deep breath. "I'm not interested, Dean. I do appreciate the effort. But I'm in a relationship, and I do believe you misconstrued what you overheard."

He held his hands up in supplication. "I didn't mean to upset you. Your man talks loudly. I heard him talking to a woman, and he sounded like a man explaining himself."

"My boyfriend is in law enforcement, and sometimes the job calls at odd hours. He works with women." I raised my brow.

He ducked his head. "Of course. I may be projecting my own relationship disaster onto you. I've been reeling for a while now. I'll leave you in peace. I've caused you enough trouble for the night." He started to rise.

He looked so downtrodden that I felt terrible for being rude and abrasive. "No. Listen, it's okay. I've not seen you around before."

He settled back on the bench and smiled. He had a friendly smile. "I have a confession to make. Courtney pointed you out to me when I first arrived in town."

I cocked my head toward him, leery once more. "Courtney Hampton?"

He nodded. "Well, Daniels now, but yes. I only got a glimpse that day. You were stunning in that vintage dress. Took my breath away."

I turned on the bench and studied him, his profile illuminated by the streetlight. "You were at the party?"

He smiled again. "I was, but not for long. My date got sick, and we left before the shooting." His eyes softened. "I read in the paper that you tried to save that woman."

"Yes." I repositioned myself, facing forward, and crossed my legs. "But I would rather not talk about it."

"I get that." His phone pinged, and he leaned toward me to dig it out of his pocket. His shoulder brushed against mine. And this close, I realized his cologne was a little overwhelming and a tad offensive. He tapped on the screen. "Well, again, I'm sorry if my advances were unwelcome. Won't happen again. I wish you the best of luck, and I hope I'm wrong about your man." He startled me by putting a hand on my shoulder, and when I met his gaze, he seemed sincerer in his well wishes. He had the look of someone who'd experienced many difficulties in his life.

"Have a good night." He rose and stretched. "Maybe I'll see you around before I leave."

"Maybe. Have a good night too." I watched him walk up the sidewalk and cross the train tracks, bypassing the pedestrian crossing path, before I checked my phone. Brad hadn't texted again or called. I battled with annoyance and a dash of humiliation.

Sighing, I glanced around the parking lot. I had no idea what was taking Mel so long. Not that I would pester her. She'd been kind enough to agree to pick me up, ending her date with Wyatt early. I'd insisted I'd get an Uber, but she wouldn't hear of it.

The night was cool but not overly so. I took in my surroundings—the town center lit up with lights, people coming and going, laughing. I didn't have all the answers to my current trials, but I would if I took a minute. Sometimes I needed to take a step back. I popped in my AirPods and decided to listen to *The Therapist* by B. A. Paris. I'd bought it to listen to while hiking. I needed it now.

I was a chapter in and completely engrossed when my phone pinged. Startled, I nearly jumped out of my skin. I laughed, feeling much better as I glanced down to read Mel's text.

I'm across the parking lot.

I stepped off the curb and scanned the lot. Melanie stood leaning against her car with her phone to her ear. She waved urgently at me when she saw me. The closer I got, the more I became convinced that something was wrong. Her posture went stiff. "Wait a minute, Nanna, calm down. I can't understand you. You're talking too fast."

My phone started buzzing in my hand with Gran's tone. I read her text as I weaved through the lot toward Mel's car.

I'm at Maria's Mexican Bar and Grill with Elaine and Kathy Smart.

The little blue dots came across the screen.

Rosa is here in an official capacity.

I glanced up to watch for cars when the dots reappeared.

Hurry!!!!!

I quickly responded.

On my way.

Melanie grabbed my arm the second I reached her. "No!" she said sharply into the receiver. "Stay right there. I'm coming. No, Nanna. I'll be there in less than two minutes. Tell

Lyla's gran that she's with me. We're by the bridge at Ate Track Bar."

A police car drove past us with its light flashing.

"I see them. We're coming!" Melanie said over the sirens.

I shoved my phone back into my bag and started to jog, my booted heels pounding against the pavement.

"Wait! Lyla, let's take the car."

"No time!" I shouted over my shoulder. When I made it around the corner of the square, dodging cars and people who had begun to gather, gaping across the railroad tracks at the other side of the square, I saw Gran, Elaine, and Melanie's nanna. Gran was wagging her finger in Rosa's face while Miss Kathy guarded Elaine. Miss Kathy wouldn't allow Rosa closer than two yards from the upset woman. The sight would have been comical if it were anyone else and the situation a different one.

"Ladies, I don't mean any disrespect. I understand that you are all upset. But I have a job to do, and I'm going to need you to step aside," Rosa said calmly yet firmly. "We are going to take Mrs. Morgan over to the police department just to have a chat."

"A chat my behind, Rosa Landry," my plucky gran shouted. "You are targeting this sweet senior citizen, and we won't stand for it." Gran folded her bony arms, indignation written all over her pale face. "Someone should tan your hide."

"You tell her, Daisy," Miss Kathy thundered as she gesticulated wildly. "This is injustice. Plain and simple." There was no doubt where Melanie had inherited that particular trait. Miss Kathy's wrinkled face was flushed with excitement, her warm brown eyes full of fire. She was on the shorter and the rounder side, but a formidable creature nonetheless.

"Get out there and hunt down the person responsible and leave this poor woman alone." Gran's white hair bounced around her head as she continued to wage war.

"Slow down. Sheesh, my thighs are burning." Melanie struggled to catch her breath as she caught up with me. Melanie wasn't the athletic type though petite and lean genetically. "What in the world is Rosa doing?"

"Looks like she's planning on arresting Elaine."

"I can't believe it. I thought Nanna must be mistaken or perhaps overreacting." Melanie looked aghast at the sight before us.

"Lyla!" Gran spotted me the second I threaded through the crowd in front of the restaurant. "Finally, someone who will set you straight."

Gran had forgotten diplomacy worked way better than insults or threats. I sidestepped Harry, who stood with his hand resting on his gun. I bristled and gave him a dead-level stare. "There will be no need for that, Harry."

I took a deep breath when he made no move to remove his hand from his service weapon. My heart thundered—another tragedy in the making.

"My God. These are upstanding older women of the community. There's no need for this show of force. Right?" I pleaded with Rosa's more reasonable nature as I made eye contact with my friend.

She seemed to take a minute to focus on me before she took notice of her officer's overly aggressive posture and shook her head. "Of course there's no need for force. Stand down, Officer Daniels." Rosa's voice was commanding.

"Sergeant, there is a mob forming behind us." Harry sounded amazed and affronted.

I couldn't believe my ears and positioned myself between Harry and the senior women. When Rosa didn't immediately respond, I interjected, "No, there isn't. These people are simply curious."

"Yes, and these curious folks are going to take several steps back." Rosa aimed her voice toward the people gawking and videoing with their phones. "We have a warrant for Elaine Morgan's arrest."

"An arrest warrant?" They must've found the murder weapon.

"She will come along peacefully, right, Mrs. Morgan?" Rosa took a step toward the three seniors huddled together.

Gran opened her mouth to protest. I could tell by the exasperation written all over her face that she'd further attempt to prevent the arrest. I intercepted Rosa and whispered, "Two seconds. Please." I searched my friend's dark gaze, hoping to discern where we were. I wasn't happy with what I found there. Her usual assured demeanor had vacated, and she looked, well, desperate. "Rosa, please."

Upon her reluctant nod, I turned to my grandmother. "Gran, Elaine has to go with them. This is nonnegotiable. But—" I glanced over at Miss Kathy and Elaine, thinking quickly. "We will make sure a lawyer meets her at the police department. Rosa," I said over my shoulder before turning back to Elaine. "Mrs. Morgan is formally asking for a lawyer, aren't you?"

"Y . . . yes. I want a lawyer." Elaine's voice came out broken and shaky.

My God, this is insane.

I glanced at the crowd around the Mexican restaurant's outdoor dining area. Mel stood out front, flabbergasted, with both hands to her mouth. Rosa's face glistened with sweat, even in the coolness of the night. And I could tell how angry Harry was with my interference.

I couldn't fathom why Rosa had made this a scene. She could have waited until Elaine got home to arrest her. Rosa was aware that Elaine was staying with my parents. Realization struck. That was precisely why the arrest would happen here. My father would have insisted on calling his attorney. He was known for his deep belief in representation when it came to dealing with law enforcement.

"Gran, call Mr. Greene." I glanced down at my phone, which opened with facial recognition, and handed it to her. "His number is in my favorites. I'm sure he'll be willing to represent our friend."

Gran's head bobbed up and down, and she stepped aside to make the call.

I crept slowly toward Gran's contemporaries. "Ladies, Mr. Greene is the very best in his field. He'll get to the bottom of this. Elaine, I swear to you that you'll be in the best of hands with him. He's represented my family for decades. And I'll offer to assist him and do everything I can. I know this is difficult, and I'm sorry it has to be this way, but if they have a warrant for your arrest, there isn't anything else I can do. Don't say a word until Mr. Greene arrives."

Elaine nodded slowly and gripped my arm, pulling me closer to her. "I found the gun and turned it over to the police. I should never have picked it up. I should have called and reported it instead. What have I done?" Her eyes were full of water, and my heart nearly broke. This sweet old lady had never been in trouble a day in her life.

The murder weapon had her prints on it. Had they checked her hands for gun residue that night? Because they hadn't checked mine. Or those of anyone else in my club that I was aware of. An argument to be made in court. Still, it looked terrible. "It's going to be okay. Tell Mr. Greene everything. Leave nothing out." I took Elaine's arm after I squeezed Miss Kathy's hand.

Melanie rushed forward and took her weeping nanna in her arms. The daggers she shot at Rosa were lethal.

Reluctantly, I led the shaking senior over to Rosa, who had her cuffs out. I met Rosa's stern gaze, staring her straight in the face. "There's no need for that." There would be no moving me on this one. If she pushed me, I'd make this even more of a scene. One call to Piper and she'd have a news crew here in minutes.

Protests from the crowd became audible.

"Good God, the acting chief is going to handcuff an old woman?"

"What's this world coming to?"

"Hey, Harry! Where's your cousin? Someone needs to do something about this."

Rosa's defiant eyes held mine, and for a second, I thought she would cuff poor Elaine anyway. And I could tell she was considering it. Flexing her authority here could backfire. I gave my head a tiny shake and glanced out to the crowd. I did not like that it felt like we were on opposing sides here. Hated it. But right was right. When she put the cuffs away, I let out a sigh of relief.

"This way, Mrs. Morgan." Rosa gently took Elaine's arm and led her to her cruiser.

The crowd had grown, a lot more phones were out now, and I was sure this arrest would hit YouTube in the next five minutes. Good God!

Elaine hadn't even been in the ballroom when the murder occurred. Her staff would corroborate her story. This arrest seemed like a haphazard one. What in the world was the DA thinking?

Lots more muttered murmurs and shouts echoed around us.

"Release Elaine!"

"Elaine is innocent!"

"I'm calling the news to report this injustice!" someone from the increasing crowd shouted.

Gran handed me my phone and shook her fist into the air to encourage the crowd. "Elaine is innocent," she shouted before she looped her arm through mine. "William is on his way. These folks won't stand by and let this happen." Despite her brave performance moments ago, I could feel the tremor in her limbs, and she kept sniffing and patting her eyes with the tissue in her hand.

I hugged her close, listening to the roars of protestors. It sure didn't appear that Sweet Mountain would stand for this. Melanie and Miss Kathy huddled close to us as we watched Elaine's small brown head bow in the back seat as Rosa pulled away.

Piper was right. I would be calling Quinn tonight.

Chapter Fifteen

"It took me forever to calm Nanna down. She loves deeply. Thank God we got there when we did. I can't even imagine how bad things could have been." Melanie handed me a cup of tea and settled next to me on my white tuft sofa.

"Yeah." I blew on the surface of the steamy hot tea, still in disbelief. Melanie and I hadn't even attempted to reach out to Rosa. We both understood we had to let the process play out now.

"It was really sweet of Daisy to stay over with Nanna tonight. They'll be able to comfort each other."

"Rile each other up is more like it." I could see Gran and Miss Kathy scheming to bust their friend out of jail. An honest-to-God Lucy-and-Ethel type of scheme.

Melanie laughed when I told her my vision of our two grandmothers bulldozing down the side of the jail and rescuing their friend. "Yeah, with Sally Anne at the wheel."

I nodded and laughed. Gran's friend Sally Anne was a character for sure. It was the levity the evening needed.

"Have you heard from Amelia?"

I shook my head. "Not since she called to tell me they arrived safely and her sister received a fifteen-year sentence."

"Wow. I can't even imagine." Melanie's eyes were wide, and she gave her head a shake. "I still feel awful about the way I acted at Nobles. She said she forgave me, but I haven't forgiven myself yet. I get so carried away sometimes that I forget that I can come across as a raving witch."

"Melanie Smart, you are the farthest thing from a witch. Stop beating yourself up. Amelia understood, and she was in a mood too. Emotions were running high."

Mel bowed her head. "I've debated calling, but I know she'll be focusing on Sasha. Ugh, the guilt."

I squeezed Mel's arm. "She wouldn't want you to feel that way. I think it's best if we wait to hear from her."

Melanie smiled. "You're right. She'll be delighted when we tell her about your mother's fund raiser. Amelia has nothing to worry about with Frances Moody tugging the purse strings of the county's most wealthy donors."

"So true. Mother is serious about her philanthropy."

"I can't wait for Amelia to come home. Life seems weird without her here. Like part of our family is missing. And she would flip her lid if she knew what happened tonight. How Rosa went all O.K. Corral on us."

That was a little extreme, but I got her meaning. And we were a family—one with some issues at present, but a family nonetheless.

Mel exhaled loudly. "Life is out of sorts, and I hate it."

I nodded, feeling the same. "Tomorrow we should know more. Mr. Greene will find out what the police have." I felt a tremendous amount of gratitude toward our family attorney. He'd told me on the phone that the police were stonewalling at present. He'd chuckled then and told me to wait to hear from him. And that Elaine had requested that I specifically be assigned to her defense team. This whole situation would be a sticky mess, since a friend of mine was at the helm of the investigation. I mentioned the conflict to Mel.

Melanie placed her mug on the coffee table. "Yeah, but justice must be served. And we both know Elaine isn't guilty. Besides, you know, even before tonight, Rosa hasn't been herself. Something is up with her."

I nodded and told her about the phone call Gran had witnessed and how Rosa had nearly bitten my head off when I mentioned it.

"See! That's what I'm talking about—and tonight." Melanie shook her head. "I mean, I get she's doing her job. I do. And she must have her reasons for arresting Elaine. Evidence and all. Maybe someone is trying to frame Elaine, I don't know. And I don't want to jump to conclusions, like I usually do, and pass judgment before I have the facts. But it's little Elaine." Melanie scrubbed her face with her hands. "How insane is the notion?"

"Pretty insane." I sipped from my mug. "There isn't any motive I can see, and I've racked my brain." It had been instinct when I offered to reach out to our family attorney. I shifted and gave Mel part of my chunky blue chenille blanket.

"Her cousin was the disgruntled gun-waving lunatic, not Elaine." Mel pulled the blanket higher on her lap. "Although now I feel a little guilty for speaking ill of the dead."

We both swallowed, and I could tell we were both reliving the moment we'd seen the poor woman on the floor. Where had the gun been all that time? And where exactly had Elaine found the weapon? That could lend itself to suspicion.

The prosecution could present a scenario in which Elaine had hidden the murder weapon. But then why wouldn't she have gotten rid of it instead of turning it over to the police? Ugh. I rubbed my forehead and let Melanie in on my thoughts.

"Clearly, it shows her innocence that when she found the weapon, she turned it in. Someone counted on her honest nature to throw the scent off them."

"Yeah, and Elaine had no concerns that the police would suspect her, or she wouldn't have turned the weapon over. It's plain as day."

My stomach swam. Elaine had been aware of the risk, though. She'd mentioned it to me the day I'd gone by and searched the ballroom. Elaine had worried that Rosa blamed her for Patricia's murder. She'd also said it might be best if the weapon never surfaced. Huh . . .

"What? I can see the wheels turning." Melanie looked concerned. "You don't actually think—"

"No, no." I waved my hand.

"Good. Because as you just mentioned, the fact that Elaine did turn the gun in should have been enough to rule her out. She isn't a criminal mastermind."

I kept my musings to myself. Now my concerns for Elaine deepened. There'd been witnesses everywhere. Witnesses who'd overheard the cousins arguing. People who'd seen the stress Patricia had put Elaine under, and now the murder weapon had miraculously appeared with her prints on it. I put my mug on the end table and rubbed my temples.

"What?"

I could have kicked myself. Why hadn't I already called the medical examiner? I needed more information to make any other deductions. "I'm just curious to see the forensic and coroner's report. I'm sure Mr. Greene will have access to it soon."

Melanie gave me a solid head nod. "I feel better knowing you're helping her. Not that I don't trust Mr. Greene; I just trust you more."

"Thanks for the vote of confidence." I gave my best friend a smile and squeezed her hand. Melanie's opinion of me professionally carried a lot of weight.

A text came through, and I gaped.

Inundated with work. Can't talk.

Chapter Sixteen

Mel leaned over and read Brad's excuse. I put the phone on the end table.

"You texted him about the arrest?"

I nodded numbly. "When I got home." I took a deep breath and rubbed my face. Even after he'd understood my situation, Brad hadn't called. He'd texted me. A terse text at that. Not exactly a sign of romantic love.

"I'm sorry, hon." She wrapped her arm around my shoulder. "What a horrible night you've had. I can't believe you're even sitting upright. You are so strong." Her voice lowered into hostile territory. "I could murder him."

I wrapped my arms around my knees as I pulled them to my chest and leaned my head on her shoulder. "No, I'm fine. I should cut Brad some slack. He didn't run out. He had a case. He texted me."

Why did I feel the need to defend him?

Melanie scoffed. "No. He left and stuck you with the bill. I'm sorry, I liked Brad in the beginning, but now he's on my shit list."

"It's work. We have an understanding when it comes to our work." I let out a long-drawn-out sigh. This was not me.

"Um." Mel coughed. "Are you sure it's work?" She stiffened, and I sat up straight, turning to directly face her.

"Wine?" She got up and clapped her hands together. "Let's have some wine."

"I don't want any wine." I slid to my feet, following her into the kitchen.

"Sure you do." She kept her back to me. "Red or white? Do you have both?"

Oh. My. God. Why had everyone, including a stranger, seen what I hadn't? "Mel."

She opened the refrigerator and stuck her head inside. "Hmm?"

She still didn't turn around, and I made a token attempt at blocking the deluge of fear and doubt.

"Melanie Jean Smart." My tone held a warning.

"You're out of wine." She came out with two beers and giggled. One of her typical Melanie giggles. Oh no. She opened both bottles with the flip-flop bottle opener magnet stuck to the fridge. I took the beer and stared at her.

Melanie, my boisterous, chattering, never-at-a-loss-for-words best friend, fell silent. And that terrified me. She couldn't hide things from me. No, we'd been inseparable since the first day of kindergarten. We'd been through everything together—first loves, first heartbreaks, major family issues, and her divorce. We always had each other's backs, no matter what. Figuratively and quite literally. Not only was her business right next door to Cousins, but her townhouse butted up against mine. She got me like no one else. And right now, she'd know I would not let this go. I waited while she tipped her bottle back and guzzled.

My nerves were doing somersaults, and I was glad I hadn't eaten much. Had I been in denial because I hadn't wanted to see what was right in front of me? I did not want to be that woman. Ever. I didn't need a man. But Brad was different. Or at least I'd believed he was.

She put the half-empty bottle on the bar with a clunk and covered her mouth when a little belch escaped. "Excuse me. Now, listen. Like I said, I know I was totally Team Brad in the beginning. And he seemed great. We all thought y'all were the perfect match. I could envision your wedding and my amazing maid-of-honor dress. I even had a few picked out just in case." Melanie wouldn't meet my gaze.

"Mel, quit stalling." I perched on the barstool and took a sip from the bottle. "It's me. Shoot me straight. Like always."

"Okay." Melanie leaned on the bar, fiddling with her hands. "Remember when Wyatt went to that work convention in Atlanta and Brad said to give him a shout one evening when he was free, and they'd meet up for a drink at a bar he frequents?" Upon my nod, she continued, "Well, Wyatt did reach out, and they scheduled to meet, but there was some confusion. Wyatt thought Brad said Friday night when the text clearly read Saturday. Brad had sent him a calendar invite, and Wyatt got the date mixed up." She took another gulp from the bottle.

I tore at the label on the bottle, waiting for her to drop the bomb. With all her dithering, I knew what she was going to say. That stupid guy at the restaurant had warned me just tonight. And Mel wouldn't act this way otherwise. "Who is she?"

Melanie shook her head, her eyes full of pity. "I'm so sorry. Wyatt didn't know. She and Brad were playing pool, and Wyatt approached and noticed how"—she sucked her bottom lip into her mouth—"familiar they acted with each other."

The emotions threatened to overwhelm me. Eviscerated. Betrayed. I stared at my empty hands. Blinders. *You wear blinders.* Rage.

I slid off the stool, my fists clenched at my sides. That was why Brad had been so distant. Why he hadn't been able to make it to town and acted oddly when I offered to stay over at his place. Come to think of it, I'd hardly ever stayed at his apartment. He said my place was much nicer and far roomier. It was undoubtedly quieter. I glanced around at my two-story, fifteen-hundred-square-foot cookie-cutter whitewashed brick townhouse, my open floor plan, and agreed his place was smaller. Still, it was in the village and had exposed brick and higher-end appliances.

I'd bought it. *I'm such an idiot.*

"Has it all been a ruse, Mel? Have I wanted the life I created so much that I willingly ignored warning signs?" I paced and ripped the band from my hair.

Her shoulder rose, and her hands were to her mouth. "Maybe. But I don't think so. I don't want to think so, but—"

"Did he honestly believe he could keep me tucked away in Sweet Mountain while he kept another woman in the city? I've read books about men like that. We've read loads. Hell, just last month we watched that Masterpiece show."

"Mrs. Wilson." Mel cringed.

My tone sounded venomous as I stomped across the room to grab my phone. "Like hell will I be a Mrs. Wilson." My fingers got busy.

It's over, Brad.
We're done.

I tossed the phone against the couch and flung myself onto the other side of it. I wasn't one of those women who couldn't be alone. I didn't sit around dreaming of a knight to come and whisk me away. But I'd enjoyed sharing my life with someone. No. I'd enjoyed sharing my life with Brad.

"I'm a blind, stupid fool!"

"You're not blind or stupid." Melanie marched in front of me and took my hands. "You are wonderful, and he is a giant ass. He will rue the day he made his awful choices. He missed the boat on the best thing that could ever happen to him."

I kept my eyes wide, so I wouldn't cry. The pain went so deep that the wound was hardly discernible. I know it wouldn't be later.

Mel frowned. "You had no idea. Not an inkling?" She knew I'd need to hash this out. Knew I'd need to scour my brain for clues.

I thought deeply. "We'd had a few conversations about moving to the next steps of our relationship. We were still trying to figure out what that looked like, but I never picked up on a cheating vibe."

Melanie nodded her sympathy.

"Some guy in the bar tonight had a better read on him than I did." I let her in on the encounter with the man in the bar.

Mel's face flushed. "That's just like a man. Air his dirty laundry out in front of strangers and not expect any consequences. He never even considered you! You have to live here. What if that guy tells people? Brad Jones is at the top of my shi—"

"Wait." I stared at my oldest friend in the world, and my heart nearly stopped. "You said this happened last month."

Mel nervously dropped my hands. "I wanted to tell you. It was literally killing me. But Wyatt said Brad had some elaborate excuse. That Brad didn't even seem rattled when he saw him standing there. I didn't want to be the friend that spread gossip and caused a rift in your relationship."

"You tell me everything." I ran my fingers through my hair. "You have no filter. Why did you decide to start withholding information now?"

"Don't be mad. I meant well. And nobody is beating themselves up more than me, right? God, I'm really striking out in the friend department lately," Melanie said morosely. She looked so grieved that I felt like scum.

I got up and hugged her. "I'm sorry. I'm just all jumbled up. None of this is your fault. And you're telling me now."

"I honestly didn't think more about it until the party."

I released her. "What happened at the party?"

"When he arrived, I was in the covered courtyard chatting with a couple of members from one of the other book clubs. I overheard him on the phone. He was standing over by the hedges away from everyone else. He sounded upset." She shook her head. "Or maybe angry. I don't know."

"What did he say exactly?"

Mel took a deep breath. "He said, 'Jennifer, be reasonable. I'll be back in the city first thing in the morning. I'm going to tell her tonight.'"

Jennifer? Oh. My. God. Jennifer Mitchell, his ex. I sat down on the edge of the sofa. My phone pinged, and I glanced over at it, cringing. It wasn't Brad. Piper texted, letting me know she had some news and would be coming by in the morning.

"So he planned on ending it with me that night. He just couldn't do it because of Patricia's murder." All the signs were there. I just hadn't wanted to see them.

"I don't know." Melanie sat down next to me. "When he saw me, he was all smiles. Acting like nothing was amiss. He behaved as if I hadn't overheard his conversation when he knew I had."

"Are you sure he knew you overheard him?"

She half laughed. "Absolutely. I threw my drink on Brad's shirt."

The stain on his shirt that awful night. I smiled and hugged my friend. My mind went back to Nobles the morning after the murder. Mel had tried to bring up her issues with Brad, and I'd shut her down. "I'm sorry I doubted you."

"You have nothing to be sorry for." She rubbed my back.

"I hate men," I grumbled into her shoulder, feeling petulant.

"I know, honey. We all do. Men are the worst."

Chapter Seventeen

"Night," Melanie called as she stumbled toward her house next door. "Remember, bros before h—. No, wait, that's not it."

I laughed as Mel kept tapping her forehead, as if that would bring the phrase she searched for to her mind.

The chill felt good against my warm cheeks. "Night, you crazy woman."

"Wait! I got it." She held up her finger as she turned back around to face me, sniggering. "Chicks before d—"

"Melanie!" I bent over, laughing. Mel tended to get a little crude when she drank. She never held her alcohol well.

She cackled loudly and began to walk backward. "I've got it now. You ready?"

I nodded, still fighting a fit of giggles. I was so thankful for my best friend. Life wouldn't be worth living without my girlfriends.

"Pearls before swine!" Mel stumbled backward over the azaleas and went down hard. Her shriek echoed through the night.

"Oh my God." I held my hand over my mouth to muffle my loud bursts of laughter. I stumbled over to where she lay on the ground and held out my hand to her. "Are . . . are you okay?"

She was laughing too hard to answer. Her loud cackles exploded into the night like rapid fire.

"My God, y'all are trashed." I glanced over to see Piper as Melanie went on all fours and peeked over the bushes. Piper stood with her arms crossed, shaking her head at us.

"No, we're not." Melanie managed to get to her feet. She had dusted her backside off.

"Uh-huh." Piper pointed to the twigs sticking out of Mel's hair.

Mel messed with her hair. "And if we are drunk, it's only because Lyla needed a blowout." She cupped her mouth with her hands and said way too loudly, "Brad's cheating on her."

"Mel. Shout it from the rooftops, why don't you." I scowled.

"Sorry." She yawned loudly. "I'd stay and chat, but I got to get to bed. I've got to be at the shop at ten."

Piper stood next to me as we watched Melanie trample the bushes on her way to her front door. "Sorry about Brad."

I shrugged, having no desire to go into it. "What time is it?"

"Quarter till six. I guess you have no recollection of my text from last night."

I rubbed my eyes. "I do. Come on. I need some coffee."

* * *

"Who is this woman? The one giving the interviews," I asked Piper after a hot shower and my third cup of coffee.

We'd just finished watching the video footage from Elaine's arrest. As I'd suspected last night, the scene hadn't painted the police department in a positive light. A petition to remove Rosa from active duty had already started making the rounds. I didn't know how much weight it would carry, but Quinn wouldn't be happy either way. His entire department had seemingly gone to shreds the moment he'd left for his honeymoon.

"Her name is Judy Galloway. She attended the party. She belongs to one of the other book clubs y'all invited. And as you can see, she pulled no punches. Click on the news folder on the home screen. That's what will go live in about an hour." Piper rinsed out her cup and put it in the sink.

I used my index finger and thumb to zoom in on the woman's face speaking to a reporter on the screen. I couldn't place her at the party. She was a middle-aged jowly woman with a tiny mouth, which she'd painted bright red. "I don't recall her, and I believe I spoke to every club. Have you met with her?"

Piper nodded. "Yes. She checks out."

Hmm. A couple of taps on the screen, and the front page of this morning's *Sweet Mountain Gazette* came into view.

"*Sweet Mountain Police Department's acting chief, Sergeant Rosa Landry, botched the investigation by allowing guests to contaminate the crime scene. Her arrest of Elaine Morgan is a cause of concern. Elaine Morgan is portrayed by those close to her as an upstanding member and pillar of our community*," I read aloud and glanced over the iPad at Piper, who sighed.

I glanced back down at the article of the witness's accounts.

"*Several others have come forward with complaints that Sergeant Landry physically shoved people around and had a difficult time managing her temper.*" My voice rose on the last word. "That isn't true, is it?" I couldn't recall that taking place. Granted, I'd been sort of out of it.

"It is. I have it on more than one account."

I returned my attention to the screen.

"*Sergeant Landry spoke derogatorily to her officers and wouldn't listen when guests insisted the investigation should not target the owner of the bed-and-breakfast, Elaine Morgan.*"

I shook my head, as if the motion could help me make sense of the words. I continued reading the quote from Judy Galloway. "*If anyone crosses Rosa Landry, she puts a target on your back. I know from personal experience. I felt in fear for my safety, which is why I decided to come forward. Elaine Morgan is innocent, and Rosa Landry has framed her.*"

I couldn't believe the words printed before me. "Why would Rosa frame Elaine? It makes no sense." I rubbed my eyes, which felt like they were filled with sandpaper. "How? Elaine told me she found the gun and turned it over to the police. That's why her prints were on it." My eyes went wide, and I held up my hand when I realized my blunder. "That is off the record, Piper."

Piper pursed her lips. "It's off the record until I get confirmation from another source."

"Fine," I agreed. "This Judy Galloway knows Rosa?"

She shrugged. "Claims to. And I didn't print their names, but two from your own book club are quoted in that article. Tammy and Joel."

I blew out a breath and shook my head. "Well, Rosa's certainly up to her eyeballs in the muck." And I would be speaking to those club members.

"Yes. The speculation as to Rosa's fitness to serve on the police force isn't just from the Sweet Mountain residents. We didn't print it, but there was a quote from another source about Rosa's past."

I waved my hands, signaling for her to elaborate. This just kept getting worse and worse.

"The source claims Rosa was almost dishonorably discharged from the army because of some violent incident. That she should have never been allowed to serve on the force in the first place. Several terms were floating around, *psycho* being the most frequent."

"Piper, that's akin to slander!"

"I know, we didn't print it. We weren't able to verify the claim in time to run it with the story."

"But you plan to?" I gave her a pointed glare.

"If we get corroboration. Not the psycho part. And don't shoot the messenger." Piper rubbed her forehead, and I noticed how tired she looked. Her hair was smoothed back into a ponytail, but there was evidence of dry shampoo she hadn't blended well enough. Though her skin was moisturized, the lines around her eyes were pronounced.

"I'm sorry, Piper. You're good at your job. The best. I didn't mean to question your abilities. This situation is, well, a lot." I set the iPad down. My head began to ache, and I held both sides in my hands, bracing my elbows on the bar as I massaged my temples. *First someone kills Patricia, a woman I investigated. Then the woman who hired me is arrested for the crime. Now the conduct of one of my closest friends, Rosa, is being called into question via the press and public opinion.* I thought back to Rosa's body language last night. She'd seemed edgy and unsure of herself. Not like Rosa at all.

And when I tried to reach out, she'd not been receptive. Why? We always discussed our troubles. I would've cried on her shoulder about Brad the same as I had Mel's. I felt an intervention coming on. Rosa could only avoid us for so long, and her life was blowing up.

We settled into silence as the sun began to rise, shining through the floor-to-ceiling blinds in my living room, bathing everything in a warm yellow glow. Wearily, Piper moved into the room, kicked off her Brooks running shoes, and curled up on the chaise end of the sectional.

"And just so you are aware, I've tried Quinn a few times. I hope you've had better luck reaching him than I have."

I shook my head. "Voice mail is all I'm getting."

"Well, keep trying. I think it'd be better coming from you." She meant because I'd found the body, not because she'd been dating Quinn right before he started seeing Courtney. Quinn had felt badly burned by Piper. He should have known her career would always come first. Double standard, if you asked me. He readily admitted that his job was part of the package. But when she'd leaked something she believed wasn't off the record, all hell broke loose, and their relationship crashed and burned.

I got up, shut the blinds, and took a seat on the other end of the sofa, resting my arm on the back. "I hear you. What a mess."

"Yep." Piper leaned her head back and closed her eyes.

My copy of *A Murder Is Announced*, sitting on the end table, caught my eye. I picked it up and flipped through the pages. An eeriness overtook me.

Someone is toying with us. They were trying to manipulate the murder at Magnolia Manor to mimic the one in the novel. And not for fun like we were. *For real* this time. I had to get to the bottom of this, and fast.

"Piper, you awake?"

"Barely." She yawned, and her eyelids cracked open. She stared at the book I held up.

"We might have a bigger problem. I'll be trying Quinn again. He must have spotty coverage or have his phone off since he's on his honeymoon. But that doesn't seem like something he'd do. I'll leave him a more urgent voice mail this time if I can't get him."

Chapter Eighteen

"Thank you for taking a minute to speak with me." I smiled at Tammy as she took a seat at the table. "I didn't know you were working here too."

"Yeah, just for a little while. I'm trying to save up for a down payment on a house." She glanced around, looking for her best friend. Fatigue was written all over her. "I don't know where Joel is. He said he'd be here. You'll have to make it fast. If we pick up, I'll have to get back to work."

The market and deli had only a couple of booths filled. Tammy had mentioned on several occasions that two o'clock in food service was the lull of the day. Tammy sighed, looking a little put out.

"Have I done something to upset you? Are you worried I'm angry that you spoke to the press?"

She gave her head a shake and scratched her long thin nose. "No. You're here because you wanted the truth, right?"

I nodded. "Okay, if that's not it, then what is it?"

She blurted, "You said to go for that guy last night, and then I saw you leave with him."

"Oh." She'd taken me by surprise, and I gave a little laugh. "I didn't leave with him. He followed me outside."

"Maybe, but"—her eyes narrowed—"you were all cozied up with the guy on the bench. I followed him out and saw you."

I pursed my lips, feeling a little annoyed. "It wasn't like that. The man came to tell me that he'd overheard Brad on the phone with *another* woman. He caught part of their conversation and it didn't sound professional. Can you even imagine how humiliating that was for me?"

She sat back against her chair, and her face flushed. "Oh. Oh God, hon. I'm so sorry. Was he right? Is Brad cheating?" Her voice trailed off.

I lifted my shoulders. "It looks like it. But I don't want to get into it. I'm still processing."

She squeezed my hand. "Sure. Let me grab you a glass of tea."

"Thanks." I took a sip from the glass she deposited on the table. She'd also put a basket of their famous cheese muffins within arm's reach. "I'm fine. Just feel like an idiot. Can we get back to why I'm here?"

"Absolutely." Tammy nodded with a smile, and I appreciated her willingness to let the subject drop.

"Okay. Well, I'll be brief, then, and get right to the point. I'm assuming you heard about Elaine's arrest."

She picked up a muffin and nibbled it. "Yes. Terrible."

"Well, I'm aiding in her defense."

"That's so good of you." She took another bite and swallowed.

"Do you recall seeing Elaine in the ballroom when the shooting took place?"

She shook her head. "I already told the police that I didn't. But it isn't me you should really be talking to." The bell above the deli door jangled. "Oh, there he is." Tammy waved to Joel. He didn't look like himself. Joel always seemed to be happy. When he'd first started attending our club, I'd thought he put on his cheer, but I'd later discovered it was just his natural disposition. Mel and I had discussed how lucky it would be to be born with a cheery outlook on life. Though Joel didn't look cheery today. Today he looked anxious.

Another waitress I didn't know came over and refilled my tea glass. I thanked her while Joel got settled at the small veneer table. When the waitress left, Tammy said, "Like I said, I didn't see Elaine. But Joel did."

Joel removed the scarf from around his thin neck and puffed out his cheeks. "Do you really think it's a good idea?" He leaned closer to Tammy and scratched his jaw. "We were threatened."

I frowned. "I'm sorry, who threatened you?"

They exchanged a worried glance before Tammy's pale, freckled hand covered his deep bronze one. "She's working for the defense, right?"

When she cast a quick glance my way, I nodded and said, "That's correct." I understood she wanted Joel to hear it from me.

"I trust her."

Her vote of confidence hadn't exactly settled Joel, but he'd talk.

Joel's head bobbed forward as he said, "Okay, maybe it will be better to tell someone else, just in case."

Just in case. That sounded ominous.

"Joel, you *can* trust me. I won't betray you, and I'll do every-thing in my power to make sure these threats, wherever they came from, stop."

His eyes locked on mine as he chewed on his bottom lip. "Okay. Let me get this out before I change my mind." He took a deep breath. "I went to the restroom, hoping I'd get back before the mystery kicked off, and ran into Elaine washing her hands. We chatted for a few minutes about the history of the property."

"Joel is a real history buff." Tammy smiled encouragingly.

"I am." A brief smile creased his lips. "Anyway, we got caught up chatting and continued our conversation into the hallway." He shook his head. "We missed everything."

"You're certain this was during the shooting? When the power went out?" I jotted down what he'd said in Notes.

"Definitely." He swallowed. "The lights went out while we were in the hallway. I heard the shots and was agitated I missed it. I made my apologies to Elaine and hightailed it back toward the ballroom."

"Did Elaine accompany you to the ballroom?"

He shook his head. "Not immediately. She had her own troubles. One of the maids had approached her before I left, alerting Elaine about a leaky faucet in one of the rooms."

"Do you recall the maid's name?"

He shook his head again.

"You didn't notice a name tag?" I asked.

He furrowed his brow and seemed to think it over. "I don't think she wore one. Sorry."

"What happened next?"

"Before I made it into the ballroom, the sirens went off, and all hell broke loose. The next thing I knew, Elaine was behind me telling everyone to go down the corridor and sit on the floor."

I nodded and glanced between them, a bit confused. "At what point were the two of you threatened, and by whom?"

Tammy wrapped her arms around herself and rubbed her thin shoulders. I got the impression they hadn't mentioned the threat to the police.

"Okay. I'm going out on a limb here by telling you this. I do trust you. It's just, well, Rosa is the police."

A chill overtook me. "Rosa threatened you?"

Tammy and Joel slowly nodded in unison. Tammy kept glancing around as if worried we were being watched.

"I overheard her telling one of her officers to search everywhere for the gun. And to make sure to check under the credenza on the left side of the ballroom for it. The statement caught me off guard, and I asked if she'd seen the gun go under there." Tammy swallowed, looking uneasy. "She scowled at me and told me to join the others. I sort of slinked out of the room. But later, when I'd gone outside, she grabbed me from behind and slammed me into the building. I was terrified. She said to stay the f-word out of her investigation, or I might be next."

My spine went ramrod straight. "What?" That didn't sound like Rosa at all. Sure, she'd been a bit on edge. And yes, she'd arrested Elaine when I couldn't see cause. But unprovoked violence toward a fellow club member wasn't her MO and struck genuine fear within me. She'd never threatened to harm another person. Not the Rosa I knew. And I knew her pretty darn well.

Joel took Tammy's hand. She seemed to draw strength from the gesture. "I couldn't believe it either, and I know she is one of your closest friends and a core member of our club. But the malice that rolled off her was real. I swear."

She swallowed. "The day I was supposed to give my statement at the police station, she was sitting in her cruiser outside my apartment. Almost as if she dared me to make a complaint. Of course, I didn't go after that."

"And after I heard what happened, I didn't go either." Joel rubbed his arm.

I massaged my forehead. "Are y'all sure you didn't misconstrue why Rosa was at your apartment?"

"The only thing I'm sure of is that she wanted us to steer clear."

"You believe us, right? I mean, we're talking to you at your request. We could have kept our mouths shut like we have been all this time." Joel's eyes shifted toward Tammy, unsure now of his decision to speak with me.

I hated to see them so frightened. I leaned over and squeezed Joel's arm. "I believe you."

And as much as I hated to admit it, I did believe them. Whatever was going on, Joel and Tammy clearly felt intimidated.

Chapter Nineteen

I met Mr. Greene outside the county jail, where he'd just visited with his client. He eagerly awaited my findings, and I proudly delivered. "According to Joel Adler, he can place Elaine outside the ballroom at the time of the shooting. And from his account, other eyewitnesses can as well. And I spoke to four other employees on the phone before arriving here who will also testify to that fact. I haven't spoken to a couple of others on my list, but I will. These"—I handed him the images I'd had printed—"are the crime scene photos I took the other day. It might be good to compare to the originals."

"Outstanding work, Miss Moody." Mr. Greene turned in his seat to face me as he looked over my notes. We were sitting in his Cadillac. "And quite expedient. When we spoke this morning, I never expected such results. My usual investigator would take at least a week to produce his findings. I might throw a little more business your way if you're interested."

"Definitely interested." I smiled at the older man, who'd been our family attorney for as long as I could remember. "How's Elaine holding up?"

"As expected, she's a gentle soul. I feel certain she'll be released tomorrow. We'll be attending a preliminary hearing in the morning. I don't believe they will be able to make the case to warrant a trial. Everything they have is circumstantial and incredibly weak. Quite frankly, I'm shocked they managed to get a judge to sign off on the arrest warrant, which begs many more questions. The most pressing is what they could have presented the DA to give him probable cause." Mr. Greene scratched the top of his head. "If the case proceeded as Sergeant Landry planned, surely the acting chief would know we'd request all her supposed evidence during discovery."

"Well, some of the witnesses might've been afraid to come forward or be honest."

He raised his bushy gray brows, and I told him about Rosa and her alleged intimidation tactics.

"Hmm." His lips compressed into a thin line. "I want to get their statements on the record. I don't believe we'll need them, but if we do, I won't have them intimidated."

"Okay."

"This Sergeant Landry is a good friend of yours?"

I nodded and told him about our relationship—how we'd met, her active role in my club.

"If the case moves forward, will this be an issue for you?" He held my gaze, and I could see why prosecutors didn't want to meet him in the courtroom. This man did not like to lose.

I lifted my chin. "No, sir. And just to show you I mean it. I spoke to Quinn on my way to meet you here." I wouldn't allow my personal relationships to come before the case. This was a serious charge, and even though my heart and head didn't agree about Rosa, I was determined to do everything in my power to get to the truth. My thoughts went round and round until I felt nearly dizzy. I'd be trying Quinn again this evening. Like I'd told Mr. Greene, I'd finally managed to get him on the phone. The conversation hadn't been productive because cell coverage was poor, but he'd gotten the gist. And he'd be returning early.

"I'm glad to hear it." Mr. Greene checked his cell phone, which had buzzed. "And it is good news for Mrs. Morgan that you facilitated the introduction. Suppose I hadn't raised such a fuss. This might have gone entirely too far. Cost the taxpayers a lot of unnecessary expense, not to mention the continued mental anguish Mrs. Morgan is suffering."

Anguish. That sounded like a term used to lay the groundwork lawsuit for monetary damages.

"I also plan to have a word with the mayor."

Oh boy.

"Your father and I have a round of golf scheduled with him next week, and he'll be getting an earful from me. I would have gone straight to him if he was in town. This could have been over before it even began." He glanced at his watch. "I hate to rush you, but I have a dinner engagement to get to."

I smiled at the confident man with gray bushy eyebrows that always looked to be waving at me.

"You've grown into quite a capable woman."

"Thank you, Mr. Greene. Enjoy your dinner."

He'd paid me the most welcome compliment. A real confidence booster.

*　　*　　*

The parking lot of my favorite specialty foods market had emptied while I'd been inside paying for my groceries. I always put off grocery shopping for as long as I could. After the long night and even longer day I'd had, I'd barely finished up shopping before the store closed for the night. My phone had rung several times while I was shopping. Still, after the dirty looks I'd received from a couple of employees ready to clean up and end their shifts, I'd neglected the calls. Boy, was I dead on my feet.

I dug through my bag after closing the trunk and leaned against the car. My breath puffed out in white clouds under the fluorescent lighting in the dark parking lot. I checked my phone to see I had two missed calls. One of which was Brad, and I felt heartsick. I didn't want to hurt, hated that I did, but I still couldn't deny that Brad Jones had wounded me. My finger was hovering over the callback icon when I spied Rosa's name next to his. I hit her name instead.

"Lyla, this isn't a good time," Rosa said without preamble.

"I'm returning *your* call." I didn't appreciate her tone. *God!* Life was literally unraveling all around me.

"Look. I know things are crazy right now. I have a murder on my hands, Lyla. A case that is falling apart, and I'm doing everything I can just to keep my head above water." She sounded out of breath. "And you're not helping the situation."

"I'm doing what you should be doing." I felt like stomping my feet in indignation, yet resisted. "And I think we—"

"And what would that be?" Her tone came out bitter and resentful. She'd cut me off before I could alert her to my growing concerns about a crazy person toying with us.

"Searching for the truth! God, what's gotten into you? I hardly recognize this person you've become. Your tactics will be scrutinized."

"My tactics!"

I puffed out a breath. "Listen, we need to talk. If something is going on, you need to get ahead of it. Do something now before too much damage is done."

"I have no idea what you're talking about."

"Yes you do. Have you lost your senses?"

She let out a frustrated growl. "I don't have time for this. I think it's best if we cease communication. I'm in the midst of a murder case. I don't have time for frivolous things like a book club or puerile gossip. Don't call me again." Click.

Cease communication? What in the world? I wanted to scream. I leaned against the car and stared up into the night's sky. Everything indeed did seem to be unraveling at the seams. Everything.

A text came through, and I expected it to be from Rosa containing an apology.

Please remove me and all the Book Babes from the Jane Doe Book Club. We've left all club social media outlets.

Not from Rosa. From Tammy. I stared down at the text in confusion.

What? Sheesh. Had I crossed a line with her a few hours ago? Had I come across as if I didn't believe the two of them? No. I didn't think I had.

My fingers moved across the screen. Tammy answered on what had to be the last ring. I'd almost given up and readied myself to leave a voice mail.

"Hello?"

"Tammy, it's Lyla. I just got your text. What's going on?" I opened the car door and paused as a pink flyer caught my eye. I pulled it from the windshield.

"This isn't what we signed up for. We never agreed to this, and it isn't funny. Especially after what I told you today. You know how scared Joel and I were—are! I'm all in for creepy Halloween parties. You know that, but this"—she gave a bark of bitter laughter—"is not funny. And as the president of our original club, the Book Babes, I've been asked to speak for everyone. We're cutting ties, effective immediately."

"I honestly don't have any idea what you're referring to." I fisted the flyer. "I know how—" The cheap clip art image of the old game of hangman caught my eye. My Gran had played paper games like this with me before we were all glued to screens. I relaxed my grip and smoothed out the page. There were ten dashes beneath the hangman art and an announcement that read:

A Murder Is Announced: The Jane Does, your host for the evening, is informing everyone that a murder will take place on Friday, October 22nd, at Oak Mill Cemetery, 15 N Erwin Street. Come for a night of Halloween fun where a book club member will die!

Ten dashes for ten letters. My breath came out in a whoosh. "Sweet Lord." The phone slipped from my fingertips and crashed against the ground.

"Lyla! Lyla, are you okay?" I could hear Tammy shouting.

Stooping, I picked up my phone, glancing around in fear that someone could be watching me. "Y . . . yes." I cleared my throat and got into my car. The engine roared to life, and I turned the heat up full blast. My chill had nothing to do with the cold. The phone switched over to the Bluetooth car speakers. "Did all of you receive this flyer? Someone put one on my car while I was buying my groceries."

"Yes, and you scared me."

"I dropped my phone." I couldn't believe what I was looking at.

Someone is toying with us, and I have proof.

"Tammy, I can tell you with absolute certainty that neither I nor any other founding member had anything to do with this." I started to wad up the flyer and thought better of it. I sat it in the passenger seat and snapped a pic.

"I believe you. Can you say for sure Rosa didn't?"

"I just spoke to Rosa, and she doesn't have time to pull any stunts like this."

"So, who did? Oh no . . ." Tammy's voice trailed off.

"Don't jump to conclusions. I don't know who is behind this, but I plan to find out." Someone was walking across the lot, and my breath caught in my throat. "Hang on a sec." I put the call on mute. The person came straight for my car. My heart hammered against my rib cage. My hand went to my purse, which held my Kahr Arms P380 handgun.

The man smiled and lifted a hand when he reached my car, and I recognized the store manager. I rolled down my window.

"Miss Moody, is everything all right? Not having car trouble, are you?"

"No, Mr. Simms. I had a phone call." I smiled and then thanked him for checking on me.

"No problem. You have a good night now, and drive safely." He patted the roof of my car and left. When I turned around to see where he was going, I spied an old Ford pickup at the end of the lot.

Even more spooked that someone might be watching me and the other Jane Does, I decided to warn everyone. I unmuted the call and put the car in drive. "Tammy, can you call a meeting? Tonight, if possible? I think we should all speak in person."

"Hang on a sec." I heard hushed voices in the background before she put me on mute. I should have known they'd all be together. "Okay. But not Rosa."

"No. Not Rosa." My stomach swam as I slow-rolled to the stop sign. I wondered if Rosa had any idea the damage she'd done to her reputation. Eyewitness accounts were difficult to refute. Especially when they came in numbers. I didn't believe she'd had anything to do with this stunt, but whatever had caused the change in her behavior gave me a heavy sense of foreboding.

"It'll be just Mel and me. Amelia is out of town. Text me where, and we'll be there."

"We're all at my house, but, um, we'll come to yours, if that's okay."

That she didn't want me to come to her house told me how afraid they all were. "That's fine. I'll head home now."

Chapter Twenty

A half hour later, a cacophony of shrills and shrieks and murmurs of deep concern vibrated around the first floor of my townhouse, which was crammed with club members. I'd asked my questions regarding where and when they'd all received the flyers. I'd prefaced the questions with the point that someone had been impersonating our group with some awful gag. Still, these were mystery readers, educated by genre fiction.

"I think everyone should calm down. I believe the case against Elaine will be dropped and the police will have to direct their attention elsewhere. I don't think we have anything to be overly concerned about," I said. "Not that we shouldn't be vigilant and keep our eyes open." It wasn't a stretch for everyone to suspect the flyer threat might be linked to the murder at Magnolia Manor. And with Elaine being cleared, or potentially being cleared, that meant the perpetrator was still out there. Still, we certainly didn't need everyone panicking and making it more challenging to get the facts. Hysteria could lead us on wild-goose chases. And after the flyer, we hadn't the time for that.

Tammy had no compunction about calling me out. "Lyla, you know we have a problem. A serious one. Now isn't the time for well-intended placation. We need to know what the hell we're dealing with here, and it isn't a gag."

I understood her stance; still, cautions were needed. I wouldn't create a state of pandemonium, and I wouldn't spread rumors. The difficulty in solving Patricia's murder came from the chaos surrounding the crime scene. If this turned out to be a real threat, the same situation could disrupt an otherwise strategic investigation. A thought occurred to me. Perhaps that had been the plan all along.

Tammy pierced me with her green gaze. "I'm just going to say it. Rosa Landry is a threat to us."

"She isn't!" Melanie piped up for the first time since the meeting had kicked off. She'd been sitting back and chewing her lips and shaking her head.

"Don't be so sure. I spoke to Judy Galloway, the one who did that interview with Piper Sanchez," Joel said. The man's face was contorted with worry. "She insists we are all in danger. That Rosa isn't who she claims to be and we should give her a wide berth."

"Hold on a second." Melanie was on her feet. "I won't sit by and listen to y'all bad-mouth our friend. None of us knows how we would handle this impossible situation." I had yet to tell Mel of Rosa's request to sever our friendship until the case was over. At least, I assumed it would be until our case was over.

"Look, Melanie." Tammy turned to face Mel, her cheeks flushed. "We like you and Lyla. And Amelia is the sweetest. Our beef isn't with the three of you. But forgive us if we aren't as convinced as you are about Rosa. Her behavior at the party was reprehensible. She shoved me against the wall like I was a common criminal. All I did was ask a question." Nods went around, and Mel and I shared a rueful glance. "And I know Lyla doesn't want me to bring this up, but I must! If Elaine isn't guilty, who is?" She held up the flyer in her fist. "And what does this mean?"

Her words left the room in silence. The unspoken reality that we might all be targets hung in the room. *Targets.*

"We're not sure it means anything yet," I said as calmly as I could manage.

"Please don't treat us like we're morons." Joel's thin lips stretched impossibly thinner, and the woman to his left sniffed. She'd been over in the corner of the room, exchanging low-voiced comments with three other members. I believed her name was Christie or Kelley. I felt terrible that I had a hard time recalling her name. Not that I could ask her now. She rose, and the members she'd been conversing with earlier did as well. "We're leaving. Tammy and Joel can represent us. They know everything we do. This is all too much, and we have to get home."

I stared at the faces filled with concern. "I'm not being condescending or treating you all like fools. I've been in the investigative field for a few years now. And one of the things I've learned is not to assume anything. Facts are what we count on." I held my hands out, making eye contact with each one of them. "I'm so sorry you all feel threatened. And you have my word that I won't stop digging until I get to the bottom of things and make the person responsible pay for their crimes. Sweet Mountain has always been a nice, safe place, and I plan to keep it that way."

"I wonder if we all were simply naïve," the woman said. "I don't believe any place is safe anymore. All you have to do is turn on the news."

Kate Young

She had a point, but I couldn't take that perspective. I would do everything in my power to make my little part of the world a better place.

Joel said, "Christie had a drive-by from Rosa too."

Ah, Christie, not Kelley. I jotted the name down and made a mental note.

Christie told me a story similar to Tammy's. She'd spotted Rosa's cruiser outside her residence. She had gone to the press instead of the police.

"I'm sorry you were frightened. But you can't be certain as to Rosa's motives." I raised my hands. "I'm not making excuses for her. You had every right to speak to the press if that makes you feel safer. And to prove that I am willing to do whatever it takes, Chief Daniels has been informed and will be back here in Sweet Mountain earlier than expected. I will be meeting with him the second he arrives."

Hearing that I was on their side seemed to simmer them down. Mel simply sat staring at her hands in silence.

"Thank you for your hospitality." Christie and her friends moved toward the door. "We'll be on our way. We appreciate you hearing us out."

Everyone looked fatigued. And I *hated* it. This wasn't what I wanted for my book club. A wave of anger raged through me like I'd never experienced. The person's audacity to torment my friends meant only one thing: that person had no conscience, no feelings whatsoever. What we were dealing with here was an author of confusion—a true mastermind.

There weren't more words to console my group. I'd already sworn to ensure the apprehension of the responsible party. I simply watched them go out the front door. Joel and Tammy hung behind.

Mel cast a glance toward Tammy, who'd put her empty coffee cup on the bar.

"I'm sorry I bit your head off," Mel began. "It won't happen again."

"It's okay. You are a loyal friend. I get that. I would be the same if someone accused Joel of misconduct."

Tammy took my hand. "I believe you will get the guy. Perhaps we'll just pause our club meetings until you do. There is no Book Babes club anymore. We're all Jane Does."

Well, that was something.

Chapter
Twenty-One

Thursday morning, after yet another fretful night, I knew it would be a three-cups-of-coffee kind of day. For Mel too. She'd needed to carpool this morning after her car wouldn't start. Mel and I were silent as I parked. We were both feeling a little melancholy after last night. The idea that one of our best friends was on her way down a destructive path grieved us. Melanie had tried Rosa three times before giving up and resigned herself to the situation.

I understood Mel's pain. When you're running down an investigation and someone you care about comes up as a person of interest, the struggle to look other places—any other place—is unimaginable. Neither one of us believed Rosa was involved in the murder. There had to be another explanation for the suspected terrorizing of the Jane Does. But we did see the misconduct and the potentially unethical way she'd handled the case. We forced ourselves to examine the accounts.

Mel sat up straighter. "Who is that?" Seeing the way she'd quickly checked her lipstick in the visor mirror, I knew she'd spotted an attractive man.

I put the car in park and adjusted my sunglasses. The man I'd met the other night at the bar stood between my office and Mel's shop. I couldn't help the warmth that rose to my cheeks. He'd been right about Brad, and I'd behaved like a typical female in denial.

"I don't know exactly. He's the guy from the bar. Dean, I think his name is. Courtney sent him my way."

Melanie's eyes went wide. "Wait a minute. I think I saw him at the party the other night. He was leaving with some woman when I threw my drink on Brad."

"He told me he'd attended but left early. Did you recognize his date?"

She shook her head. "He was kind of trailing after the woman, and she didn't look well."

"That's what he told me." I cleared my throat as I reached behind the seat for my purse and computer bag. Melanie kept grinning at me.

I knew that look. "No, Mel. I am not interested in going out with anyone right now."

"Why not?" Melanie blinked at me with angelic eyes.

"I haven't even spoken to Brad yet. Heard his side of things. So we're sort of in limbo."

"You tried to call him back last night, and did he answer? A big fat no. So again, I ask, why not?"

I gaped at her. Her mention of Brad ignoring my callback stung slightly, even though I knew she was only trying to help. "Mel."

Melanie leaned closer. "What is it you always say to me?" She straightened up and lifted her chin and said in mock falsetto, "Melanie Smart, you've got to stop pining after that loser and get back out there. He never deserved you anyway."

"I don't sound like that."

"Okay, whatever. But I don't see the issue. Seriously, that guy is smoking hot!"

I opened the car door. "I'm in the middle of an investigation, the Jane Does are terrified, and I'm not ready to get back out there."

As I locked the car from the key fob, the sequenced beeps caught his attention, and he glanced up from his phone. An easy smile creased his face, and a wariness came over me. What was he doing here? This couldn't be a coincidence. I wondered what he wanted from me, other than the obvious.

Melanie leaned closer and whispered as we approached our places of business. "Look at him, yum! There's no harm. Think of it as a pleasant distraction, an ego boost, and"—she contorted her face in an exaggerated conspiratorial expression and spoke out of the left side of her mouth, looking absolutely ridiculous— "maybe a little stress relief."

I lost control and chuckled to myself. Melanie made it challenging to stay serious. "Go to work, Melanie Smart."

She laughed loudly, using her practiced seductive laugh as she hurried her pace and raced ahead of me. She extended her hand. "Hi there. I'm Melanie Smart. I own this shop."

"Hello, Melanie. I'm Dean." He glanced up at the colorful striped awning and the shiny Smart Cookie sign before turning his attention back to me. "I'm here to see Miss Moody."

"Oh." Melanie drew out the word with a smile.

I cast a warning glance her way before turning to Dean. "Good morning. Is there something I can help you with?" I said, using my professional tone of voice.

"I sure hope so," Dean said, and Melanie giggled.

We both cut our eyes in her direction, and Dean's lips twitched. "Someone has a dirty mind."

Melanie giggled again. "No, not us. We're good girls." She winked. "Well, mostly."

"My God. Good-bye, Melanie." Everyone needed a Mel in their lives most days, but not today.

"I've got a couple of minutes." Melanie smiled mischievously. "So, Dean . . ."

I turned my back on them and went inside my own office. Mel meant well, but sheesh. She wanted me to get over Brad. We didn't feel over yet. Yes, I had technically ended it with him, or maybe he'd ended it with me and I'd made it official. Either way, it felt messy, and we both would need closure. A heaviness settled in my shoulders, and I sighed as I started the coffee machine.

No, I hadn't the time for this. Today was a big day. Elaine would be arraigned, and I had to focus and wait to hear the next steps from Mr. Greene. I had to get to the bottom of what was going on in Sweet Mountain and directly see what this man wanted. I was done feeling sorry for myself for today. There was no room for my love life woes. My coffee finished brewing, and I took a couple of sips from the steaming-hot liquid. *Ahhh.* My brain slowly began to wake.

The door opened, and in walked Dean.

I turned to my guest and forced a smile. "Coffee?"

He shook his head and took a seat in the chair in front of my desk. "No thanks. I already had a travel mug full."

I sat at my desk, sipping more caffeine. "Okay," I said, then took another sip. "My brain has fired awake. Tell me how I can help you."

He took off his denim jacket and folded it over his arm. The tattoo on his exposed forearm caught my eye. It reminded me of one I'd seen before. Military, perhaps?

"I'm looking for Calvin Cousins. You're his niece?"

I cocked my head, wondering why he wanted to speak with my uncle. "I'm his partner."

His brows shot up. "Oh. Partner." He hitched his thumb toward the door. "Blondie out there told me you were his niece."

Blondie? Huh. "Partner and niece."

He smiled a slow, easy smile. He was an attractive man. Very attractive. Ugh. Melanie had gotten into my head. "Ah." I cleared my throat. "What do you want with Mr. Cousins?"

"I've recently become a civilian and was looking for work. Courtney mentioned he hired a lot of ex-military and might be hiring." He glanced around the office with interest. "I thought I'd come by and see."

"I'm sorry, Mr. . . . ?"

"Dean is fine." His smile was still fixed in place. I noticed he had slightly crooked but white teeth.

"I'm sorry, Dean. Mr. Cousins is out of town on business until next month. And—" My phone pinged, and I glanced down at it. It was from Rosa. She'd received my message. One I knew she couldn't resist.

Fine. I'll meet you.

Dean had glanced over at my phone too.

I met his gaze with a scowl. "And I'm not the one in charge of hiring."

He instantly sat back. "Sorry. I guess I wondered if it might be from your boyfriend. Blondie said you'd ended things."

"Blondie talks too much." I covered my phone with my hand and slid it closer to me on the desk.

"Well, I guess I'll get going then and come back when Mr. Cousins is back in town." He rose and put his jacket back on. "Don't be mad at your friend. I think she just wanted to take your mind off your troubles. I would like to take you out sometime, if you're interested."

I rose and walked around the desk. "I'll mention to Calvin that you're looking for work when he gets back. You can send your résumé to the email on our website. Though I don't think we're looking to hire anyone."

"Fair enough." He smiled. "Thanks."

"Uh-huh." I folded my arms, not exactly sure why I felt the need to keep my guard up.

He shook his head in a bemused fashion. "The women in law enforcement in this town. Wow."

"I beg your pardon."

"I don't mean any offense, and I wasn't even going to bring this up, but since you asked . . ." He dug into his pocket and pulled out one of the pink flyers. "You're also the leader of that book club, right? Jane Does?"

"Where did you get that?" My skin prickled.

"That cop who botched the investigation at Magnolia Manor."

"Sergeant Landry?" I felt ill.

He nodded; his brows drew together. "Are you okay? Your face looks pale."

"I'm fine." The room spun a little.

He helped me into the chair he'd vacated. "Water?"

I nodded and pointed to our little fridge by the coffee bar.

Dean handed me a bottle and went down on his knees in front of me. "I take it this flyer is more than a party invitation."

I took a couple of sips and didn't respond. When I raised my eyes to meet Dean's, they were alive with curiosity.

"They're right, aren't they? The press about Sergeant Landry."

I took another sip from the bottle. "I'm not sure what you mean."

"Yes you do. And now I think you need to know something." He rose, his face serious. "This Landry"—he pointed to the flyer—"she stopped me at the square and gave me a jaywalking warning the night they arrested that old lady. The one you're trying to get out of the jam. It was right after I left you, in fact. She seemed to be standing around looking for a reason to stop me. Rude and extremely unprofessional. I'm shocked she still wears a badge." He shook his head, looking disgusted. "She got a call while in the process of ticketing me. She let me off with a stern warning. She acted shady and a little jumpy. I'd seen PTSD behavior many times, so I followed her. Curiosity." He shrugged a shoulder.

He gave me a shy smile. "Then I saw you. You disarmed what could have become a volatile situation. I even considered stepping in before you arrived, but I feared I'd only end up in a cell with the old woman."

Our eyes held for a few beats. Dean's words sobered me right up. I shook myself and stood. He moved back to let me rise. I cleared my throat, feeling like an utter fool and behaving like one. "When did Sergeant Landry give you the flyer?"

He held my gaze. "After she gave me the warning. She had them in her cruiser. She said her book club was hosting another party if I was interested and that this one would be mind-blowing." He handed me the flyer. "Suspicious of her to invite me after she just reprimanded me. Anyway, I blew it off." He took a breath. "But when I heard around town that a lot of people are going, it raised my hackles again. I guess they all want to see if someone gets killed again. Stupid people."

I stared down at the hangman game, and it hit me like a two-by-four in the face. His account gave credence to the claim that Rosa hadn't been scrupulous in her position. As much as I hated to face the facts, there they were. And even more shocking—if I'd had any doubts before, I no longer did. This flyer was a clue. A clue to who would be murdered. And who was behind all of this. I studied the blank dashes below the hangman clip art, and chills like icy-cold fingertips crept up my skin.

"Lyla."

"Huh?" I stared up at him.

"If you need any help with this, I'd be glad to offer my services."

"I told you I'm not authorized to hire anyone." I kept staring at the pink paper.

"No. I mean, I could help *you*. I'm ex-SEAL." He lifted his big broad shoulders, his hands so strong and large they could easily choke the life out of someone.

Why am I thinking this way?

"With the police situation in this town being what it is, and you going at this alone—I could stick around and help."

"I'm not alone." My tone came out bitter.

Dean took a step back, his eyes so wide the whites were showing. "I didn't mean to offend."

"No, of course not." I blew out a breath and unfolded my arms, allowing my hands to drop against my thighs. "I appreciate it."

"Okay. I'll stick around just in case. I'm staying at the Holiday Inn if you change your mind. I'll leave my number." He grabbed a pen off the desk and jotted his number down on a sticky note.

I did a little deep breathing after he left. I had two clients to speak to this morning, and I couldn't put it off. Uncle Calvin trusted me to keep the office running while he was away. Despite the overwhelming sensation that the world was crashing down and someone was planning on using my book club as a catalyst to commit another murder, I had to slow down. Not get ahead of myself. Patience and meticulous planning were critical.

Chapter
Twenty-Two

It took longer than I expected to wrap everything up, and I had to work straight through lunch. I scarfed down a bag of pita chips with hummus at my desk with a Diet Coke. I'd been at it so long, my eyes were crossing staring at the screen, but I had to keep at it. As I worked, it dawned on me that perhaps Rosa had been laying a trap for the killer. It'd be an ingenious strategy. And Rosa was clever. Disparaging her character might be part of the plan, like being undercover. Apologies could easily be made to the club members after she apprehended the guilty party. They'd understand. But that didn't explain her arresting Elaine. Thankfully, she'd been released today. Mr. Greene's call had been a welcome one.

I rubbed my eyes and checked the clock. I'd have to leave to meet Mel and Rosa in a bit. I yawned and stretched before I leaned back over the computer. Our online group had been hacked, and a flood of new members had been accepted. I'd made sure I'd contacted everyone I knew via text, ensuring they knew about the security breach and to steer clear of the so-called party. I hadn't reported the hack. I combed through the messages, looking for clues.

JB Rollins: *Can't wait for the party!*
Kelley Smith: *Should be lit!*
Christy Dale: *Y'all, I think this page was hacked. I spoke to one of the Jane Does, and they aren't hosting another party.*

Well, finally, there was someone with a bit of sense. I took a sip from my can.

JB Rollins: *Don't care, Christy! It'll be better than there lame party.*

I had to fight my instinct to correct JB's grammar. He seemed to be the instigator of this whole dialogue. His chants down the feed of *Party, Party, Party* were monotonous. I wondered who this JB was. I clicked his profile. Looked like a college kid. About twenty-two or twenty-three. He'd studied at the college in the neighboring town. Hmm. Not much about his profile seemed suspicious. I'd run a background check on him just to make sure.

I reported the hack and posted my declaration that neither I nor any other Jane Doe member had sanctioned this rave—which was what it sounded like these kids were attempting to turn the party into. Dumb kids. They had no idea what they could be stumbling upon. If possible, I planned to put a stop to it.

I sat back and stared at the flyer. It could have been printed by any home printer. I'd called around town and checked our local printers and office supply stores. They hadn't had any orders, so it must have been a home printer job or from a store out of town.

My phone rang, and Quinn's face came up on the screen.

"Hey, I'm so sorry for disturbing you while you're on your honeymoon. I wouldn't have called again, but I wasn't sure if you were able to hear me clearly on the last call." Not understanding Rosa's motivations and Dean's statement about her was the reason I'd called him again this afternoon. He hadn't answered, of course. But I'd left him a message stating the urgency of the need for a callback.

"It's okay. I knew you wouldn't have called unless it was an emergency." His voice sounded groggy with sleep, and my stomach fluttered.

Did he stumble out of bed and call me?

What time was it in Italy? I did quick math after a glance at the time. Wow, it was the wee hours of the morning there.

"You sure you're up for talking now?"

"Yes. Get to it."

"Understood." After a deep breath, I spilled my guts. I told Quinn everything. He got the condensed version of the murder. The complaints regarding Rosa's conduct from club members. The concern about the false party announcement, and finally, what I'd learned from Dean.

"Harry's concerns are warranted, then?" He sounded wide awake now.

I should have known Harry would be contacting his cousin as well. "I'm not sure what's been going on inside the precinct, but there are enough concerns to go around."

"The press?" He gave out a derisive snort.

"Yes."

"What does Brad think?"

Irritation overtook me. Brad? Why did it matter what Brad thought?

"Lyla, are you still there?" There was a bit of crackling over the line.

"I'm here." I closed my laptop and began to pack my bag.

"Harry told me Brad helped out with the witnesses at the crime scene. And we both know Brad isn't closemouthed when it comes to his opinions."

That was true. "Brad had issues with the initial cause of death. He hasn't commented on the investigation." I took another sip of Diet Coke. I did not want to get into this.

"Why not?"

"He has a case."

"Since I'm out of the country and can't get back for at least two days, it would be good if I had another seasoned cop who can insert himself into the investigation. Brad's presence wouldn't raise any eyebrows."

I closed my eyes. "I haven't spoken to Brad, since, well, we're"—I cleared my throat—"we're not together anymore."

Silence.

"I also should tell you that from my conversation with Mr. Greene, a lawsuit is brewing. And Quinn, he plays golf with the mayor."

"Shit!" I heard his hand slam on something. Maybe a table. "I'll have Rosa's ass for this!"

"Don't overreact. I'm leaving work to meet Rosa now. There may be things we don't yet know about." I didn't want him to destroy my friend's career. I had a hard time believing Rosa was anything but the honest, caring, tough chick I'd grown to know and love. If she wasn't, I'd take her down myself. The deceit would be unforgivable.

I heard Courtney in the background. "Quinn, are you on the phone?"

"Go back to bed, babe. It's work."

"Work? Who is it? Oh my God! You're talking to Lyla! You just can't stay away from your old girlfriends, can you? Lyla can't leave you alone. Not even when I send another man for her to focus on. How could you? First Piper called this morning, and now I find you sneaking arou—" The phone went dead silent. I wondered why Quinn had taken so long to put me on mute. So Courtney had sent Dean as a diversion. And evidently, Piper had wanted to make sure Quinn understood the seriousness of the situation, sending Courtney into a spiral. Well, we'd deal with the fallout. I stopped myself from focusing on Quinn's wife's ludicrous games and resumed contemplation about the case.

Piper had been right to call. Two voices were more potent than one. And even though Quinn heard it all from her before, he'd listened intently to every word I'd said as if it were new information. He'd become an excellent cop.

"I'll be home as soon as I can." Quinn was back. "Stay close to Rosa. I'm counting on you to be my eyes and ears while I'm away. You can work with Harry. He's still wet around the ears, but he's trustworthy. I'll let him know we've hired you on. The case against Elaine will be dropped, so there'll be no perceivable conflict of interest."

Phew. Quinn had apparently already laid down the law on the case against Elaine. Perhaps that was why Rosa had sounded so stressed. "Okay. I'm sorry again. I hated to call you."

"Never hesitate to reach out to me if you need me. Never." Now things were getting weird. "I'll see you in a couple of days."

Chapter Twenty-Three

G ran's ringtone blared over my car speakers as I drove home.
"Hi, Gran."

"Hey, sweetie pie."

"You sound better." I smiled, glad to hear her sounding like
herself.

"Oh, yes, I am. Right as rain after I coughed up all that gre—"

"TMI, Gran." I cringed. I didn't have the strongest stomach
when it came to illnesses.

She chuckled. "Well, Mr. Greene worked his magic, and all
the charges against Elaine have been dropped."

"Yes, I heard. He called me with the news earlier today." I'd
expected the announcement after my conversation with Quinn.
Mr. Greene had said the case had been a joke. An absolute
embarrassment to Sweet Mountain's police department. "I'm so
happy things worked out."

"Mr. Greene sang your praises to your father when he came
by for coffee."

"I didn't do much. Chatted with a few people and reported my
findings." I waved to the security guard as I turned into my complex.

"Don't be modest. You were his secret weapon. He said so."

"I doubt that." I laughed. Gran was having a good time with this. She'd always been my biggest fan and loved to celebrate everything. I loved her so.

"Well, I might have stretched the praise with the secret-weapon part, but he did say he planned on offering you a job. Frances seemed quite pleased by the idea. You'd make a lot more money than you do working for your uncle, I bet. Get to wear all those pretty clothes of yours to the office and such. Go to his fancy meetings with him."

Gran didn't exactly understand what my job entailed, I supposed. Fancy meetings weren't in my usual job description.

"It'll be something to think about. And it's nice to be considered." I couldn't imagine not working for my uncle. But I'd not rule any opportunity out.

"And I hear he's going to have a word with the mayor. Elaine is thinking of suing the police department. Don't that beat all. I bet that the Daniels boy will be fit to be tied."

"Yeah. I bet Quinn will be." *He already is.*

"Yep. And it does make one wonder who did the shooting and why the police didn't find the person. I'm betting you're hot on their trail. I told William that."

I spied Rosa's cruiser as I pulled into my designated parking space. "I appreciate the vote of confidence, and I think I'm getting closer."

"I knew it! Mum's the word."

"I gotta run. Love you."

"Love you too, sugar."

Melanie came out of her townhouse as I got out of the car. She'd gotten a ride home with her cousin after they closed the shop. Before she left, Mel had popped in to tell me she was leaving, and she'd fumed when I told her about my conversation with Dean. Judging by her posture and the way she was tapping her foot at my front door, her arms crossed, she was still fuming.

Rosa followed us inside without a word. When Melanie closed the door, the three of us stood in my living room. Rosa finally spoke. "Listen, I know y'all are furious with me. But there is so much y'all don't understand."

"You're right. We don't understand what in God's name possessed you to go after poor Elaine Morgan." Melanie unfolded her arms. "We don't understand why you've decided to shut us out. Or why you're behaving like a crazy bi—"

"How dare you?" Rosa's nostrils flared as she faced off with Melanie. "You have no idea what the hell you're talking about. I never should have come here. I knew it would be a mistake."

"Stop this!" I stepped between them, doing a little huffing of my own. "Insulting each other won't help us solve this crime."

"Us?" Rosa snorted.

I pulled the flyer from my bag and slammed it into her chest. "Can you explain this?"

Rosa gripped the flyer and stared down at it. "What's this?"

"Don't play dumb with us, Rosa Landry. We've been your friends—no, your sisters—for years." Melanie folded her arms again. "Tell us what you've done. You owe us that much."

Rosa threw her hands in the air, her face red with anger. "What I've done? What *I've* done? All I've been trying to do is protect this town from a killer."

"Oh, swell job there," Melanie snarked. "The flyer?"

"I have no idea what this is." She threw it at us. "Are you seriously wasting my time with some bullshit Piper Sanchez stirred up?"

I took a step toward her, my blood near boiling. "Do you deny distributing the flyers? Or taking out an ad in the *Gazette*?"

Rosa's head whipped back as if I'd slapped her. "Yes, I deny it. My God, I've been working my tail off. When do I have time to print flyers or solicit advertisements? This is all Piper's doing. She's trying to stir up more trouble to break a story. And at my expense."

"Bull! You've been working your tail off to make yourself look like a fool, you mean. Arresting poor Elaine, harassing club members, not to mention physically assaulting Tammy! You should have seen how scared they all were." Melanie was on the verge of tears. "I don't even know who you are anymore. Where is my friend?"

Rosa's gaze skated from Melanie's face to mine and back again before she deflated onto the sofa and placed her face in her hands. "I didn't assault Tammy. She exaggerates. And the reason I arrested Elaine was that someone set me up. Or sabotaged me is more like it."

"You were set up? Spare me." Melanie wiped furiously at the tears that tracked down her cheek.

Rosa dropped her hands. "It's true. I received intel from an anonymous source that pointed to Elaine Morgan. I had documented proof of Elaine threatening Patricia. I had her prints on the murder weapon, and I was hell-bent on proving myself. Especially after Officer Harry Daniels's incessant undermining. I got ahead of myself." She scrubbed her face and shook her head, looking disgusted. "I screwed up. There was a backup in the lab, and I didn't wait to get the audio back from being analyzed before seeking the warrant. I told the DA the case was a slam dunk. I've tanked my career with three lousy words. *A slam dunk.*"

I sat down next to her. "The recording had been fabricated?"

She nodded in three slow motions. "The entire recording had been tampered with. Elaine's words were modified. Your folks' lawyer, Greene—he shredded my case until there wasn't anything left. He had his tech guy turn the job around in under an hour."

"It's a good thing. Elaine would have suffered horribly if the case had gotten drawn out. A sweet little old lady, Rosa." I stared at my friend. She had dark circles under her eyes; her uniform hung looser on her frame. She couldn't be eating. Or sleeping.

She ran her hands through her shoulder-length dark hair and gripped it, tugging slightly. "*I know.* I could make excuses for myself, but I won't. I was only trying to do my job, and I probably won't have a badge for much longer."

I didn't want to say that it might be a good thing. I honestly didn't want to think it. But the mess Rosa had made gave me pause. This behavior was so unlike her.

Melanie sat down on the other side of her. "Why did you go off half-cocked like that? Why didn't you work the case?"

"I thought I was working the case. Don't you see what is happening?" Rosa's watery dark eyes searched mine. "Someone is trying to ruin me."

Wasn't that what Patricia had said Elaine had done to her? The thought gave me a sick feeling in the pit of my stomach. I didn't want to be suspicious of one of my closest friends. But I could not and would not go through life with blinders on. I didn't know what was going on with Rosa. My gut told me she wouldn't do anything to hurt anyone on purpose. But there was a change in her. Something was off that I couldn't put my finger on.

"What about Tammy and Joel?" Melanie asked. "They weren't trying to ruin you. They were terrified."

Rosa fought annoyance. "When it all went down at the manor, you remember what a chaotic scene that was. Tammy was all up in my face shouting. Everyone was. I had to secure the scene the best I could. No one would listen to what I was telling them. People were rushing around, and I had a shooter on the loose and no control over the crime scene. But I overreacted and told her to shut her mouth and butt out. I'd speak to her when I needed to hear her voice. I'll apologize."

"She claims you slammed her into the wall," Melanie said, more softly this time.

Rosa genuinely looked confused. "I didn't lay a hand on her." She closed her eyes and stood, pacing. "I have to get to the bottom of this case. I have to find out who is screwing with me and who killed Patricia Donaldson. If I can catch the guy, maybe, just maybe, I can save my job."

She looked a little wild-eyed as she turned to face me. "I need your help. People in this town won't talk to me now."

"Have you considered allowing Harry to revisit the witnesses? I know you don't like him, and yes, he may be trying to use your failings to elevate his career, but he might be able to discover something you can't."

"I told you how he undermines me. I'm not certain he wouldn't botch the investigation just to lay it all on me." Rosa sounded desperate. I wouldn't dare lay out the fact that Elaine had a valid lawsuit because of her mistakes. Nor would I mention that Quinn had brought me on tonight. It might break her. She needed sleep.

I picked up the flyer. "A man visiting said you gave him this flyer."

Rosa's eyes sharpened. "What man?"

"Dean," Melanie supplied.

"Dean who?" Rosa's body went completely rigid.

"Willis, I think. He said you gave it to him after you issued him a jaywalking warning the night you arrested Elaine." My words hung heavy in the air.

Her thick brows drew together, the single line between them deepening. "I did not issue a jaywalking warning the night of Elaine's arrest. Nor did I give that flyer to anyone. But that someone is out there disparaging my character alerts me that my suspicions are true, and that guy must be involved."

"How do you figure?" Mel asked.

"I figure I don't have any other leads, and this guy might be the first. Maybe he's even involved."

"That sounds a little farfetched. I mean, why in the world would this Dean guy stick around if he had something to do with the murder?" Melanie kept shaking her head.

I glanced back down at the flyer and studied it, counting the dashes. Realization stomped all over me, and I believed Rosa. Perhaps not all her theories rang true, but someone somewhere had definitely set their sights on her. How had I not put this together before? Tens dashes for ten letters that spelled *Rosa Landry*.

I checked the date on my phone, and a cold chill ran up my spine. "Rosa, I think someone is trying to do more than ruin your career."

Chapter
Twenty-Four

The following day, I stood at the front desk of Holiday Inn across town. Today was October 22, the Friday referred to in the announcement, and I'd decided I couldn't wait another second for Dean to call me back. I'd left him several messages, and after no callback when he'd seemed so eager to chat me up before, I feared that perhaps Rosa's suspicions were warranted.

"Thanks so much for doing this for me," I told Joel.

Joel tapped away on the keyboard, pausing to pick up his reading glasses and perch them on the end of his nose. "It's not a problem. You know I'm always glad to help." More typing. "Hmm. I don't have a guest registered with the name Dean Willis. Are you sure he said he was staying here?"

I fiddled with the piece of paper Dean had given me. "That's what he told me. See, he wrote it down here."

Joel's thin lips turned up in a wicked smile, and he gave my hand a slap. "Lyla Moody, did you have a tryst with an out-of-towner?"

I felt a flush come into my cheeks. "No. It isn't anything like that. I just need to find him. Maybe you've seen him around the hotel. He's about six and a half feet tall, broad shouldered, with dark-blond hair and deep-blue eyes."

Joel laughed wickedly. "Uh-huh. Not a tryst, my patootie. You're hunting that man down." He leaned closer. "Must have been unforgettable."

"Joel." I shook my head but couldn't help the smile that creased my lips. Even though I hadn't taken Dean up on his offer to go out, he had traipsed across my mind a time or two before my conversation with Rosa. Therapy for a wounded heart.

"If he's staying here under an alias, I haven't seen him. And honey, the man you're describing would draw interest. We don't get a lot of those type of men staying at this hotel."

"Okay. Thanks."

Joel's expression lost its playful edge, and he stood up straighter. "Yes, sir, what can I do for you?"

"Checking out," the man behind me said.

"Thanks, Joel." I gave him a wave good-bye.

Rosa lit up my phone the second I left the hotel, as if she were tracking me. I got right to it. "Either he isn't staying there or he's staying under a different name. Joel hasn't seen him around."

"I knew something didn't sound right about that guy. Can you come by the station and sit down with our sketch artist?"

"What are you going to do, put an APB out on a guy because he handed me a flyer?" I took a left onto the highway.

"No. I just want to know who I'm looking for. I need some idea to work with." She sounded stressed to the max.

"Calm down. I'm going to try Dean's number again. Last time it just went to a generic voice mail. We need to talk anyway.

Let's sit down when I get there. I won't be long, but I need to scope out every possibility first—especially that cemetery mentioned on the flyer." I was expected at the police station in an hour as it was; she just didn't know it yet. It'd be better to have that sort of conversation face-to-face.

"No! No, you don't. Leave that to me."

Annoyance overtook me. "Don't bark orders at me, Rosa Landry. I'll do whatever I have to do to keep you and this town safe."

She groaned. "I appreciate your concern. Just help me, will ya?"

"I am helping. I spoke with Joel, didn't I? But you have to take this threat seriously."

"Yes. I'm sorry, and I am. That's why we need to find this Dean guy. See if he's involved. We could be dealing with a serial killer."

A cold chill overtook me. I'd never actually uttered the words *serial killer*. I'd thought them, of course, or at least feared them. "All right. But it might not even be him. And I racked my brain trying to find a connection between him and Patricia."

"I did the same. There isn't an obvious one. But don't worry about it. I have it in hand."

"You're not keeping anything from me, are you?"

"No." She didn't sound very convincing. I'd push more when I saw her.

"You should send a car out to the cemetery. With a police presence—perhaps it will deter any persons with the wrong intentions—but you should stay away."

"I don't want to alarm anyone yet."

She was hiding something from me. "Maybe just send Harry, then."

"I don't want to deal with *Harry*." Her tone edged on hysteria. "Sorry. Just trust me on this, okay?"

"I'll be in touch." I disconnected the call and planned on speaking to Harry myself. I understood Rosa's desperation. But utilizing the department's sketch artist would surely bring unwanted attention. And I simply couldn't contribute to another false arrest. As much as I loved my friend, I honestly wondered if she was fit for active duty in her current state of mind. Nevertheless, I planned on keeping her safe.

* * *

A train was crossing the road when I made it downtown, and traffic had backed up. I put my car in park and used the time to try the number again. The phone rang through my speakers in time with the train whistle, and I tapped my fingers against the steering wheel and waited.

"Hello," a deep male voice said.

I sat forward. "Hi, is this Dean?"

"Yes, speaking."

"Hi, this is Lyla, um, Lyla Moody." I gripped the wheel, feeling nervous all of a sudden.

"Hey, Lyla, what can I do you for?" He had a little chuckle in his voice.

His folksy demeanor didn't put me at ease. "I left you a couple of messages. I just had a quick question for you."

"Oh, I lost the charger for my phone and just went by Target to pick up another one. I haven't checked my messages yet. Sorry about that."

That explained the no callback. "No worries. Like I said, I only wanted to ask you a question."

"Shoot."

The jarring way he'd said *shoot* caused me to jump. Sheesh. I had to rein in my emotions. "You mentioned the officer that gave you a warning and the flyer about the party was Sergeant Landry. Are you positive?"

All the humor left his voice then. "Absolutely. It's tonight, right? You worried about it?"

"I'm worried about a lot of things." Hopefully, that was ambiguous enough. The last thing we needed was for him to take it upon himself to show up at the cemetery tonight.

He sounded like he was swallowing, and I could imagine him holding the phone with a cup of coffee in hand.

"I ran by the hotel you mentioned and was going to see if you wanted to grab breakfast." I gazed down the tracks and saw this was going to be a long wait.

"I'm here. Did you have the front desk call up to the room?"

I spied a news van going over the flyover bridge on the other side of the square and got a sinking feeling in the pit of my stomach.

"Lyla. Did you have the front desk call?"

"Oh, sorry. I planned on it, but the front desk couldn't find you in the registry." Another news van caught my eye as I craned my neck around to get a better view of the bridge. One van could be a coincidence but not two. The touch screen on my dashboard alerted me to another call coming in. Piper. Definitely not a coincidence.

"At the Holiday Inn Express on Highway 20?"

He was on the other side of town at the Holiday Inn Express. His note had just said Holiday Inn, and I'd made an assumption. My instincts had been right; there was no need for a sketch artist. "My fault. I guess I got mixed up with the Inn and the Express."

"Well, I'm flattered you went searching for me." I could hear the smile in his voice. If he had any suspicions about my motivations, he hid it well.

"I felt bad for being rude to you when you came by the office. I wanted to apologize by showing you around town." I heard a television in the background. The news.

"Something is bugging me, though. Why would you need to double-check? Does Sergeant Landry say otherwise?"

"She does."

The volume on the TV in the background turned way up. "Well, she would, wouldn't she? There's a press conference going on at the police station. That's her, all right. I'm positive."

"What?" Alarm shot through me like a jolt of electricity.

"Yeah. Wow. It looks like the sergeant is holding a press conference."

I grabbed my phone, checked my local news app, and found the live news conference. Rosa had called an impromptu news conference. A press conference she'd told me nothing about. Trust her, she'd said. Not withholding information, my ass. "I have to go."

"Hey, wait. You mentioned the sergeant denied giving me a warning."

I didn't want to discuss this now. "I'll have to talk to you later." My hand hovered over the disconnect button on the touch screen, and I silently willed the train in front of me to end.

"I have a picture of her I can send, if that helps."

"What?" My hand dropped.

"A picture of the sergeant. I'm always worried about police impropriety. My background, I suppose. A convenient body cam malfunction or abuse of power. I make it a habit when I'm pulled over to take a picture of the officer. Get their badge number. Sergeant Landry's conduct concerned me. I tried to capture the badge number on her uniform."

"Did you file a formal complaint?" I tried to listen to the conference and Dean at the same time, failing miserably.

"No. When I found out Sergeant Landry was a friend of yours, and seeing I was interested in getting to know you better, I let it drop. I'll text it to you."

Rosa's rigid posture in front of the small audience informed me I was missing quite a lot. "Okay. Thanks. Listen, I'll call you back." I turned up the volume just as Rosa, red-faced and agitated, said, "We ask that the press be careful in their representation of the investigation. It is imperative with an investigation such as this one that the press does not engage in fearmongering. Sadly, some of the local media have been guilty of such tactics to sell subscriptions."

"Isn't it unusual for a person in law enforcement present when a murder occurs to head up the investigation?" Piper ignored Rosa's directive.

Rosa ignored her as well and attempted to take a question from another member of the press. I chewed on the side of my thumb.

"Isn't that a conflict of interest and perhaps the reason there is a potential lawsuit against your department?" Piper did not back down.

"Piper Sanchez, I'll have you know that this investigation is aboveboard. You better watch yourself."

My God. Rosa, no!

"Are you threatening a member of the press, Sergeant Landry?" The ever-unflappable Piper stepped forward. A challenge.

"I'm merely stating facts." Rosa wiped her sweaty brow. She looked guilty as sin to the accusation of misconduct. *What in God's name is going on with her?*

My phone pinged, and I clicked the text from Dean and inadvertently cut off the news feed. I blew up the image he'd sent and checked the length of the train. God, this train crept and was forever long. Sighing, I glanced down at the picture and froze. The quality wasn't the best, but the woman in the image did look like Rosa. A quote floated through my head.

Very few of us are what we seem. Agatha Christie.

My heart sank.

Chapter
Twenty-Five

The police department was in total chaos when I arrived. Rosa, insulated by a couple of her officers, stayed holed up in the office. Licking her wounds, I assumed. I managed to have a quick word with Harry before driving home to change. I couldn't believe how in a matter of weeks, my happy world had imploded. When my phone rang, the ruins crumbled a little more.

"Hey." I hit the speaker icon and sat down on my bed, sock in hand.

"Hey. Are you okay?" Brad sounded tentative and uneasy. Good. At least he cared.

"I'm managing."

"I saw the news. Someone really needs to step in and relieve Rosa from duty. It was a real circus act today."

I sighed. "Yes, I know. Quinn is on his way back."

"Thank God for that. Are you working on the case? I assume . . ."

I rubbed my head, listening to him go on and on with his questions and assumptions until I couldn't take it a second longer. "Brad." I gripped my sock. "Enough. Who was the woman, and how long has this been going on?"

There was silence for a few long beats. The weight on my chest was unbearable. But I would not be the one to break the silence. Would not beg him to do what was right and come clean.

"She's a coworker. Was a coworker. We've worked together for a long time. We, my division, and some from forensics were celebrating her early retirement party. She's going into teaching and getting out of fieldwork. That's what Wyatt walked in on." He cleared his throat.

Jennifer Mitchell, just like I thought. Something had to be going on. He would have told me they were working together otherwise. Plus, he hadn't been himself. And he knew how upset I was. And still he hadn't driven to Sweet Mountain. Hadn't come pounding down my door declaring undying love for me. God, my fantasies sucked sometimes.

"What's her name?" I twisted the sock in my hands.

He cleared his throat. "Jennifer."

"As in your ex?" My pulse sped up.

"Yes."

I laughed. *God, I am so stupid.* "The Jennifer you had all that history with. The one you almost married but decided it would never work out because you both were in the same office and dealt with the same crimes? Now she's leaving. Isn't that perfect?" I jerked the sock onto my foot. "How long has this been going on?"

"It isn't like that. Whatever you've concocted in your mind isn't what's going on. Yes, there are feelings between us. You can't spend years with a person and just cut your emotions off toward them."

Of course not. But he'd said they'd both decided they were through. Guess they'd both decided otherwise. I could throw up.

"Yes, I should have talked to you before now. I'm a jackass. But I didn't want to have this sort of discussion over the phone. There isn't anything going on, I swear. But"—he blew out a loud breath—"to be honest with you, I've been clear on what I've wanted, Lyla. We've had several discussions over the last few months that ended with you dismissing me. I—"

"No! You will not turn this around on me." I shoved my left foot into my trainers. "I'm not the one with feelings for another person. I'm not the one who's at fault here. You know what, Brad"—I snorted—"it doesn't matter. It's over. We'll work together on the cases as we need to. The Jane Doe cases are important. And I'm still going to advocate for them to Calvin. But, like you, I have a case right now. And I need a clear head."

"I get that." His tone sounded monotone, empty. "I'm sorry."

"Yeah, me too." I disconnected the call.

* * *

"Do you really believe Rosa could be involved?" Melanie asked as she pulled down a dark Erwin Street leading to the Oak Mill Cemetery. We'd ridden in silence the entire way over here. I'd not told her about my call with Brad. I wasn't ready to discuss it yet. Too fresh. Too painful. Work—work was good.

I had my night vision binoculars out and began scanning the landscaped area. I was determined to put an end to all this madness. "She's involved. I'm not sure how. She wouldn't even see me today. And she'd been hell-bent on me sitting down with a sketch artist not a half hour before. And that picture Dean sent isn't the best, but a jury might find it interesting. I don't know if it's the threat against her that has her so rattled and unstable acting or that she's done something that could get her arrested. She won't be coming out here tonight. Harry will be keeping her busy until he does a drive-by later."

"That's good. I guess. Rosa admitted to making some serious mistakes. I hope they aren't the life-changing kind like that new conference. God, it really blew up in her face. I cringed during the entire thing, watching through my fingers like a full-on collision that I couldn't turn away from."

"It was bad."

"Piper shouldn't have been so awful to her. It was as if Piper could see Rosa's cracks and fissures and decided, who cares about her mental state? Let's apply pressure and see what happens."

"That's her job." I glanced over at Mel. "Rosa should have been prepared for that. Not that I'm not worried for her. Something crazy is going on here. And honestly, if someone is baiting her, I can't imagine how'd I react if I were in her shoes."

"I've been trying to—"

I reached across the cab and grabbed Mel's arm, and she squeaked in surprise. "Slow down. I see movement." We slow-rolled around the bend, passing giant angel statues by headstones and creepy weeping child ornaments. I saw a few cars parked in a row.

Melanie giggled, sounding quite hysterical. "Sorry." But the giggles continued. I motioned for her to park behind the last car, several yards back.

We got out of the car as quietly as we could manage, being careful to close the doors lightly. I had my sling pack tucked to my side, carrying my loaded piece. Melanie kept herself low and behind me. Laughter erupted up ahead, and I could smell smoke from a fire. When we got closer, I spied a rusty barrel and flames coming out of the top. Those dumb kids had shown up despite the warning. I shook my head. I didn't want anyone else to get hurt.

I pointed, signaling that we should go around behind the activity and sneak up to see what we were dealing with. I had no intention of going in with Mel guns a-blazing. I'd wait for the police.

Not that the activity I spied warranted such actions. From here, it looked like kids taking advantage of a Halloween prank by partying at the cemetery. Their loud voices carried. The wind chill made me glad I'd worn my fleece hoodie as we scurried around headstones and grave markers. Melanie had a death grip on the back of my sweatshirt. For someone who loved haunted houses and horror movies during this season, she sure freaked out when she got anywhere near cemeteries.

Mel stumbled and nearly choked me.

"Sheesh, let go." I jerked my shirt out of her grasp.

"Sorry. I just think this might not be the best idea. I mean, maybe we should call this in. The psycho might be waiting to see who shows up from our club and, when it isn't Rosa, pick you or me." She ran her finger across her neck.

I halted by a large stone a reasonable distance from where the youngsters had gathered and glanced over at a panting Mel. She pointed at me. "See! I'm onto something, aren't I? We should go back to the car."

A shriek echoed around us, and we both froze, clutching each other. When laughter followed, I relaxed a little. It would settle my mind to think tonight could turn out to be nothing. Maybe I'd been wrong and the flyer had been a prank. And perhaps the situations surrounding Rosa were completely unrelated. I loved my friend dearly, but I couldn't deny the unusual behavior she'd exhibited. She'd gone on and on about someone attempting to sabotage her, and then she'd gone on live television and sunk her own battleship.

I motioned to Mel to follow me out to the tree line where we'd established our little stakeout camp. I had driven out here earlier today to set up a spot where'd we be able to scope out the only tree resembling the one on the flyer. Better safe than sorry. Best case scenario, we'd get a little chilly hanging out and watching the kids party.

I began moving the branches away from the camp we'd set up earlier.

Mel began pacing, wringing her hands. I could see she was spiraling, getting herself so worked up that she'd not be able to sit still. "I don't know about this. I'm getting an awful feeling. And you know how my gut is always right. When I get a bad feeling—watch out!" Her words came out frantic, barely a breath between them.

I grabbed her by the shoulders and said in a low, pacifying tone, "Listen. I know you're scared, and I understand. I don't know what I was thinking."

She gripped my arms in return, nodding her head in agreement.

"I'm so sorry I allowed you to come with me. I have no idea what I was thinking bringing you along. Your poor thing." I poked my lip out. "I know how delicate you are. I won't let anything happen to you. I will protect you."

Mel's face contorted with indignation. "Delicate?" she spat. "What are you talking about? You didn't allow me to do anything." Melanie jerked away from me and wagged her finger in my face. "And I don't need you to protect me. I'm a grown woman and fully capable of taking care of . . ." Her voice trailed off as she studied me.

I smirked, and she slapped me on the arm. That tactic always worked with Mel. It was like her reset button. I winked at her.

"You're incorrigible."

I tilted a shoulder, turned back toward the party, and lifted my binoculars. "It worked."

Melanie laughed softly behind me. "Yeah, okay. Next time just slap me. You know, like they do in those old silent movies when the female protagonist gets hysterical. I'd much rather be slapped than patronized."

"You got it," I said over my shoulder. "Slap first."

"Thanks." She settled next to me inside the tent. "Are they doing anything suspicious? Oh." She leaned forward. "Maybe it's one of them. You know, that JB kid you were telling me about. The one egging everyone to attend."

"I don't think so. All JB has is a couple of speeding tickets, and he plays college ball. From his social media posts, I gathered that he's hoping to make the pros."

"Huh. So what are they doing?"

"Just defiling some sad souls' resting places. They're smoking, drinking, and dancing around their rusted-out old burn barrel."

"This is going to be a long night." Melanie groaned.

Long and boring, I hoped.

Chapter
Twenty-Six

We sat watching drunk college kids act like fools for what felt like hours in the two-person camo instant pop-up tent Melanie had ordered from Amazon. The portable little tent folded down neatly and fit into a small backpack. I'd commended her for her choice.

Mel had brought snacks, or "sustenance," as she referred to her petits fours and biscotti and a thermos of coffee. About an hour in, I'd expected to see a patrol car roll by and run the kids off, but it never came. Earlier today Harry had agreed to make a run out here. He'd been much more accommodating since my conversation with Quinn. I hadn't even had to bring it up. He was in the know, as he called it. I shot him off a quick text.

Kids partying on the grounds. A drive-by would be nice.

I slid the phone back into my pocket. Harry's delay made me wonder if this whole party thing might have been a diversion. This entire situation had me second-guessing my second guesses.

I'd had so much coffee that I'd had to do the unthinkable and dash behind the tent and do my business primitive-style. Thank God Mel had brought napkins. She kept snickering and saying, "Watch your jeans, and don't sprinkle as you tinkle."

I was sanitizing my hands with a double dousing of the alcohol-based gel when Mel whispered-railed, "Holy smokes! It's Joel and Tammy!"

"What?" I took the binoculars from Melanie's outstretched hand. A little too quickly, I panned the area. I thought I caught a flash of light. Maybe movement. Slowly, I scanned back.

"I can't believe it," Mel gasped. "Wasn't it Tammy who first brought the flyer to your attention?"

I nodded, still scanning, and found them several yards from the teens. There they were. Tammy and Joel wearing black hoodies and carrying flashlights. I watched them creep slowly up behind the group and lost them behind a grouping of large headstones. I crept out from the covering of the bushes and trees, trying to get a visual again.

"Lyla!" Mel whispered.

I kept moving forward. Closer.

Another whisper-shout. "Lyla, wait!"

Something dropped from the tree. A scream went up. One of the girls was on the ground and scrambling backward. A couple of kids were running away. I dropped the binoculars, allowing them to fall around my neck. I ran, stumbling and fumbling in the darkness, toward the only illumination ahead. I had my hand on my sling pack when I arrived on the scene. My gun was within grasping distance.

"Everyone remain where you are." My voice came out thick and raspy.

"The cops!" one boy said and bolted.

The kids who remained were rolling on the ground laughing. Drunk out of their minds.

"He did it!" a boy shouted, pointing in the direction of another boy.

I glanced up at the swinging oversized rag dummy that dangled from the tree and blew out a breath. Both my knees throbbed, probably skinned from my stumble to the ground. My chest ached from the battering it had taken from the binoculars as I ran. I bent down, grabbed the gallon of water on the ground, and doused the fire.

"All right! The party is over." I used all the authority of a professional investigator. "Each of you is breaking several ordinances, and I should call the cops and have you all run in."

Blue lights appeared, and a police siren blipped a few times. *Finally.*

The laughter stopped then, and they all stared up at me with wide eyes.

"Go! Now!" I pointed to where they'd parked.

Mel reached me, huffing and puffing, her hand over her heart. "I've got to start exercising."

Piper stood next to me, shaking her head. "I was with Harry when you texted."

From her state of dress, she didn't have to say in what capacity she'd been with him. I wouldn't comment. It was her life.

We stood while Harry gave the kids that remained a stern warning. He'd been able to prevent the ones too drunk to drive from the possibility of ruining their lives and potentially someone else's. He wrangled an unruly heavyset boy who'd taken a swing at him into the back of his cruiser.

"I'll be hitching a ride back with you and Mel." Piper tied her tan trench coat tighter around her. "It's freezing out here."

"You're telling us," Mel said. "We've been staking this place out for hours. Any sign of Tammy or Joel?"

Piper glanced at Melanie, who had busied herself cleaning up the beer and spiked seltzer cans littering the ground.

"No. We saw Tammy and Joel here earlier," I told Piper, who raised her newly threaded brows. "I lost them after the screaming commenced."

"What were they doing?"

I lifted both shoulders in an exaggerated fashion. "Probably exactly what we're all doing here." Though I'd made myself perfectly clear to my club that they should steer clear tonight. As frightened as they'd seemed over the last few days, it gave me pause that they would go against my instructions.

I glanced up at the dummy swinging from the tree.

"I've got to run this kid in." Harry rubbed the side of his jaw. "From what I gathered, one of the kids saw the posts online and decided to have a little fun with it."

"Yeah. I've been watching it and tried to shut it down." This *had* turned out to be a stupid hoax. Someone had a horrid sense of humor. But I felt immensely relieved.

"Dumb kids," Piper grumbled.

Still, that didn't explain the flyer.

"Did they say if they knew who printed and distributed the flyer?" I stared at a perplexed and agitated Harry.

He rubbed the back of his neck. "Not yet. But they will."

A deep guttural bellow came from down the hill toward the road. Piper nearly fell into me, shouting, "Holy shit!"

Harry shined his light in that direction.

"She's dead! Oh. My. God. Rosa's dead!" a male voice wailed.

"Stay here," Harry demanded, and charged through the cemetery toward the remaining cars.

Not a chance! I ran ahead of him, my heart hammering in my ears. Joel sat on the ground several feet from a gray Mustang. *The gray Mustang.* His hand was over his mouth, his arm extended and pointing. I froze beside the car, and Harry, huffing, pushed me aside. The top was down, and he went over to the driver's side, where Rosa slumped, shining his flashlight on her body. I could only glimpse part of her arm as Harry blocked my view. He radioed in as he leaned forward.

My vision swam, and I thought I was going to be sick. Rosa wasn't supposed to be here. She didn't drive a Mustang. My God . . . I stumbled toward Joel.

Joel's wide-eyed gaze latched on to mine. "She's dead," he gasped. "I . . . I can't believe it."

Slowly I made my way around the car to see my friend's body. Harry barked into his phone. I heard him calling for backup. It took a couple of beats for me to get up the nerve to raise my eyes to Rosa's face. I heard Piper saying something behind me but couldn't make out the words.

There were boot prints in the soft red dirt around the car. The bluish-gray uniform had patches of dried mud on the arms. I tried to swallow; my throat was dry. Thunder boomed overhead in a loud, ominous warning. I wanted to shake my fists toward the sky and shout, "Too late!" The warning had come too late. I lifted my gaze, tears streaming down my cheeks. I noticed a deep wound to the cleft in Rosa's chin, and my pulse quickened. Her nose had been broken, her face bruised and streaked with dried blood. I leaned forward, being careful not to touch the car or the body. My shoes sunk into the soft earth. Something was caked to the side of her face. Even with all the distortions, I was one hundred percent certain.

"It isn't her." My voice sounded unrecognizable. I cleared it and said over my shoulder, "It isn't her!"

Harry turned around. "What?"

"It isn't Rosa."

"What?" Melanie managed to get out around sobs. She and Joel were clutched together on the ground, and it occurred to me that I hadn't noticed when Melanie had followed us over.

I shook my head. "It isn't Rosa. She's dressed in a uniform, her hair is the same color, and the resemblance is remarkable, but it isn't her." I moved away from the deceased.

This had to have been the woman in Dean's photo. This had been the woman roaming around town impersonating a Sweet Mountain police officer. A sergeant and acting chief at that.

Bold. Callous. Daring enough to shoot a woman in the middle of a party?

"Everyone remain exactly where you are. Once the other patrol car gets here and the scene is secured, we are all going down to the police station. Everyone will give a statement and an account with the reasons why they are here. You"—Harry pointed at Joel—"don't move."

Joel's bottom lip quivered. Melanie wiped her face with a shaky hand, still feeling the aftereffects of adrenaline.

I stared at the car containing our Jane Doe. *My God.* Rosa was right. Someone had been trying to sabotage her, and they'd received a death sentence.

A quote floated through my mind. *Three can keep a secret if two of them are dead.* Benjamin Franklin.

Jane Doe hadn't been working alone.

The mastermind is still out there . . .

Chapter Twenty-Seven

The next morning when my alarm went off at six thirty, I practically had to drag myself from bed. Too many sleepless nights were catching up with me. My mind raced with theories and conjectures regarding the woman impersonating Rosa. Who'd killed her? Why had she persisted in terrorizing the town and my book club with her flyers and threats? I hoped to have those answers this morning.

I scanned my news feed while I had my cup of coffee. Snippets from last night were all over the media. I nearly dropped my mug when I saw a quick panned image of myself. Piper must have videoed it from her phone. The video cut off when you saw my profile—the part where I was saying it wasn't one of my best friends who'd been bludgeoned to death and left on display in a graveyard.

Piper appeared on the screen, freshened up and with much better lighting. She reported from the scene, telling the audience how a disruption-of-the-peace call had turned into the discovery of a Jane Doe dressed in a Sweet Mountain Police uniform.

I turned up the volume as Piper said, "Lyla Moody, a local private investigator working in conjunction with the Sweet

Mountain Police Department, was on the scene behind me when the body was discovered. It was Miss Moody who recognized the impostor and alerted Officer Harry Daniels. The police are working to identify Jane Doe and hope to have an ID shortly."

I hit Piper's contact icon as I hurried out the front door.

"Are you on your way here? It's all hitting the fan. We're setting up for the press conference."

"What?" I waved at the security guard as I passed. "Please tell me Rosa didn't call another one."

"Not Rosa. Quinn's back, and from the look of him, this is going to be worth the lack of sleep." I heard a lot of background noise and a man talking. Piper responded, "Dammit, Gene, I told you to set up on the left side. Now I'm going to have to add lots more concealer, and we need another ring light." I heard rustling. "Sorry about that. If Gene hadn't been with me since the inception, I would fire him."

"I'm betting Gene would probably quit, too, if not for the same reason." I crossed the railroad tracks, thanking God there wasn't another train, and took a left onto Eagle Street.

She laughed. "Yeah. He doesn't mind my witchy side. Anyway, I heard from a source that Rosa has been put on leave. It was Quinn's first order this morning. And a lawsuit has been filed."

I made another left. "I had a feeling that was coming."

"The lawsuit or the leave?" I could hear Piper spraying her hair.

"Both. Listen, I'm coming. ETA five minutes."

The outrage at the police station last night hadn't helped Rosa. Even with Jane Doe impersonating her, public perception had been solidified. The late night had contributed to everyone's foul mood. We'd been up practically all night giving our statements. Answering the usual questions. Why we'd been at the cemetery. How long we'd been there. What we had witnessed, no matter how inconsequential it seemed to us. If we'd ever had contact with the victim, and if so, what the interaction had consisted of.

Piper, Melanie, and I sat with the rest of the group and weren't singled out. I answered the same questions as everyone else, even though the officers knew why I was at the cemetery. The station was overcrowded with college kids, their outraged parents, and the attorneys of those whose parents believed as my father did and had lawyered up. From the few times I saw Rosa, I could tell some of the parents weren't pleased to have her questioning their child. And maybe she'd gotten the same reaction from Joel and Tammy as well.

Joel had asked for an attorney straightaway. He wanted Mr. Greene, but I supposed our family attorney's fees were too steep or Mr. Greene wasn't interested in representing him, because another attorney showed up as Mel and I were leaving. Not that Joel had been officially charged with anything. Not that I knew of, anyway.

The parking lot of the Sweet Mountain Police Department looked as I'd expected. There were more news vans this time, and a lot more reporters. A stage of sorts had been set up on the cement porch of the station. The reporters stood close to the base of the brick steps leading up to the building.

Our town hadn't needed a large building. When the Baptist Church had moved locations around fifteen years ago, as their congregation had outgrown it, the city had renovated it and the police department had moved in.

As I parked, I received a text from Dean, asking if I was okay and saying he'd changed hotels if I needed him. On my short drive over, several calls had come in from Gran and my mother. Not knowing what to tell them yet, I'd let them roll to voice mail. I nudged my way through the crowd to get closer to hear better. I'd seen Quinn give a press conference only once, and he'd looked about as uncomfortable then as he did now, standing there in his official blues. Piper stood out front, her camera guy right behind her. My pulse quickened. A couple of what looked to be state officers stood behind him, but Rosa was nowhere to be seen.

Oh, this is not good.

Not only were the news outlets present, but I recognized many locals as well. Everyone wanted to know what was going on and how our chief of police would be handling things.

"Effective immediately," Quinn was saying, "Sergeant Landry will be put on suspension while the Sweet Mountain Police Department undergoes a thorough internal investigation into these claims. Make no mistake, any and all misconduct complaints are taken seriously and will be dealt with swiftly. The investigation into the death of Patricia Donaldson is ongoing. A separate investigation will be conducted into the death of Jane Doe found in Oak Mills Cemetery last night. We've called in a special investigator from Atlanta to help. And with that, I'll take a few questions."

"Chief Quinn, who has taken over the Donaldson murder case?" a reporter asked.

"I know you've noticed these officers behind me." Quinn motioned to the two people behind him. "With a potential lawsuit pending, Georgia State Police will be assisting with the

investigation into the brutal murder of Patricia Donaldson."
Quinn pointed to another reporter. "And rest assured, we will
find the person responsible."

"Has the case against Elaine Morgan been officially
dropped?"

"Yes. The DA has decided not to pursue a criminal case
against Mrs. Morgan at this time. Mrs. Morgan has also received
a formal apology from our department for any anguish she suffered as a result of her unfounded arrest."

Anguish. There was that word again.

"Are the two murder cases linked?" a reported shouted.

"At this time, we have no reason to believe the cases are
linked." Quinn pointed to Piper.

"Are you taking the claims that we may have a potential
serial killer in our town seriously?"

Audible gasps went up, and grumblings began. Followed by,
"Chief Quinn, are we in danger?"

Before Quinn could respond, another rapid-fire question
came.

"Chief Quinn, should you put out a public announcement
to warn the town? A serial killer could be in our midst." Piper
kept her head held high.

Quinn's eyes flickered with anger. "Miss Sanchez, it's buzz-
words like those that create panic. We have no reason to believe
we are dealing with that sort of criminal. Rest assured we are
investigating every lead and leaving no stone unturned. At this
time, I'm asking the residents of Sweet Mountain to come forward if they have any information on Jane Doe. In particular, if
they interacted with her or saw anything suspicious the night of
her death. Thank you."

Piper raised her voice. "With the Jane Doe impersonating one of your officers and a flyer inviting residents to attend yet another murder, how can you possibly say the cases aren't linked?"

Quinn made direct eye contact with me and angled his head toward the building. Good, he wanted to speak with me too.

Reporters continued to shout questions, but Quinn stepped away from the podium and went inside the building.

The crowd reluctantly began to disperse, and I waded my way toward the steps. Piper stood with her cameraman in a deep discussion. When she saw me, she gestured for him to wait for her back at the van. She looped her arm through mine and leaned her head closer. "Hey, how worried should I be?"

"Concerned but not terrified." I glanced around. "Not cool, inciting panic."

"I'm just trying to give the department the kick in the pants it needs. If I hadn't asked the questions, another reporter would have."

"Probably so. Although Rosa must accept her part of the blame for her suspension, she isn't wrong about someone coming for her. And I'm darn well going to find out who and why before they make their next move. She still may not be safe."

Piper nodded. "Are you sure it's Rosa and not just your club that's being targeted?"

We separated for a moment to allow a couple of camera crews to pass. I held Piper's gaze and, once people were out of earshot, said, "I'm not sure of anything. But I'm leaning toward it just being Rosa."

"What can I do?"

"I'll call you. I need to get inside and speak with Quinn." I turned and started up the steps.

"Hey, Lyla."

I glanced over my shoulder.

"FYI, *he's* inside." Her face told me exactly who *he* was.

Chapter
Twenty-Eight

A flurry of activity buzzed around me when I walked through the white double doors of the police station. The new desk sergeant sat behind an enormous mahogany desk in the poorly lit front room with a phone to her ear. Her hair looked disheveled, and her face flushed when I walked up to the glass separating the desk from the waiting area. She held up a finger when she noticed me. I stepped back, realizing there weren't any vacant seats available, and stood to the side, glancing up at the plaque that hung over the glass. I knew it by heart, but I read it every time I came into the building anyway.

It read:

The Sweet Mountain Police Department's focus is:
To protect and serve our citizens with a high level of
   integrity
To utilize a community policing philosophy
To strive for excellence in all that we do
To become less incident driven and more proactive in
   preventing crime

"Is that the woman from the news this morning?" a voice behind me said.

I kept my head down.

"Yeah, yeah. I think it is."

The closed security door between the waiting room and the office buzzed open, and the girl at the desk waved me through. A wave of gratitude washed over me. An uproar began from impatient people waiting to be taken care of, and I hurried through the door before my entrance provoked a mobbing. Concern agitated my insides like a butter churn.

The state officers were conversing with Quinn at the back of the room. The tension radiated around us like thick heavy humidity. The air almost felt too stifling to breathe. I had never encountered this sort of activity in Sweet Mountain before. People I'd never seen before scurried around the tiny office.

Brad stood with his hand on one of the partitioned walls at Harry's desk. My pulse quickened.

A man loaded down with a portfolio, a heavy-looking bag slung over his shoulder, and a thick wool coat tried to get by me.

"Oh, sorry." I stepped out of the doorway to allow him to leave, intending on making my way to where Quinn stood.

Brad raised his head then, and our eyes met. My feet were nailed to the floor by creeping dread. I'd known I would be facing him. Steeled myself for it. It made sense that they would be bringing in the most experienced investigator handling the state's Jane Doe cases. But the brief distraction in the lobby had thrown off my concentration. The door closed behind me with a solid thud, and I jumped. Thankfully, it shook me out of my momentary discomposure. I cleared my throat, straightened, and broke eye contact.

"Lyla!" Quinn called curtly and waved for me to follow him to his office before disappearing inside the small room. Harry rolled back in his chair and watched me as he chewed on the back of his pen. I gave him a nod of acknowledgment, and he returned it. I'd seen a different side of Harry at the cemetery. As much as he attempted to be a senior officer on the force by default because of his cousin, he wasn't. Quinn had mentioned that he was green. And that he definitely was, but there was a great strength within him as well. The scene and Jane Doe had shaken him. More so than he'd thought it would. He'd held it together, though. Secured the scene and gotten everyone down to the police station promptly. He'd be a good cop one day.

I navigated around the beige room with its ratty, green, threadbare carpet, giving Brad a wide birth. As wide as I could manage in the small space. He didn't make a move to stop me, and for that, I felt appreciative, or perhaps slightly disheartened. I didn't know for sure. We'd pretty much said everything there was to say on the phone. Still, it felt uneasy.

By the time I rounded the water cooler, I'd concluded that it didn't matter. My whipsawing emotions had no bearing on why I was here. I would compartmentalize anything and everything. To do my job and secure Sweet Mountain's safety, I had to.

A wise decision with the press nearby. I pushed open the door with *Chief Daniels* stenciled on it.

"Close the door," Quinn said as he settled into his chair and removed his uniform cap. His office had wood paneling and an artificial plant in the corner. Other than that, it still lacked any descriptive pieces, which surprised me, because Courtney had mentioned to Melanie that she would be redecorating it for him.

"Not an ideal way to come back from your honeymoon." I moved my bag from my shoulder to the floor. "I hated to interrupt your trip. If I'd had any other choice, I wouldn't have. Was Courtney terribly upset?"

He shifted in his chair and ran a hand over his cleanly shaven face. Without his goatee, he looked younger. I hadn't seen Quinn clean-shaven in years. "She's fine. Honestly, I wished you called sooner." He ran both hands through his short salt-and-pepper hair. "Maybe I could have managed this case better. I would have reined Rosa in, avoided a lawsuit, and kept the staties out of town." He let both hands settle on the desk. "Greene mention anything to you about terms of the suit? Perhaps what they'd be willing to settle for to make this go away?"

"No. I didn't think Mr. Greene was handling the lawsuit."

"Someone in his office is." He stretched. "Okay. Listen, you're going to be working with GBI Jones on this Jane Doe situation. He was brought in by the state, not me."

"That makes perfect sense to me." I appreciated his use of Brad's formal title—clear boundaries.

"Is that going to be a problem for you?"

"No. No problem at all."

He rummaged around his desk. "Good. The department is packed, and moving some of the work to your uncle's office would help. Jones will have all the clearance needed for the two of you to access databases."

I nodded. There were a lot of people who bought Hollywood's portrayal of private investigators. In fact, PIs were valuable assets in criminal investigations and often worked with the police and other law enforcement agencies when the situation called for it. Unlike the police, whose actions might be restricted as officers and enforcers of the law, a PI, as a private individual, might not be as limited. A private investigator could go and do things they couldn't.

"I'll introduce you to the two state police working on the case." He opened and closed a few drawers. "It should go without saying, but I must say it." He gave up on his search and lifted his head. "Rosa isn't to be consulted on anything to do with this case."

"Of course." I leaned forward. "Are you taking the threat against her seriously? Someone impersonated her for a reason, and whatever that reason was, it may have gotten her killed."

I reminded him about the flyer.

"I'm on it. I don't want you to concern yourself with anything to do with Rosa. Focus on the Jane Doe." His voice had an edge to it. "Are we clear?" There was a knock at the door, and he didn't wait for my answer. "Come in."

Chapter Twenty-Nine

B rad walked into Cousins Investigative Services later that afternoon. I'd made up my mind that I would keep all our interactions professional. We had a case to solve, and nothing in our personal life should interfere with the job. I flipped the sign to CLOSED.

"You can use the desk." I'd cleared the desk off in anticipation that he'd need it. He liked to spread his work out, use multiple screens and have plenty of elbow room. I was good working from the seating area. The coffee table would be adequate for my printouts and such.

He made no move from where he stood. His blank expression unnerved me more than anything else. He looked good, though, dressed in his gray slacks and navy sports coat. I'd put that outfit together for him several months ago and convinced him to purchase it.

I gave myself an inward shake. "Coffee?" I kept my back turned and began making myself a cup at the coffee bar.

"Are you actually going to pretend that everything is fine between us?"

I turned and stared him straight in the face. "Yes. We have a job to do. My friend's life may be in danger. In fact, I'm almost certain it is." I'd sent Rosa a text asking her to please take care and be extra vigilant. It'd been clear to me that some of the alleged accounts of her activity at the manor hadn't been Rosa herself but the impostor. "Our personal relationship has ended. Plain and simple. Let's focus on what's important." I felt proud that my tone was steady. Confidence oozed from my pores, even though I felt the opposite.

His eyebrows pulled together. "Closing your eyes to reality won't change things. It'll make them worse."

A flush crept into my cheeks—hot and tingly.

So we were doing this then. *Fine.*

"I'm not closing my eyes to anything. My eyes are wide open. I see you, Brad Jones. I know what you did and who you are."

He didn't flinch. Didn't move. "I told you what that was about," he said, quick and low.

Anger built up in the pit of my stomach. "Yes, you told me. You went dark while I was dealing with this mess. And when you finally crawled out of your hole, you told me that your ex, the one you planned on building a life with but didn't because you worked together, changed jobs." I threw up my hands. "Now you can crawl back into her bed. She did exactly what you wanted."

He snorted and shook his head. "I see plainly what you think of me. That our understanding about work only applies when you deem it relevant. If roles were reversed, you'd expect me to sit back and wait until you finished your case with a smile on my face. It's happened. And she and I closed a case right before her retirement party. Yes, we were celebrating."

Celebrating. I could spit nails.

"And honestly, Lyla, why do you care? You made it abundantly clear that you didn't see us moving to the next phase in our relationship."

I felt unsteady. Brad's words caused me to momentarily falter, but I rallied. "The next phase? We both agreed things were good as they were. I thought—"

"No. You shut me down every time I brought it up. *You* physically shuddered when I discussed marriage or living like a civilian family."

Did I? I scanned my brain and suddenly recalled a conversation we'd had at dinner with my folks. Somehow Little League had come up. I thought my father had mentioned something about his colleague's grandson playing or something. Mother had brightened at Brad's comment that he'd love to coach T-ball or Little League one day. The inference had been there. I'd cringed at the idea of being a minivan-driving mother. Laughed at the notion, even. Why? Because Brad had expected me to quit my job and find something less dangerous. And his ex had done just that.

I sighed. "So it was already over, and I had blinders on."

Brad gave me a sad smile. "You've made it clear we want different things."

I'd thought we were perfect together—both career driven, enjoying the freedom of being untethered. I sighed as I recalled a couple of instances where I'd pushed away his references to a future that had me home with kids or in another type of job while he continued working in law enforcement. Perhaps I'd have looked at the idea more fondly if he'd painted a world where I'd still be working in my chosen field. I should have discussed it with him. I'd chosen to ignore it instead, afraid to find out he wanted more than I could give him.

Ugh. I'd never wanted to be a person who denied the facts. Denied what was right in front of me.

"Why ice me?" Anger gave way to remorse. "You could have told me. Should have."

"I had a sensitive case." He moved to the desk then and put his briefcase down. He leaned against it, looking weary as he folded his arms. "I left my phone at my apartment. I couldn't chance it being discovered. And as soon as I got back, I called. I planned on coming down and speaking with you face-to-face. Then I got the call about the Jane Doe here. I'd been pulled in and knew you were wrapped up in it. I hate this. *Hate* it, Lyla. I don't want this to end. I love you. But after knowing where I stand, do you?"

He waited for me to speak. He shifted his feet. The first sign that he, too, battled inner turmoil. The lines around his eyes looked deeper. Granted, I felt I might have overreacted in my anger, misreading the situation. A case I could understand. Would have if Mel hadn't clued me in on what Wyatt had witnessed and Dean's interjection. Still, I felt betrayed. He'd admitted having feelings for his ex.

Resentment burst out of me. "You agreed our arrangement worked. You convinced me it was what you wanted too!"

He closed his eyes and took a deep breath. "I'm getting older. Dealing with the worst this world has to offer day in and day out makes me want a safe haven. A little place I can shut out the world—my work. I want a family before I'm too old to play with the kids. Can't you understand that?" His voice was soft and reasonable, a tactic to both reach and calm me. I'd heard him use it before.

He opened his eyes and waited for me to speak. People like us didn't have the luxury of living under the pretense that the world was a perfectly safe place. The world we lived in would seep into the imaginary life he'd envisioned. And how could it not? We held people's lives in our hands every day, whether it be a mother searching for a missing child, a Jane Doe whose life had been brutally ripped from her, or a club member I loved dearly whom I believed to be in danger. No—either he understood my calling was just like his, or he didn't.

"Think on it, Lyla. Think hard. We'll put a pin in this until after we close this case. And either way, I can still work with you. You are a capable investigator growing into a stellar one. You're right. Our cases are too important to allow any personal drama to affect them." He held out his hand. "Deal?"

I searched his face. His dark gaze was serious, a look that I was sure struck fear in the hearts of those he went up against. A look that had warmed mine. He was right. I owed it to him to consider what he'd said and not give him a flippant or knee-jerk answer while my emotions were stirred up. I'd read somewhere once that there's a time to think and a time to lay fallow. Now was a fallow time.

I closed the distance between us and took his hand. "Deal."

* * *

A couple hours later, we'd gone through the coroner's initial findings. The Jane had most likely died of asphyxiation. We'd have to wait for the final report to know for sure. Dental records were being searched, and we'd have to wait on those as well. From the initial findings, it didn't appear she'd spent a lot of time in the dentist's chair.

We couldn't run her prints because someone had tampered with them. A grotesque and calculated act. We couldn't use my go-to facial recognition software with her nose broken and her left cheekbone shattered. It would be futile. We went through missing persons and found several hits that could be her. Anyone could get a uniform, it seemed. There were companies online that made them but didn't keep good records. Or at least they didn't want to share their records. We'd have to get a court order to access anything. That would take time. Brad and I had both come to realize we were dealing with a person with psychopathic tendencies.

"Another dead end." I stretched, leaning forward on the settee, after I ended the call I'd been on.

Brad lifted his head, but his fingers were still moving on the keys. "What did you find?"

"The missing person in Savannah didn't have a cleft chin. That and the fact that the Mustang was stolen more than three weeks ago in Alabama, and we've got nothing." The VIN number had gotten a hit immediately. Our Jane must have pulled the plate and replaced it with a cardboard tag.

"Savannah was our best lead." He rolled back in the chair.

"Yep. Now we got bupkis."

"Hmm. This Dean fellow. The one that brought you the images of Jane. Do you think he has any more pictures we could use?"

I rose. "That's a good question. Maybe. Dean's staying over at Holiday Inn Express. No, wait—" I recalled him texting me the other day. I scrolled through my texts and found his. "He's changed hotels. He's staying at the other Holiday Inn. I think I should pay him a visit. I've been thinking about him and wondering why he's stuck around. He came by here looking for work. Ex-military." I took a deep breath. "Something is off about him."

"Off how?" Brad rose and grabbed his sports coat off the back of the chair.

"He's too helpful. I get he might be attempting to prove himself to land a job, but he's too attentive."

Brad pursed his lips. "That's not something off. That's being male. He's attracted to you."

"Maybe." I shrugged and grabbed my purse. "Let's take a ride. I don't want him to have time to gather himself. I want to catch him unawares. See what his deal is. If he's into me, I can use that."

Another snort from Brad, which I ignored.

When we pulled up to the hotel, there were a couple of press vans. It looked as if the hotel had emptied itself of all its guests. People were everywhere, and car horns blew. People were fleeing like bugs from a trap.

Police and ambulance sirens bellowed in the distance.

"What the hell?" Brad hit his lights on his unmarked black Lincoln and pulled up to the front, parking by the curb.

Joel came through the automatic doors holding a tan blanket to his chest, his expression ghostly. He proceeded to wrap the blanket around the shoulders of a woman sitting on the curb. I recognized her from the article. The jowly woman who'd loved attention sat with her arms wrapped around herself, rocking.

Brad unclipped his badge from his belt. "Police. Everyone, back up, please."

Judy Galloway lifted her watery gaze. "There was so much blood. Blood everywhere."

Alarm prickled my scalp. I moved over to Joel, who clutched me like a barnacle. His hands were shaking.

Brad bent down and had a low discussion with the woman.

"What happened?" I asked Joel softly.

"You know that guy you asked me about? Dean something or other?"

I nodded, searching his thin face, his eyes so wide they were mostly white.

"Well, he and I were chatting at the front desk, and Judy Galloway called about a disturbance." He cleared his throat, looking shaken. "From the room next to hers. She complains a lot, and most of her issues are resolved within minutes, so we . . ."

He didn't have to finish his statement. I could read it all over his face that they'd ignored her complaint.

"I waited for Dean to leave before going up, and that's when I found her."

"Who?"

"Judy. When we didn't respond swiftly, she'd gone to the room next door herself and found a massacre."

Chapter Thirty

There was so much blood.

Judy's words rolled over in my mind as I stood right outside the hotel room. Quinn and Brad were inside, and all I could see was red. Smeared bloody handprints on the wall and red-stained carpeting. The two state officers I'd met earlier rushed onto the floor, and I stepped back, a sinking dread in my stomach.

A text from Piper came through, asking what I knew and if she should run the story.

Brad came out of the room, shaking his head. "It isn't blood."

I hadn't expected that. "What?"

Quinn came out and rested his hands on his hips. "Looks like another damn prank. It says *Happy Halloween* written in fake blood above the wall. A concoction of corn syrup and food coloring. I've seen it before."

I left them to converse and walked into the room, now that it wasn't technically a major crime scene. The sheets were slashed; the sweet smell of fake blood was pungent. I detected a slight hint of chocolate as well. Beer cans were strewn all over the place. I shook my head and noticed that the idiots had left their college hoodies on the floor beside a backpack. I toed the opening wider and found a bottle of chocolate syrup. Ah, there was the source. I used my knuckle to open the bathroom door wider. On the mirror was another one of those terrible hangman games. But in this game, someone had drawn a little stick figure dangling from the noose, wearing a star—presumably a police badge. The responsible party had also filled in the dashes with letters spelling *Jane Dope.*

Idiots.

* * *

I made my way back down to the lobby. I texted Piper, told her not to run the crime scene story, and gave her the scoop on the vandal incident. Joel stood giving his statement to Harry, and I went over to them once I'd finished texting. What I'd given Piper would be generalized, but she could work with it. "It was a prank. The room was staged with fake blood."

"My God." Harry rubbed a hand over his balding head. "These unruly kids. Like we don't have enough on our plates. After the cemetery BS, I'm running them all in this time. Their parents can fight it out in court."

"Keep me posted."

He gave me a clipped nod and went to see the scene for himself. Joel collapsed into the chair, his hand over his heart. "Stupid kids. I swear, I've had it up to my ears with all this anxiety. I can't take much more. We've had rooms full of them staying here from that college party at the cemetery. I should have known when Miss Galloway said someone banged on her door screaming bloody murder. Like literally shouting the words 'bloody murder.'"

"Make sure you make a full report to Harry. They'll face vandalism charges, and maybe Harry can scrounge up a couple of other things to slap on them."

"Oh, don't worry. How could kids be so heartless? They should be terrified staging a murder scene like that with a real killer on the loose. It's like asking for trouble. Drawing the attention of a crazy person is never a good thing."

"They're young and feel invincible. I used to be that way." I gave him a smile.

"Used to be." Joel laughed. "You are the bravest person I know. I want to be like you when I grow up. You got it all together."

"Not hardly." I rubbed my index finger between my brows. My life was in shambles at the moment.

Joel took my hand. "I think you're doing great."

"Thanks." I smiled at him and ran a hand through my hair, neatening it behind my ears. I didn't like the feeling of being idolized. I hadn't any idea Joel thought so highly of me.

"Any luck with the Jane Doe?" Joel cleared his throat and took a sip from the bottle of water next to him.

"Not yet. Hey, what did you say you and Dean were talking about?" I tried to get myself back on track: finding the identity of our Jane Doe and getting rid of the uneasy feeling I got from Joel. Surely I was overreacting. Adrenaline aftereffects. It happened.

I debated asking to see Dean's room. I had no cause, and I didn't want to put Joel in a position to lose his job. If only there were a reason to gain entry. I racked my brain and came up empty.

"He was asking about jobs in town. He wanted to know if there were any other PI shops like your uncle's nearby. I told him to try Google." Joel seemed to shake himself and stood as he pulled his cell phone from his pocket. "I have to call the owner. He's on his way over, and he'll be glad to hear it was only a prank. After all this, I'm not sure I even want to live here anymore." Joel stepped away.

* * *

Melanie lit up my phone as soon as the news spread to town. The cool fall air felt good on my cheeks. "Hey, Mel."

"Hey. What's going on? Rosa and I are going mad here."

Rosa?

"Hey, Lyla. I came by Smart Cookie to see Mel, and we both heard the news."

Melanie cleared her throat. "You're on speakerphone."

"Full disclosure," Rosa began, "I drove by the hotel when I heard the 911 call come over the scanner. I saw the commotion and read what the witness Judy Galloway had to say." Someone had published her bogus story. What had happened to competent journalism?

Judy was becoming a major pain in the neck. I would be doing a little more digging into her background. I told Mel and Rosa about the discovery. There wasn't any harm in it. This had nothing to do with the investigation of our Jane Doe.

I gave them a brief account of the incident.

"Oh my God. Kids?" Melanie said.

"Looks like." A pickup truck flashing its lights caught my eye. "Hey, y'all. I'll call you back."

I hiked my bag higher on my shoulder and hightailed it across the lot. I recognized Dean sitting in the driver's seat. "Hey."

"Hey yourself." He nodded over to the hotel. "What's happening? I heard something about another murder."

God. Rumors in this town. "Nope. This time it really was a prank."

He nodded. "I wondered. There were a group of kids making a ruckus on the floor this morning. I think they were up late drinking and lost their brains down the toilet with the contents of their stomachs."

"Yeah." I leaned against the car and smiled. "You wouldn't happen to have any other pictures of the Jane Doe on your phone, would you?"

"I might. Having trouble IDing her?" He leaned over and pulled his cell phone from the holder on the dashboard. He scrolled through and handed me the phone.

I frowned. There were three pictures, none of which were any better than the one he had sent me. In fact, they were much worse. Grainy. Blurry. Completely out of focus. "Thanks anyway." I handed the phone back to him.

He nodded. "Sorry they're not better quality. I really should upgrade my phone." He sighed. "Anyway, the offer of my help still stands." He smiled then, and I could clearly read his interest in me.

"I appreciate it." I smiled in return. "But I'm working with the police department now. And with the sensitivity of the case, I couldn't bring anyone new on that hasn't been vetted by Calvin first."

"Any idea when he's coming back?"

"A week or so. I'll mention your interest to Calvin when he calls in."

His eyes lit up. "That'd be great. I'd even be interested in more of a freelance thing." He glanced over at the hotel. "I'm going to be checking out in a few days to head back home.

You can have Mr. Cousins give me a call if he's interested. I'm flexible."

I stepped back. "Okay."

"I truly regret the way things worked out with Sergeant Landry. I should have kept my mouth shut about the warning. And I certainly shouldn't have ever discussed my concerns with that nut, Judy or whatever her name is, in there." He nodded toward the hotel.

"You didn't know the Jane Doe was impersonating Rosa. You can't take that on yourself."

"I guess." His window started to roll up. "Good luck with the Jane Doe case."

"Thanks."

He gave me a tight smile, and the window paused midway. "One more thing, and it may be nothing at all."

"Anything could be helpful." I folded my arms. "Shoot."

"Back to that woman. Judy Galloway." He nodded to the hotel, then gave his head a slow shake as he said, "Something isn't right about her. I saw her at breakfast this morning; that's where we spoke. She told anyone who would listen that Sergeant Landry was the devil incarnate and would kill us all if she had the chance."

He had my attention.

"She worries me. Lord knows my opinion doesn't matter much to you yet. And you don't want another ex-military butting their nose into police matters, and I've already done enough, but I have a bad feeling about that one." He met my gaze. "I couldn't live with myself if I didn't warn you and something happened to you."

"To me?" My heart rate sped up.

"Judy made me wonder. How well do you know Landry? Is it possible she isn't who you think she is?"

I stood stone-still, staring into the eyes of this stranger. A man who was either trying to warn me or positioning himself as the outsider who could step in and see what I couldn't.

"I know her well." I did. I might not know every detail of her past, but I knew deep down she was a good person who cared for her friends and community.

He let out a little sigh. "Good. I'll sleep better knowing that."

His window rolled up, and he gave me a small smile.

Judy Galloway seemed to be an attention hog. What was she still doing in town anyway? I planned on finding out.

Chapter
Thirty-One

M elanie and I were having takeout at my dining room table when Amelia FaceTimed. She had an adorable little doll on her lap that could have been hers. We were astonished to see the spitting image of Amelia in miniature form—same eye shape and high cheekbones and bow-shaped lips.

"This is Sasha." Amelia beamed.

"Hi, Sasha," Melanie and I said in unison and waved.

The little girl giggled, melting our hearts.

I'd never seen a more precious child. "I'm Auntie Lyla, and this is Auntie Mel."

Another round of giggles before she squirmed from Amelia's lap to play with her pink Duplos on the floor. "She's full of energy. We should be coming home as soon as the adoption is finalized. I can't wait for you all to get Sasha snuggles."

My thoughts drifted to my conversation with Brad. Amelia looked positively radiant in her new role as mommy. I pushed it from my mind. Now was not the time to be thinking about motherhood. "I can't wait either. We miss you so much."

Melanie scooted her chair closer to mine. "And just an FYI, you're never allowed to be gone this long again. Or at least not with any frequency. We're having withdrawals here."

Amelia laughed. "I miss you guys too. We have so much to catch up on." She got up and moved to the other side of her hotel suite. I could tell from where she sat that she could still keep her eyes on the little girl. "I saw the recorded news conference on my feed this morning. I can't believe Rosa is suspended and that Jane Doe impersonated her." Amelia shook her curly head. "I was literally mind blown. Do we know who she is yet? Can you help Rosa at all? Or is she to blame for the lawsuit?"

"No, we haven't identified her yet. Someone went to great lengths to ensure that wouldn't be an easy feat. We're working on getting to the bottom of this. Some of the complaints made against Rosa can be addressed and put on Jane Doe. But others she'll have to own. She arrested Elaine without real cause. The investigation is in shambles, and even when they find the perp who did kill Patricia, the defense will have no problem poking massive holes in the case."

"Wow." Amelia looked as perplexed as I felt. The door in her room opened, and we saw Ethan with takeout bags. Sasha's squeals of delight added the levity we all needed. "I'll see you guys soon."

We waved good-bye, and I sighed as I disconnected the call.

"I'm so happy for Amelia and Ethan." Mel wiped away a little tear that had escaped and tracked down her cheek.

I gave her a little squeeze. "You got that baby bug now?"

She shrugged. "Maybe. But having my nieces spend the night will remedy that."

We both had a good chuckle. But I could see Mel was considering it. She'd make an unbelievable mother, and I told her so.

"You know you don't have to be married to make that sort of decision. I mean, I've been married, and it didn't work out so well. A child of my own would be with me forever. She'd have us." Melanie gave my hand a pat, and I watched her swallow. My mother wouldn't agree with her, and I bet her old-fashioned nanna wouldn't either.

"She? Melanie, is there something you're not telling me?"

She shook her head, smiling. "No, nothing like that. It's just something I've thought about. Anyhoo, back to our conversation about Brad. Dish."

I explained to Melanie the situation as I saw it. How I planned to take the time to consider what he'd asked and how I realized he was right about my selective vision. Melanie frowned several times, but she allowed me to finish without interruption.

"So." Melanie poured us a glass of wine. "He didn't actually say he wasn't cheating. He alluded to it and said the relationship had run its course since you wanted different things."

"No, he did. He said nothing had happened." I took my glass and tucked my legs underneath me as I reclined on the sofa. "But he also told me that he and Jennifer still had feelings for each other." I took a sip from the glass.

"The jerk!" Melanie wound her long blond hair into a bun and secured it with an elastic band. "If he and Jennifer"—she curled her lip—"had feelings for each other, then why not come clean before now? Why be cryptic about it? No, I think he's pulling this"—she used air quotes—"'we want different things' to soothe his guilty conscience."

"I don't think so. But Brad's right, Mel. I have been pushing him away. Not intentionally, and only when he nudged for more. I just don't see a future where I'm not pursuing my career. Is that so terrible?"

"No. It isn't. It's your life, and you should be able to live it however you see fit without guilt and pressure from others."

"It isn't that I'm totally against the idea of having a family." I thought back to the giggling little Sasha and smiled.

"Of course not." Melanie propped her arm on the back of the sofa and her head on her hand, turning toward me.

"I just think my life is on a different trajectory." I frowned. "Am I a horribly selfish person?"

"No."

"Then why does it feel like I'm being annihilated for taking a different path?"

Melanie nodded her sympathies. "I get it. Why are we expected to live by the expectations of others? Not everyone has to live the picket-fence life with two-point-five kids and a dog. There are many different versions of a family. Lots of mothers work in law enforcement. That could be your life."

I nodded.

"But the question is, can it be Brad's?"

"Yeah. That is the question." I sat my glass down. I knew the answer.

* * *

Harry called shortly after Mel had left. I was towel-drying my hair as I hit the answer icon. "Hey, Harry."

"Hey. You wanted an update about the vandalism. Is this a good time?"

"Perfect. Whatcha got?" I placed my damp towel on the table next to my open laptop. Sleep would elude me again tonight, so I planned to work late.

"The two kids I rounded up gave us something. They claim they were hired to enact the fake murder scene."

"Hired by whom?" I ran my finger along the trackpad and woke my computer.

"Don't know. They're lawyered up now, and we're waiting for them to arrive. I'm sure the kids will be aiming for a deal with leniency. One of the brats did say that the person who hired them had a real beef with law enforcement, Rosa in particular."

"Was it our Jane they were referring to? They could have crossed paths with her."

"Maybe."

My fingers slowed over the keys. "You know, Harry, Judy Galloway has been slandering Rosa all over town."

"The witness?"

"Yeah, that's her. She's the one in the paper too. I tried to talk to her this afternoon, but she'd already gone down to the police station."

"Right. I talked to Miss Galloway. Nothing there."

"Huh. I've got some intel I'd like to discuss with her."

"Not a good idea. Like I said, nothing there. Hell, I gotta go. Lawyers are here." He disconnected the call.

I stared at my cell, perplexed by his quick dismissal. Not prudent policing if you asked me. Maybe he'd gotten credible information he hadn't been able to share with me. I still planned on speaking with Judy. She seemed to be everywhere, spouting her mouth off. But what would be her motive to pay college kids to trash an empty hotel room?

I rubbed my face with my hands. How did the Jane Doe fit into all of this? And had Judy been working with her?

Chapter
Thirty-Two

The following morning at six, I was back at the hotel. I'd called Joel the night before, and he'd clued me in on Judy's early-morning eating habits. I strolled into the breakfast room and picked up a plate at the end of the line. The hotel impressed me with its continental breakfast offerings. I couldn't cook to save my life, and this, by my standards, was a feast.

I went through the line and placed a muffin on my plate, then a spoonful of decent-looking scrambled eggs. The server refreshing the fruit gave me a sideways glance as I waited a little too long to choose my fruit. Judy was finishing up her selections at the end of the buffet. I wanted her to be settled at a table before I moved on.

"Morning." I smiled at the server before continuing down the line. I took my time making my cup of coffee, doctoring it to just the right creamy consistency. Seeming too eager might make Judy believe she was under suspicion.

"Is this seat taken?" I stood next to the small round table where Judy sat, really digging into her waffle. If she was guilty of something, it sure hadn't affected her appetite.

She glanced up and wiped the back of her mouth with her sleeve. "Nope. Go ahead and take it."

"Thanks." I laid out my food and put the tray on the empty seat next to me. "I'm Lyla." I held out my hand. "I don't think we've officially met."

She put her fork down and shook my hand. Hers was a bit sticky. "I know who you are. You're the one working for the cops. I'm Judy."

"I know who you are too. You're the one talking to the press who had that horrible incident with the college kids yesterday," I said as she released my hand.

"Yep, that's me. You here to talk to me about Rosa?" she asked around a bite of waffle. My mother would have had a fit. Manners were something she'd insisted on since kindergarten.

"If you don't mind." I took a sip from my mug.

"Don't mind a bit. I've been waiting for you to hit me up."

"Oh?" I raised my brows.

"Definitely. You've been going around town talking to every-one but me." She cocked her head to one side as she cut more waffle and said, "Pretty lazy detective work, if you ask me."

"Well, I'm here now, and I'm listening." I leaned back and kept my mug between my hands. *We're just two gals having a chat*, I hoped my body language conveyed.

"Good." She bit into her limp bacon. "Someone should lock that woman up. She's a nutcase. I told the paper and the police here in town. But nobody seems to be taking me seriously. And I had a run-in with Rosa about five years ago in Louisiana."

She paused, sipping from her Coke glass.

"I was dating a guy in her unit. You know she was in the military before moving here, right?"

I nodded.

"Well, after they came back from their tour, every Friday, we all had drinks at this bar. Chris, the guy I was seeing at the time, went on and on about her insubordination. How she always bucked the system and had serious anger outbursts."

"Did he give you any specifics? Like, was Rosa's conflict mainly with Chris, or an overall general situation with her superiors?" I tried not to rush Judy and allow her to tell her story in her own time. Though I was skeptical. Rosa had spoken fondly about her unit and even met up with them now and again.

"Well." She leaned in and dipped her finger into the syrup on her empty plate, swirling it around. "Let's put it this way." She sucked the syrup off her finger. "Her husband, the head of her unit, filed charges against her."

"Her husband?" I sat forward and placed my coffee cup back on the table.

She grinned widely. "Yes. She didn't tell you she has an ex-husband, did she? Nah, she didn't. I can see it all over your face. Michael didn't know what to do with her. He tried to end it with her on numerous occasions. She all out attacked him at the bar one night. I'm talking fists flying, glass breaking, the whole bit. She's a bunny boiler."

I raised my brows. "Bunny boiler?"

She nodded. "You know, like Glenn Close in *Fatal Attraction*. She had a bunny boiling on the stove when Michael Douglas and his family came home."

"Ah." I fought a smile at the woman's inference. Her face told me she believed every word she said. Piper had mentioned she thought there might be truth in the accounts of Rosa's past. She simply hadn't been able to confirm the claims. If she was going only on Judy's version, I could see why she would feel that way. But seriously, a bunny boiler? A new phrase for me. That was stretching things.

"So, her husband, um—"

"Michael."

"Right. Michael. I imagine he managed to untangle himself from her, and things settled down."

"Finally." She gave an exaggerated eye roll. "She's such a royal pain in the ass. If I'd known she lived here and was part of the book club party, I wouldn't have come. But now that I'm here, I'll be damned if I don't warn the residents of Sweet Mountain that they have a viper in their midst. I bet you anything she killed that woman at the party. Maybe it was an accident or something"—she gave a shrug—"I don't know, but the way she wigged out after arresting the poor old lady who owned the B and B speaks to her mental instability." She picked up her fork and stabbed a grape on my plate. "I saw her talking to your Jane Doe. They were at the railroad tracks. Rosa pinned something to her uniform." She ate the grape and took another. Her phone chirped, and she dug through her giant shoulder bag hanging on the back of her chair to retrieve it.

I took a sip of my coffee, which was now lukewarm, as I processed what Judy had told me.

She stood and tossed her bag over her shoulder. "I've got to go. If you want to meet up again sometime, just give me a holler. I'll be here till the end of the week, then I've got to get back home. Clean this up for me, will ya?" She pushed her tray toward me and stalked out of the room.

Wow.

* * *

I was battling a niggling headache by the time I made it to the office. Brad had retaken the desk. While he was checking the CCTV footage he'd gained access to, I pulled up the guest list we'd compiled after Patricia's murder. I decided to print it out and go at it with a highlighter before working on my spreadsheets.

I'd been a little surprised at how Brad and I had fallen into our usual work routine. I'd not been able to keep myself from glancing over at him while he worked. I consoled myself with the fact that even if we didn't work out as a couple, we'd always be a really great team. Slowly, I was adjusting to the idea, and I knew that was telling. Somewhere deep down, I'd sensed where we were heading. The thought of ending our relationship still brought a lot of anxiety. I had to discover if the anxiety could be attributed to the lack of Brad in my personal life or to the fact that I'd be alone. Or if it even mattered after he'd admitted to having feelings for his ex.

I focused back on work. Work I understood.

I highlighted Judy Galloway and Dean Willis straightaway. Judy kept showing up at all the places where crimes took place. She'd been at the party and had been the first to speak to the press, and I didn't believe for one second it was a coincidence she'd alerted the police about the vandalized hotel room. My gran always said that coincidences were God's way of winking at you. Well, I was paying attention. I didn't care what Harry thought. She could have paid the college kids to draw more attention toward Rosa. She clearly had a vendetta against her. And I wanted to know why. Was it simply bad blood? Or was there more to the story? Judy came off as abrasive and unfeeling, but maybe that was because she was hell-bent on destroying my friend.

A friend who hadn't told me that she'd been married and divorced. But she wasn't just a friend; we'd been more like sisters. If any of what Judy had said turned out to be true. That's why it would hurt so much.

As I continued down my list of out-of-towners and a few locals who raised an eyebrow, I thought of Harry's reaction to Rosa. His continual attempts to undermine her. I wondered what his motives were. Could it be he simply didn't care for her or her methods? Or did he believe she was utterly incompetent?

I dug through my bag for Goody's headache powder and washed it down with my coffee.

"Headache bad?" Brad asked as he looked up from his computer.

"It's manageable."

"You can take off. I've got this."

"No. I'm good. Our Jane Doe could be somewhere on this list, and we haven't time to waste."

He nodded and went back to work.

I started with the guests who'd booked a room at the B and B. I pulled my laptop onto my lap. I still had remote access to Elaine's database from when I was working on her defense team. I went through the records, noting when someone checked in, how many were in their party, and when they checked out. The majority of the list had checked out that night. I wasn't even sure how the staff managed to handle the rush of departing guests. One party of two had never checked out. I knew the B and B had been vacated completely that night. Either they'd never called back in to have their card charged, or . . .

"Brad. I'm going to step outside and make a phone call. Then we need to take a ride."

Chapter
Thirty-Three

Elaine hadn't reopened for business. Still staying with my parents, she'd informed us when I'd called that the state police had also asked for access, which she'd granted but only with her attorney present. She wasn't taking any chances, and after her ordeal, I didn't blame her. They planned to be out at the property later today or first thing in the morning. She had no qualms about letting me search unsupervised, and I was grateful.

When I referenced the guests that hadn't checked out, she'd said, "They probably fled without formally checking out, and our office manager quit on the spot the next morning. It's been awful. I'm trying diligently to rebuild my life and my brand. Thankfully, the lawyer Mr. Greene set me up with seems good. Mr. Greene assured me I have a case that cases are made from. The lawsuit is a slam dunk."

"Well, Mr. Greene would certainly know."

"Yes," she'd said, and I could hear the tremor in her voice. This event had caused her severe trauma. The fact that she was still staying at my parents' place brought me some comfort. She did not need to be alone. I let her go with a bit of encouragement. She took comfort in the fact that she had friends who would help her.

The groundskeeper let Brad and me in. Elaine had told me where all the keys were and informed me that her staff hadn't been back to clean the rooms yet either. Mr. Greene had advised her to leave them. That made sense. No one could accuse her of tampering with evidence. And with everything as it had been the night of the murder, hope bloomed.

The B and B still used old-fashioned room keys; it added to the novelty of staying at Magnolia Manor. We gloved up, and I unlocked the room door on the second floor, the one that the Smiths, party of two, had stayed in. The bed was unmade. My heart rate increased. A robe was on the floor in front of the bathroom. One suitcase was open on the slipper chair in the corner of the room. We might have gotten lucky.

"You check the bathroom, and I'll see if there is anything in the luggage. We might as well check the other rooms too while we're here."

"I'm surprised that we found any luggage. The state police should have bagged and tagged all this by now." Brad shook his head.

"Well, actually Rosa and Harry should have bagged and tagged it." I moved a couple of tops out of the suitcase. "The state police still haven't been in here. I told you Rosa had a one-track mind when it came to Elaine. Something she truly regrets now."

I carefully moved the pieces of clothing, shaking them out to see if something could be hiding, then dug around for secret compartments but came up empty. I wondered where the woman's purse was. I glanced around the room, searching. I opened the nightstand drawers and then moved on to the dresser. Nothing. I pulled the blankets back on the bed, and my hope balloon deflated. But there was only one suitcase, with items belonging to one woman. Two people had been staying in this room. Hmm.

Brad walked out of the bathroom with a prescription bottle. "It was in the garbage. Betty Smithson had anxiety issues. We'll need to see if any diazepam was in our Jane Doe's system."

I nodded my head. "She could have taken the entire bottle before she died, or maybe it was mostly empty and time for a refill."

"Maybe," Brad said.

I glanced at the bag. "She checked in under her actual name, just shortened it. Bold."

"Or stupid. And now that I think about it, who goes on a trip without refilling their prescriptions? Especially if you're taking two milligrams twice a day. That's a serious anxiety issue."

"Yeah, that doesn't make sense. Maybe she never knew a thing when she was killed." I told him about not finding anything belonging to guest number two. "But I haven't checked the closet yet." I opened the small closet. It contained a small ironing board and a row of empty clothes hangers. I glanced over my shoulder toward Brad. "Nothing."

Brad's eye's narrowed as he scanned the bedroom. "Either her guest didn't check in with her or they bolted after the murder. We need to get a look at the security footage and see if Betty arrived with someone. I'll call Chief and gain access."

"Yeah." I'd been thinking the same thing. I closed the closet door, and something rustled against the hardwood flooring. "That sounded like paper." We both looked like point setters on alert. I knelt beside the bed and lifted the bed skirt. A scattered stack of pink flyers shone like a beacon.

"What are the chances that Betty—or her guest—wore gloves while they were handling these?" Brad asked with a smile from where he knelt on the other side of the bed.

My God. The negligence in this case astounded me. The police missed the prescription bottle and the flyers?

Brad was watching me, reading me. "I told you Rosa's inexperience would be an issue."

"Yes, you did. But let's not overlook the possibility that someone placed the items here after the fact. The flyers didn't surface around town until after Patricia's murder."

Brad nodded and bagged the evidence. "Not that it matters if we don't have evidence to back up the claims. It seems like clear negligence. This will help Elaine Morgan's lawsuit."

And be bad for Rosa. I stood and glanced around the room once more before we cleared out. We kept our gloves on as we made our way down the staircase and through the B and B.

We paused by the ballroom to have another look. The air in the room smelled stale, almost as if Elaine had blocked the vents off and the air couldn't circulate. There was a thin layer of dust on everything. Some from the lack of cleaning, the rest from forensic processing. Agatha Christie's picture in the middle of the table remained upright. Her eyes seemed to follow me around the room. I wondered ridiculously what the Queen of Mystery would see in this room. Nothing new stood out to me from the last time I'd gone through here. If the police had discovered the murder weapon that night, Elaine might have been spared and Rosa wouldn't have career troubles. I squatted down to look under the credenza. There was no way the police could have missed the murder weapon. No way. Which was clearly another reason Rosa had taken the bait of the doctored audio recording. *Could Betty Smithson have planted the gun here before she died?*

Brad noticed my posture. "What?"

"Drop me by the office before you take the evidence to process. I need to go by and have a word with Tammy."

Chapter
Thirty-Four

Tammy was in the middle of the Sunday lunch rush when I arrived at the deli. I took a table in her section and waited for her to finish serving her last customers. "What is it?" she told me when she eventually came over. "I'm busy here, as you can see." She glanced down at the cup of coffee I'd ordered, and I realized that I might be interfering with her earnings today.

"I know. I'm sorry and just have one question, and I'll give the table up."

She nodded and sighed, rubbing her forehead. "Shoot. I'm sorry. I am just under a lot of pressure. Money is tight."

"I'm sorry to hear that, and I wouldn't be here if it wasn't imperative. I'll be quick."

She motioned for me to hurry it up.

"At the party, you said Rosa assaulted you outside the French doors of the ballroom."

Tammy nodded, and someone from one of her tables called her name. She waved to a coworker. "Trixie, can you refill my tables while you're at it?"

A tall, thin girl with sleek dark hair pulled up in a high ponytail nodded, two tea pitchers in her hands. One read *Sweet*, the other *Un*. "Sure." The girl smiled. "I'll holler at you if anyone needs anything."

"Thanks. I'll be fast." Tammy glanced around before taking a seat in the vacant chair across from me. We were seated next to the window at the front of the deli. "Yes, she was pretty brutal, and it terrified me. I reported it to the chief yesterday."

"Good. That's good." I kept my tone soothing. "It was dark out and raining."

"Drizzling by then. What's your point?" There was an edge to her tone, and I had to handle this carefully.

"Did you actually see Rosa? She came at you from behind."

"I know Rosa, Lyla. I'm not stupid enough to confuse her with the Jane Doe. Rosa pressed her hip into my lower back. I felt her gun, and . . ." Her voice trailed off as her fingers went to her lips. "Oh no."

"Yeah," I said. "Rosa wasn't wearing her uniform at the party."

"The Jane Doe." She closed her eyes. "My God. I never thought I would confuse something like that."

Now we had confirmation that Sweet Mountain's Jane Doe had been present that night. We had a witness.

"And the drive-by?"

She nodded, her lips shaping the letter O as her hand landed on her forehead. "I would have said no. Told Chief Daniels that I was certain it was Rosa. Now it very well could have been Jane Doe."

Chapter
Thirty-Five

"Daniels," Quinn barked into his cell on the first ring. I'd called him the second I got into the car. Judy's background claim about Rosa didn't line up with a false identification theory, but those of several hometown folks did. Who was this Betty Smithson, and why did she have a vendetta against Rosa?

"Hey. Has Magnolia Manor been reprocessed yet?" I slowed my breathing as I overheard him addressing another officer. I didn't want to jump to any conclusions yet. But I was onto something. I could feel it.

"We're working on it. We just gained access to the property a few hours ago. We have a few reports that I believe will hold from the previous processing, but others will hopefully be more beneficial. I know processing fingerprints has become a nightmare."

"I bet." I moved my purse to the passenger's seat.

"Harry has been going over witness statements. He and Hansen made a couple of drop-ins this morning to some locals. Why do you ask?" Quinn had that tone in his voice now. The one where he was both annoyed and intrigued by one of my discoveries.

"Have you spoken to Brad?"

"No. Why? You got a positive identity for Jane Doe?"

"Not yet. We found something that might benefit both cases. We also gained access to the B and B this morning."

"Lyla." His tone sharpened.

"We didn't touch anything. And Elaine allowed us entry without Mr. Greene being present."

He let out a long, loud exhale. He'd done it on purpose, I could tell. "Did you find something we can use?"

"Not at the crime scene but in one of the rooms upstairs." I let him in on our discovery.

"No one processed the rooms!" He sounded like he was about to blow a gasket. I heard crashing. "Harry. My office now."

"Before you go chewing any butts, I also need to tell you that I just spoke with Tammy Mason." I gave him the lowdown on that conversation.

"For the love of God! Can no one do their jobs anymore?"

I didn't remind him that I was doing mine. "We need to reexamine the security footage at check-in the night before and the morning of the party. If the evidence we found leads us down the path I think it will, we need to identify who stayed in the room we searched. And with Tammy's statement regarding our Jane, it makes sense that she was involved. And whoever roomed with her—"

"May also be guilty and still on the loose."

"Exactly. And Rosa—"

"Could be in danger." He let the expletives fly.

"That's what I'm worried about."

"We need to sit down with her. God, what a mess." I overheard Harry in the background and Quinn ordering him to close the door. "Anything else I need to know?"

"That's all I got at the moment." I started my car.

"I'll get in touch with Jones and have him get over to the medical examiner's office and lean on them."

"I can do it."

"Are you sure? It isn't pleasant."

"I'm sure. Calvin's had dealings with the man before." I tried not to take umbrage with his statement.

"Okay, if I can get anyone on the phone, I'll let the office know you're on the way. And Lyla," he began, and paused.

"Yeah?"

"Good work." He disconnected the call, and I couldn't help smiling.

* * *

My phone rang with my uncle's ringtone as I pulled into a parking space in front of the courthouse. The medical examiner and coroner's office was in the same building.

"Hello, stranger." I put my sunglasses on top of my head. It was one of those bright, crisp fall days that, under other circumstances, I'd be enjoying immensely. Fall was my favorite season.

"Hey. Checking in." His terse verbiage and the terrible call quality told me not to ask any questions. He wanted a rundown on the caseload and a status report. We had our working relationship down to a science now. I gave him what little I'd been working on. I had a couple of background checks and a divorce case in progress. I'd put one of our freelance guys on the latter. He'd sent back ample evidence of the wife's affairs with multiple partners, one of whom was her husband's business partner. I'd already sent those over to the client.

"Anything else I should know?"

"A lot is going on that you should know, but I've got to run. I can give you a quick summary if you want."

"Do." That was all I could make out with the line so full of static.

"We've been retained by local PD again. We have a Jane Doe case, and this one is a crime for the books." He could log into our system when he landed somewhere with better cell and Wi-Fi coverage.

"Did it make the papers?"

Wow, he really was somewhere remote.

"Oh yes. A lot has gone down since you've been away. Not to worry, I'm on it." More crackling sounds on the other end of the line.

He said something, but I couldn't make out what.

"Calvin? You still there?" Through the speaker, my voice echoed back at me, and then the call dropped.

"Bye," I whispered, and got out of my car.

After punching in the code Quinn had sent me, I entered the building through the side door. It was odd being inside the building on a Sunday. The security desk was empty, but still I'd left my gun, which I usually carried in my purse, in the holster in the glove compartment. I had a locking glove box, but it always made me antsy to leave it in the car. Not that I had a choice.

A man walked around the corner and blinked hard at me. "Hey, uh, no one is supposed to be here."

"Calm down." I held my hands out. "I'm here in an official capacity to see the coroner. Chief Quinn sent me." I cocked my head to one side. "Aren't you Devon, Officer Smith's son?"

He nodded as I mentioned the retired officer who usually perched at the front desk during the week.

"I'm Lyla Moody. He's friends with my uncle Calvin."

He smiled as recollection hit. "Right." He hiked his bag up higher on his shoulder. "We met at your mother's hospital fund raiser last spring. Sorry I got a little freaked out there. I wasn't expecting to run into anyone. I'm interning for Judge Riggs. I forgot a few things and thought I'd come by and grab them while it's quiet."

I glanced around. "It is eerily quiet." There were only a few lights on, and the building had a hollow feel to it.

"Where's your uncle been? Haven't seen him at the watering hole the last few weeks. I take my dad every Thursday."

"He's out of town on a job." I smiled.

"Ah. My dad is always saying he doesn't know how Calvin does it. They're close to the same age, and Dad gets worn out sitting around here all day." He took a couple of steps forward—polite yet eager to leave.

"I hear ya. Uncle Calvin has to keep busy." I got myself together.

"Well, I have to get going. Have a good day now, ya hear?"

I nodded with a smile and slung my heavy bag to the other shoulder. "Same to you."

This was the first time I'd gone to the medical examiner's office in person. I'd called and emailed to push for reports, but Calvin usually handled it if a visit was needed.

I got this. I can do this. Deep breaths.

Chapter
Thirty-Six

My nerves swam as I rode the elevators down to the basement floor. The desk clerk let me in. "Hey. Sorry, we keep the door locked when we have to come in on the weekends." She didn't look happy to be here. I didn't blame her. Not everyone's life revolved around their job.

"Make sense."

She nodded and gathered her coat and bag. "Well, I'm taking off. He's waiting on ya. Just go down that hallway and take a left at the end. You can't miss it."

"Thanks."

I went in the direction she'd sent me and stood outside the double doors for a few minutes to catch my breath. I had no idea if he'd have a body on the table or not. I'd not given that any thought. I'd assumed he would be in his office or waiting for me out front and we'd have a chat.

I can do this. I will do this.

I pushed through the doors, and the smell of chemicals and death accosted me. My eyes watered as I stood in a sterile room filled with stainless-steel tables, instruments, and what looked like power tools. A giant drain had been placed in the middle of the concrete floor. I swallowed. A sheet covered a body on a table in the center of the room. A wall of refrigerator drawers stood to my left.

A man in a white coat came through the doors, forcing me to step farther into the room.

He did a double take. "You're here about Jane Doe?"

I nodded and positioned my back toward the doors. I might need a quick exit.

"Christopher Schwartz." He extended his latex-covered hand and thought better of it. After removing the glove, he extended his hand again. "Chief Quinn said you or Jones would be coming by."

I nodded, forced a smile—the smell was getting to me—and briefly shook his hand. "Lyla Moody."

He scratched the top of his thick, dark-brown head. Suddenly his eyes lit with recognition. "Oh, right, Calvin's niece."

"That's me." I clasped my hands in front of me.

"It's nice to put a face with that lovely voice." He pulled up the surgical mask that had hung around his chin and grabbed a pair of gloves from a box next to us.

"It's nice to meet you in person too." My gaze skated around the room, landing anywhere except on the body on the table. My stomach flip-flopped a few times, and no longer able to help myself, I put my fingers under my nose.

"Your Jane Doe is right over here." He moved to the table. "As the chief requested, she was moved to the front of the line. Not that the others complained much. I don't stand for backtalk." He chuckled and started to lift the sheet. When I stayed put and didn't laugh along with him, he glanced over his shoulder. "First time?"

"Ye . . . yes." I cleared my throat and steeled myself to move forward, trying not to shuffle my feet in the process. He dropped the sheet, dug into his pocket, and handed me a menthol cough drop. "It helps."

"Thanks." I unwrapped it, popped it into my mouth, and tried not to glance toward the table. *Did I need to go this far?* I decided on a resounding no. I couldn't identify her. That had already been validated. And I'd rather not have to see the wounds on the body again if it wasn't absolutely necessary.

"You know," I said, taking a step backward, "I think I'm good here. How long until you'll be finished? I think Chief Quinn just wants to get an ID and confirmation on cause of death." I raised my hands. "Not that we think you're dragging your feet or anything." *Way to go, Lyla. Shoot rapid-fire questions at the man; that's applying pressure.* I could have rolled my eyes at myself.

I cleared my throat as he watched me with interest. "Oh, and if you'd gotten the tox screen completed, I'd love to know the results."

Christopher still had his mask up, but I could tell from his eyes he was smiling broadly. They were heavily crinkled at the edges. He sat down on the chair in front of the small wall desk and removed his mask and gloves, tossing them into the wastebasket under the desk. "I'm working on the report and haven't had the body on the table long. I'm still doing my work-up, but I can tell you that the cause of death seems straightforward. My initial report of asphyxiation by strangulation holds. From the ligature marks, I'd say she was hung."

Goose bumps broke out across my body, and I shivered. My God, that could have been Rosa. Or maybe another of our club members. I moved closer to the computer.

He clicked the mouse on his desk and scrolled down the open document on the screen. "The victim was obviously roughed up beforehand, and the fingerprint tampering was postmortem."

I leaned closer, getting a good look at the diagram on the screen. Wow. Someone hadn't been merciful in the killing. "What about the tox screen? Did anything stand out? Could she have been unconscious when the death occurred?" If she had a bottle of Valium in her, she would have been.

"I'm not sure if the results have come back, but let's have a look. I expedited those as well." He put on a pair of black reading glasses and rolled the chair closer. "Anything in particular we're searching for?"

"Diazepam." I cleared my throat, feeling slightly embarrassed at my initial reaction. This trip had been necessary, and my visits here could increase in frequency. I'd just have to woman up.

He popped a chip from the open bag on his desk into his mouth.

Yuck. Was that sanitary? I glanced back toward the screen.

"Nope." Christopher shook his head. "I'm not seeing any diazepam. And that drug would show up under the routine checks."

My heart sank a little. Betty Smithson would have had the meds in her system. "Dental records?"

"We're working on that. We've uploaded the X-rays into the database. If she's local or in the system, we should get a hit. But her teeth were in bad shape, and what dental work she had looks correctional to me."

"Correctional? Dental work while incarcerated?"

He nodded. "If she was housed locally, that'll be pretty quick."

"And if she's in the system in another state?" I swallowed the small cough drop that had nearly disintegrated.

He rolled his chair back and took another chip from the bag. "That'll take longer. If you leave me your cell number, I'll call you the second it comes in." He smiled again, and his smile sparked me to smile in return. He was a smiley kind of guy. You'd think working on murdered corpses all day long would make you a cynical person. That gave me pause. Well, Brad had said something similar about our profession and needing an escape. Mother had done her best to steer me a different way as well.

Okay, scratch that. "I appreciate it and all of your hard work." I took a card from my wallet and extended my hand. He rose, and a wave of odor hit me. The cough drop must have worn off. My hand went involuntarily to my nose.

He laughed and took the card from me. "Sorry. We can step outside."

"Oh thank God." I hurried after him and out the door he held open for me.

"I forget how offensive it is for those unaccustomed. I apologize." Christopher shook his head. "I guess that's not a very appealing thing for me to say."

"No, but I understand. Not a lot of people comprehend the trials of criminal investigations." I held out my hand and smiled a genuine smile this time. "Your work is exceedingly important. And I'm sure a thankless job most days."

He took my hand eagerly. Out here he seemed much more pleasant to converse with. He wasn't a large man but stout, with a sturdy column of a neck. He wasn't wearing a wedding ring, leaving me to conclude he was single. I bet dating for him was even more difficult than it was for me.

"Thank you so much for your time and sharing your expertise."

We parted, and though I did not want visits to this office to become routine, I had a new appreciation for Christopher Schwartz.

Chapter Thirty-Seven

I rode with my windows down all the way to the coffee shop. I didn't care that it was cool or that my hair would suffer. I needed to air out my sinuses and myself. I wasn't sure if it was possible to pick up odors on clothing in that short of a time. Still, I wouldn't be taking any chances. I picked up Rosa's favorites and was soon en route to her house.

I needed to sit down and have a face-to-face conversation with her. I had no intention of going against Quinn's explicit instructions, but like it or not, this case was personal, and lives were at stake. I would not be able to live with myself if I didn't do everything in my power to keep my friend safe.

The portrayal Judy had painted wasn't the woman I was familiar with. And now that we knew our Jane Doe had been at the party, things made more sense. The Rosa I knew would never fly off the handle to that magnitude. It still didn't account for her behaving erratically after Patricia's murder. Or the way she had arrested Elaine without covering all her bases first. I couldn't imagine how she could think going off half-cocked after an old woman with an exceptional record would work out. A woman who had never even had a speeding ticket. It made no sense. And then the press conference. I still couldn't get my head wrapped around that idiotic move. I had this deep, sinking dread that I was missing a critical piece of information.

I'd called Brad to see where things were and update him on my visit to the medical examiner. He'd pulled a few strings to get a rush on the forensics, and they had managed to get prints off the flyers. He was currently waiting in the lab. I could picture him, lording himself over the tech with that scary face of his. No one could stand silently and strike fear in hearts like GBI Brad Jones. I had loved that about him. *Had?*

I'd been pondering Brad and me when Melanie called.

"Hey, you! You, okay?"

"Fine, why?" I took a left onto Dupont Street.

"Um, I'm waiting for you at Maria's. Texas fajitas for two and margaritas ring any bells?"

I stopped at a red light, and both my hands went to my mouth. "Oh, Mel! I'm so sorry. I've had such a day. I completely forgot." At the mention of Mexican food, my stomach growled. I'd forgotten to eat.

"I'm listening."

I told her about my day minus the evidence and gave her a condensed version of my conversation with Judy.

"What!" Melanie sounded incensed. "She has to be lying. There is no way Rosa would keep that from us."

"I don't know." I stopped at a stop sign and waited for a jogger to cross the street.

"With all we've shared over the last year or so. Nah-ah, no way. She'd know that I'd commiserate with her. She and I are super close . . ." Melanie's voice trailed off. "Or at least I thought we were."

"I'm going to get to the bottom of all of this. And if true, Rosa can't hide it from us forever. And if something is going on, we need to know about it."

"You're right. Want me to meet you there?"

I turned onto Rosa's dead-end street. "No. Let me go at this professionally first. Maybe she'll be more open. She knows I'm working for the police department, and she has to be stressing about her job."

"Okay. You take a run at her as Lyla, the PI, and if that doesn't work, call in the big dog."

"Big dog?" I pulled into Rosa's driveway, and it occurred to me that we never really visited her. She hadn't offered to host us for dinner or an impromptu club meeting. I'd been here only one other time. She'd always come to Mel's, Amelia's, or my house.

"Yeah, me." I could hear Melanie smiling on the other end of the line.

I smiled. "Deal."

"You got this. Love you."

"Thanks. Love you too." I shut off the engine and stared at the late-seventies brick ranch with its attached two-car carport. A large oak on the left side of the driveway had probably been planted as a shade tree when the house was being constructed. The roots had grown under the concrete, causing little fault-like cracks close to the carport entrance. All the backyards on the street were sectioned off by chain link fences.

A miniature pinscher in the neighboring yard barked as I exited the car. The dog was around my feet, growling so loudly his tiny body vibrated. "Hey there, little fella. I'm friendly," I said in an attempt to placate the little creature protecting his territory. But he would not be consoled by the likes of me. The snarling and yapping continued.

"Sugar! Sugar, get back here." An older woman did her best to hurry over to where her dog had me pinned against the car.

I felt ridiculous. The dog couldn't weigh more than ten pounds.

"I'm so sorry." She scooped up the little dog and stroked his forehead. The motion seemed to somewhat soothe the animal, who still bared his teeth in my direction.

"That's okay." I smiled, thankful to be saved from a fate of lacerated ankles.

"Hey." The lady squinted. "I saw you on the news the other morning. You're James and Frances Moody's girl, aren't you?"

"Yes, ma'am."

She nodded, still stroking the dog. "I thought so. Those long legs and copper hair of yours are a dead giveaway. Moody through and through, you are. Your father certainly can't deny you."

"Thank you, I guess." What an odd thing for her to say. Why would he want to deny me? Oh . . . I got her point then. "No, he wouldn't get away with that one."

She chuckled heartily. "I'm just teasing you. Your mother and grandmother are good people. Your mama is something else. She does a lot of work with the ladies' shelter I volunteer at."

"Thank you. I'll tell Mother and Gran that you said so." She hadn't given me her name, and I felt it rude to ask at this point in the conversation. She certainly was familiar with my family and me.

"You're a friend of Rosa's?" Upon my nod, she said, "Poor thing has had a hard time. People think she is bulletproof." She cast a glance over her shoulder toward Rosa's house. "She isn't. Under the tough exterior, she's as soft as a marshmallow. I hear her crying out back some nights, bless her heart." She leaned a little closer and whispered, "She likes to have a cigarette when she's stressed. Not that I'm judging."

"Of course not." I glanced over at the woman's yard. It wouldn't be difficult for her to overhear Rosa. The cypress trees against her fence, creating a barrier, had seen better days. Several were brown and the lower limbs sparse looking. Though she would have to intentionally be eavesdropping.

"She doesn't eat properly either. Tons of pizza and takeout food. The delivery drivers come and go; I see them. Sometimes I take her over a plate of vegetables. I worry for her."

"That's so kind of you. I'm sure Rosa feels lucky to have a neighbor like you. It's wonderful to know she has someone close by to look out for her."

I shifted my bag higher onto my shoulder.

The woman smiled a pleased smile. "I do what I can. It's just awful what happened to her."

I inclined my head. "How do you mean?"

Her eyebrows shot up. "The police, dear. I just can't believe it. How could Chief Quinn railroad her like that?"

"Right. Well, I think the investigation is ongoing." I didn't deny her claims. She'd only clam up.

"It better be. That woman, the impostor—if she weren't dead already, she should be horsewhipped." Rosa's neighbor stepped closer and lowered her tone. "Can I trust you, or are you on their side?" Her little dog eyed me.

"You can trust me."

She studied me for a few minutes, searching my face in a scrutinizing fashion. She was so close that I noticed she had a tiny mole on her eye that she might need to get checked out. "Okay then." She solidified her decision with a single nod. "Someone has been terrorizing Rosa. It's just plain awful. I thought it was the impostor, but now . . ." She shrugged, glancing around the street. "Well, unless the impostor sent it before she died." Her eyes sparkled. "Wouldn't that be something?"

"Okay. I'm a bit confused. Why would you think someone was terrorizing Rosa?"

"Oh, I guess I am getting ahead of myself." She cleared her throat, happy to have someone interested in her story. I could read that all over her face. "Well, the first thing I noticed was a dozen black roses on her front porch there. It had one of those funeral ribbons around it that read *Rest in Peace*." She pointed to the little cement porch on the front of the house. "That was a few weeks back. Then she found a dead crow in her mailbox. She nearly had a fit when she discovered that."

"I bet she did." I stared at the little mailbox. I wondered if Rosa had reported any of this and then decided she must not have. Harry would have leaked it to Piper or me. I'd ask her to make sure.

"I would have bet my bottom dollar it was that impostor, but something arrived for Rosa today. I didn't see what it was this time. I think a gift basket or something like that. I saw her reaction, though. She bolted out into the front yard in her bathrobe."

"My God." My hand went to my throat. "What made you believe the Jane Doe sent the roses and was responsible for the bird?"

"Jane Doe?" She furrowed her brow.

I shook my head. "The impostor."

"Oh." Her shoulders rose and fell. "Who else could it be? She's not had a lick of trouble until that woman showed up. All those negative reports about her in the paper. They're blaming everything on her. Someone should help the poor dear. She's coming unglued."

"Yes. I agree. I'm here to help Rosa." My God, I'd had no idea Rosa had been dealing with all of this. She should have said something.

The woman gave me a pat on the arm. "That's nice, dear. Maybe you should insist Quinn be kinder to her."

I placated her by giving her a smile. Clearly, she didn't understand how the police department operated.

"You know"—she glanced around conspiratorially—"we should both say something. There's strength in numbers, I always say. I'm going to call him myself this afternoon. Tell him I saw that impostor on our street last week. I need to feed Sugar. It was nice chatting with you."

She started for her yard.

What? I hurried after her. "Wait just a minute, please. You saw Jane—the impostor—on this street?"

Her head bobbed up and down as she pointed to the cul-de-sac. "I saw her right there, sitting in a car in the middle of the night. I got up around three that Tuesday morning because my restless leg syndrome was acting up, and I'd forgotten to take my pills. When I walked past my living room window, I saw a police car sitting on the street there." She pointed. "The woman got out of the car and stood at the end of Rosa's driveway. Stood right there under that streetlight. For a second, I thought it was Rosa."

"Did you call the police? Report it?"

She shook her head. "That's what I'm going to do now."

I kept my face clear of expression. "Why didn't you report it that night?"

Sugar growled at me. Either he was hungry or I wasn't fooling him. He could sense my frustration toward his owner and didn't care for it one bit.

"Because if I'm honest, I didn't know it was the impostor at the time. It wasn't until I saw the news about the woman and then asked Rosa about it. Well, when she told me that hadn't been her on the street that night, I knew it must've been the impostor." She squinted and stroked the dog's head.

"It was three in the morning?"

She nodded. It would have been awfully dark out, and I had a hard time believing that at her advanced age, she'd have had the ability to identify anyone from that distance, given the lack of visibility. Not that an ID would help us now anyway.

The screen door on Rosa's carport creaked open.

The woman waved to Rosa. "Hey, sweetie. I hope you're feeling a little better today." Then she moseyed back over to her yard, stopping along the way to pick up a few fallen sticks off her well-manicured lawn.

Chapter
Thirty-Eight

"Hey." I smiled and extracted the coffees and pastries from my car. I walked into the carport, noticing how terrible Rosa looked. She wore a ratty purple terry cloth bathrobe and slippers that had seen better days. She had deep dark circles under her eyes, and her hair was an oily mess.

She folded her arms. "What are you doing here? And why were you talking to Miss Key?"

Miss Key. I made a mental note.

"I'm here to check on you, and I come bearing gifts." I held up the little box filled with her favorite Danishes. "Your neighbor's dog decided to go all Cujo on me. She seems nice." I nodded to the house next door and smiled again. I dangled the box by the little string when I reached her.

She took the box, and I thought the corners of her mouth turned up slightly. Maybe. I hoped.

"Come in." She sighed.

I followed her into the house. Her counter was littered with takeout containers and pizza boxes. Dishes were piled high in the sink, and the garbage was in a big black trash bag on the floor next to the back door. I didn't linger, not wanting to make her feel worse. I followed her into the living room off the galley kitchen, preparing myself for a disaster. I gaped.

The wall opposite her sofa was filled with pictures and time-lines. She'd used red string to connect printouts and images. I set the coffees on the coffee table, stepping closer to inspect her work. I stared at the picture of Judy Galloway sitting in her car at Sonic drinking a slushy. A couple of other shots of a few other members of different book clubs who'd been asked to stay in town. Probably asked to stick around by Rosa herself. And probably fled Sweet Mountain by now. No one could be expected to hang around a city indefinitely.

She even had included a picture of me. *Not flattering at all.* I was sitting in the car with Mr. Greene outside the courthouse. My mouth was wide open, and for some reason, I'd hunched over. "My God. Did you hire an investigator?"

"No. I'm working alone. Now, anyway," Rosa groused.

No wonder she looked worn out. I decided not to comment on my photo staring back at me on her suspect wall. Tammy and Joel were there as well, and I understood why. Rosa hadn't wanted to miss anything. But I had noticed there wasn't a single picture of Mel. My watch pinged.

"I still don't know who she is, the Jane? Or why she was impersonating me." Rosa sat down in a worn-looking recliner and took a sip of the coffee she'd taken from the holder.

We have an ID. Elizabeth "Betty" Smithson. She's in the system. I've sent the docs to your email. Christopher.

Thank you! I sent back from my watch and did a little happy dance on the inside. I still had lots of questions, but our Jane had been reunited with her name. And now that we had her, we could find her accomplice.

"But I think she's the one who killed Patricia," Rosa said. "I have eyewitness accounts who can place her at the scene. Those who mistook her for me. My guess is she stayed out of town and came in to do her dirty work."

I had an inner debate as I stared at her wall. Quinn had said not to share any details of the case with her. He'd also said we needed to sit down with her after our discovery. I turned and smiled at my friend. "I can help with that."

She sat up. Crumbs from her pastry fell onto her lap. "You've ID'd her already?"

"Just now." I pulled out my iPad and sat down next to her, moving her laptop aside. I filled her in while I tapped the screen.

Within seconds we had a mug shot and a rap sheet in front of us. "Betty Smithson doesn't look anything like me."

I raised a brow.

Rosa furrowed hers in response.

"You weren't twins or anything. But your coloring is similar, and your facial structure is close enough to pass for those not looking closely. And those who don't know you"—I shrugged— "might get confused from a distance."

She snorted.

"People see what they want to see. She wore some sort of makeup to cover her cleft chin. Not that she would have fooled any of your friends or colleagues."

"Except Harry."

"Harry doesn't know you that well."

She nodded and chewed on the side of her index finger. "Can we link her to the murder? Physical evidence?"

"I don't know. We definitely have Betty at the scene, but you are aware no prints except for Elaine's were on the murder weapon." I told her how we'd found the Jane Doe's body in the cemetery and about the condition of her fingers, concluding with what she already knew: apparently someone wanted to stall the IDing process.

"Damn." Rosa settled back against the recliner and stared straight ahead. "Betty was working with someone. She must've screwed up, and they had to take her out before she rolled on them. It's all that makes sense."

"Yeah. It's plausible." I got up and went back to her investigation wall. "Betty checked into the Magnolia Manor with a guest. Or at least registered as a party of two." I tapped one of the pictures of Judy. "How do you know Judy Galloway?"

Rosa snorted derisively. "I don't. The only thing I know about her is that she's out to ruin my life. I ran her through the system before I was relieved of duty."

I turned toward her and winced. I could tell how painful that had been for her to say. I needed her to come clean with me. To trust me enough to let me in. I couldn't get to the bottom of this otherwise. As much as I hated it, Rosa was the key to solving these murders. And she had to understand that.

She shrugged a shoulder when she raised her head to meet my gaze. "I came up empty. I see the way you're looking at me. And I get it. At first, I thought maybe she was from Louisiana and we'd crossed paths somewhere. But she's from Alabama. Maybe she knows or has family in Baton Rouge, I don't know. She won't talk to me. But she's sure talking to everyone else."

"Wait!" My brows shot up. "The stolen car is registered in Alabama."

Rosa sat up. "That's something. But not enough if you can't link her to the car."

"I'll see what I can find out."

"What is it with this woman? What would her motive be?" Rosa sipped her coffee slowly, focusing on her suspect board. I knew that look. Understood it. The determination to keep staring at the evidence until whatever was hidden presented itself. It was always there, like little bread crumbs you had to follow. But I saw something else in her tonight. A hollowness. As if something was inside her eating away and she was powerless to stop it.

"Judy believes you're the killer."

Rosa scrunched up her face. "What? She told you that?"

"This morning, in fact. We had an interesting conversation. Judy seems to think she knows you pretty well." I told her in a nutshell what Judy had said and watched her reaction like a hawk.

"She's a crackpot," Rosa exploded. "I don't know where she got her information, but she's demented."

"You never saw her before? Not even in passing? She claims to have hung out in some bar with your unit."

"No. Well, I don't know. Maybe this Judy came around and I didn't pay her any attention. I drank a lot in those days." Rosa sat up and dug a loose cigarette from her pocket, then stuck it into her mouth. "Don't say anything. Cigarettes will kill me, I know."

She was hiding something from me. I raised my hands in supplication. "Be straight with me. Tell me what's going on with you. Why your neighbor is worried that someone is threatening you." I wanted to hear from her lips exactly where she was with all this. Whatever her neighbor had witnessed could only scratch the surface of what Rosa had been dealing with. And she'd just admitted she might have met Judy before.

She pulled the unlit cigarette from her mouth and tossed it on the coffee table. She drew another one of those pink flyers in a large ziplock bag from the same pocket as the cigarette and handed it to me.

It was an updated flyer of the one I'd received and very similar to what I'd found scrawled on the hotel wall in the vandalized room. This flyer, though, had the dashes filled in with what we'd already figured out. The letters that spelled *Rosa Landry*. Under her name was written in a terrible hand, *Trick or Treat. I won't make a mistake this time.*

The killer was getting bolder with his threats. And with this daring move of delivering it directly to Rosa, he was figuratively painting a giant bull's-eye on her. I glanced up at my friend, my stomach in knots.

"My God," I breathed.

"Yeah." She stared straight in my face. "A mistake." She half laughed. "As in the killer mistook Betty for me."

"This is insane."

She held her hands out. "I know."

"You got this today? This morning?" I gripped the flyer, my heart thundering. That someone had decided to target my friend and continued terrorizing her right under our noses caused my blood to boil. I'd had enough of this. If Judy was involved, she was either the stupidest woman alive to draw attention to herself the way she had or, I considered, she could be the smartest. A hiding-in-plain-sight sort of thing. But that didn't quite make sense. Judy could have identified Rosa if she'd known her before.

"Yes. And I'm not holding out hope for prints. With Judy slandering me, the case could be made that I've orchestrated this whole thing. Hired Jane Doe"—she waved her hand—"what was her name again?"

"Betty Smithson."

"Betty to go around town creating a diversion. Then I could shoot complete strangers for no gain and stage that I'm being targeted to throw the police off my trail." She threw her hands in the air. "It'd be just my luck."

That would be smart. Rosa could easily send all the threats to herself. It would be brilliant if she was involved in the murder. *No.* I shook my head to dislodge that insane notion. "Tell me about the threats."

She leaned back, closed her eyes, and scrubbed her face with her hands. "Miss Key told you about the others?"

I nodded. "The black roses and bird."

She didn't seem surprised. "The flyer was in a gift basket filled with rotten fruit. I put it in a garbage bag and tied it up. I'll go through it to see if there is any evidence there when I can think straight."

"I'll take it."

Her head dropped forward. "That's probably best. I'm so tired, Lyla. So very tired."

"You're ready to talk to me now, aren't you?" Of all my friends, Rosa was the one who never asked for help. She'd be the first to offer it but prided herself on her strength and independence. I wanted her to trust me enough to confide in me about her troubles and not have to force it out of her. I wanted her to come to me on her own.

"Yes," she said, her voice quivering. "I'm surrendering. I need your help."

My doubts evaporated, replaced by shame that I'd ever even considered the possibility. I hadn't been wearing blinders when it came to one of my closest friends. Someone had pushed her buttons, helped sabotage her career, and painted a giant bull's-eye on her back. I went to my knees in front of the recliner and pulled her into a big hug. She didn't fight me; she held on to me as if I were her lifeline and sobbed against my shoulder.

I would tear this town apart. Use every resource at my disposal. Some lunatic thought they could get away with this—take my friend's life. Not on my watch. And by God, watching I would be.

Chapter
Thirty-Nine

B rad and I finished up the next day around five, officially
closing the Jane Doe case.

We'd written our reports, contacted Elizabeth Smithson's
next of kin. Her uncle, her closest living relative, told me he had
no interest in retrieving her remains. The family had written
Betty off years ago. She'd started selling her prescription drugs,
and that had led to stealing, assault charges, and nearly burning
down her grandmother's house three years ago, creating a rift in
the family that had never mended. Her uncle did say he hoped
she had now found peace from whatever had driven her to such
horrendous acts.

Even with the animosity I felt toward Betty Smithson for
wreaking havoc on our town, a part of me felt a touch sorry for
her. Whatever had sent her on this dark path and the demons
she faced must've been unbearable.

I still didn't have a link between Judy and Betty. There
wasn't a link between the owners of the stolen car and Judy. I'd
reached out to them, and they had no idea who she was, nor was
she from the same part of Alabama. I then searched for some

link between Betty and Patricia. It was incredibly frustrating to not find anything there either.

"Well"—Brad rose and slid his phone in his pocket—"that was Chief Quinn. My job here is officially complete."

"It's always good to close a case." I smiled.

He nodded slowly. "It is. It would also be nice not to feel so powerless all of the time."

"Crime in all forms makes folks feel powerless. Our community needs an equalizer to make a safer place." *I can't give that up.*

I didn't have to say the words. He knew it because in that way, we were alike.

"I guess I'll be getting back to Atlanta."

I rose as well and folded my arms. "Okay."

We stared at each other for a long time.

Our eyes locked—mine were stinging. Neither one of us said anything. It was clearly written on his face that he knew that I understood what he wanted and that I didn't want the same thing. His eyes were sad. And my heart ached. I couldn't help the tears, so I glanced away and wiped my nose.

Brad cleared his throat. "Great work on this case. You have grown into an accomplished investigator. I look forward to working with you more in the future."

I tossed my hair back and wiped my eyes. "It's seamless between us. I will always come when you call and will always be willing to help with any case."

His eyes were glossy too. We were both hurting. But there was no point in discussing the possibility of working this out. The canyon between us continued to grow.

When he closed the distance between us in two long strides, I didn't protest as he took me in his arms. I didn't stop the little sob that escaped my lips either. I held on to him and mourned what could have been. He stroked my hair and kissed my head.

I didn't know how long we stood there. But when we both left the office, we didn't make eye contact again. He went one way and I the other. I cried the whole way home.

* * *

I showered and changed into my comfiest pajamas and sat at my kitchen table, eating rocky road ice cream, my comfort food, and running deeper background checks. I would allow myself time to mourn more later. But now I had a job to do. I was learning to compartmentalize, and it served me well.

Rosa had allowed me access to her military records, and I found no correlation between her discharge and Judy Galloway. Another letdown. And there was no mention of a dishonorable discharge. Nor were there any records of disorderly conduct. That had been a complete fabrication. I became even more determined when I heard that the flyer and the basket's contents were free of prints.

When deep background checks fail, go to social media.

And that I found interesting. Judy's public profile held nothing back. She'd posted lots of videos of her rants about her situation in Sweet Mountain. Her friends commiserated with her and applauded her efforts to help the police apprehend a killer.

I began checking Judy's friends list to look for connections between her and Betty, Patricia, and Rosa. Something in my gut told me that everything was connected. Judy was too close to everything. Too angry with Rosa. Too involved with the press and speaking out too much about the murder. Judy's hotel room was right next door to the one that had been vandalized. It wouldn't be a stretch to link her to the flyer.

She had the maximum number of friends, and I hadn't even checked her accounts on other platforms. I couldn't do this alone. Time was of the essence.

I texted the links of the videos over to Quinn and asked if anyone at the police precinct could help me dig. When he couldn't spare anyone, I called in my club.

Thirty minutes later, the Jane Does, minus Rosa and Amelia, were all packed in my living room with their computers on their laps. I'd explained that whoever was behind this had probably eluded detection either because they had evaded the police or because this was the first time they'd crossed severe criminal lines. With the discovery of Betty's impersonation of Rosa, everyone had apologized to Rosa and offered to pitch in.

I pulled up all the photos I'd taken of Rosa's investigation and timelines. She'd done a thorough job. But she was too close to this. Too affected. Too sleep deprived. She did not even protest when I suggested she stay with Melanie. She'd understood that staying with me wasn't an option, since I was dealing with the police department and having her at my place could complicate things.

Melanie sat on the sofa next to Tammy, who sat next to Joel. Rosa had finally fallen asleep next door at Melanie's, and we didn't want to wake her. She desperately needed the rest. So we kept our voices low. The walls were thin between Mel's place and mine.

There was a knock at my front door. "Pizza's here." Joel hopped up to answer the door while I pulled some Cokes and Sprites from the refrigerator.

"Hey, Lyla, your gran is here." Joel put the pizza boxes on the counter, and Melanie went to set out some plates. I glanced over and saw my little gran standing in the foyer with a big smile on her face, holding a box of doughnuts and a rolling overnight bag at her feet.

"Hey, what are you doing here?" I went over and gave her a hug.

"Sally Anne dropped me off. Joel put the word out that the Jane Does were meeting at your place and rallying around to help our Rosa. Well, I'm a Jane Doe, aren't I?"

I laughed and kissed the top of her head. "Of course you are. I'll call Mother and tell her you're staying over with me tonight."

"Good. I knew you might want a little company, since you and Brad broke up for good."

All eyes were on me. Melanie, who'd already taken a bite of pizza, swallowed quickly and said, "What? You were eating rocky road." Of course Mel knew.

"No way! Y'all were so perfect for each other." Joel made a sad face.

"It's fine. I'm fine. We left it on favorable terms. Our working relationship won't be affected, and we still have great affection for each other. We just came to the realization that we want different things."

Gran piled up her plate with pizza and doughnuts. "And she's got me. We'll patch her up and get her back out there when she's ready. She's like her ole Gran. It's hard for us to settle down."

Everyone laughed, and I smiled gratefully at the sweetest, most supportive grandmother on the planet. She winked at me. "So where do y'all want me? I thought I'd have more of a supervisory role here. Until it's time to go out and bust some heads."

Joel snorted, and a little Coke ran out of his nose. Tammy laughed and handed him a napkin.

"I don't know what we were worried about," Melanie said. "We just needed to call Gran. She'll bust heads for us and save the day."

Everyone erupted with laughter, something we all needed. Then we settled down and got back to work.

Tammy had found a couple of people on Facebook who were happy to answer her messages about Judy. She had a good time reading out the snarky comments. Sadly, none of it amounted to anything. None of Judy's Facebook friends who spoke with us knew who Rosa was aside from what they'd seen posted by Judy.

Joel had focused on Instagram. He'd come up empty as well, though he had found someone interested in him.

"Be careful, Joel," Melanie cautioned. "You have no idea who that person is. They could be some wack job."

"I'm not an idiot, Mel. I've checked out their profile and the tagged photos on their friend pages. I'm not looking to hook up tomorrow. Just get to know them and see if I might want to meet up for a drink sometime."

I didn't want to rain on his parade, but with all the craziness going on and a target on our friend's back, I wouldn't be swapping information with anyone on social media. I decided to say something later when he wouldn't feel ganged up on. It didn't sound like he planned to do anything rash.

I'd friended several of the commenters who were eager to chat. I had three instant chats going. Two, I could already tell, were going to be fruitless. The women hadn't anything credible to relay but were full of opinions about me and the town. One woman berated me for aiding and abetting a murderer. I refrained from informing her that she had no idea what she was spouting off about. The other told me I should thank my lucky stars Judy was helping our ramshackle police department. I ended those conversations in a hurry.

Someone sent me an invitation to join a private group chat, but before I could accept, I needed a double shot of espresso. I'd have to settle for a cup of regular, extra strong.

"Oh." Melanie raised her hand from where she sat at the kitchen table with her giant Lenovo. "I've got someone on here who claims Judy stalked one of her best friend's exes and threatened her best friend with bodily harm."

I left my mug on the counter and hurried to read over Mel's shoulder.

I've been calling the Sweet Mountain Police Department to warn them about Judy Galloway. She is a stalker and a dangerous woman.

Finally, our first real lead! If it panned out. Mel and I high-fived, and I pulled up a chair. "Ask her who she talked to at the police department."

I sat while Melanie's fingers went across the keys, and we waited.

I think his name was Officer Daniels.

Melanie and I exchanged a wide-eyed glance.

"Which Daniels?" Tammy asked from behind us, where everyone, including Gran, had gathered to read.

"It has to be Harry. Quinn would have identified himself as the chief. And I don't think he'd be fielding calls. Especially with the extra help from the state police."

Melanie asked, and we waited. The little dots floating over the messenger bubble.

He didn't say, or maybe I just don't remember. But he had no interest in hearing more. He said I sounded like a disgruntled female looking to settle a score. I kept calling but to no avail. I've left six messages for the officer. He's never called me back.

"Wow. That throws up a serious red flag," Joel said as his phone chirped, and he stepped away to take the call.

"It sounds like she called incessantly." Melanie wound her hair up on top of her head, yawning. "Why wouldn't Harry run it down?"

"Maybe he did and it was a dead end. Here. Let me see that." She pushed the computer toward me. I typed a message, needing to know for sure what we were dealing with here. And maybe I just didn't want to give up our first real lead.

Well, that doesn't sound professional. My friend is a Private Investigator here in town and is working on the case with the police. She'd listen to you. Want me to get you in touch?

We waited as the tiny dots kept disappearing and reappearing. The woman must be nervous and having difficulty deciding whether she wanted to discuss this with a local PI. That didn't bode well. If she were credible and genuinely concerned, as she insisted she was, she'd be shouting it from the rooftops to whoever would listen. I got up, picked up one of the many stress balls I kept lying around, and paced the floor. All eyes were on me.

I paused. "Tell her I'd be happy to talk to her friend."

Melanie started typing, relaying the info. "Still nothing."

I did a little more pacing. "Tell her that if she's worried about privacy, I'm incredibly discreet. Give her the Cousins Investigative website information and my name."

Melanie nodded and did as I requested. "I'll set you up a quick profile and account, Lyla, since you're not on Snapchat."

We all waited, holding our breath to see how or if the messenger would respond. I kept pacing and began thinking of my next move.

"She's back!" Gran shouted.

Suddenly the bubble reappeared.

Yeah. Okay. Send the contact my IM info. My friend will message her later tonight if she's up.

"Account is all set up, and the message is sent. It could be late when you hear from HippiChic7 or her friend." Melanie checked her watch. "It's already eleven."

I leaned over Mel's shoulder and responded that Mel23's friend would be waiting to hear from her.

"What time zone is she in?" I asked, and leaned over Mel's shoulder again to begin searching HippiChic7's location, but she disappeared. She didn't have her location listed on her profile. I could find out a general area with a bit of digging. And I'd do just that if I didn't hear from her or her friend later. I'd track them via their IP address and then search the database to see if there really was something there. I'd also be talking to Harry.

I rose and stretched. Gran had moved back to the sofa with a cup of tea. "Guess we wait."

"No. It's late. I can take it from here. Thank y'all so much for coming over and helping out. We can reconvene at another time if we need to, but hopefully, this is resolved before then."

"We were so glad to help," Tammy said, and Joel nodded in agreement. "We feel awful that we contributed to Rosa's troubles."

I went over and hugged Tammy. She felt so thin and fragile. "Don't. No one would have considered Betty. My God, whoever heard of someone impersonating another person, except in the movies. And with all the chaos, the mistake was understandable. Rosa knows there is no malice between you."

"Yeah, that's what she told me. And she apologized to us as well. She looked so exhausted, and I still feel bad." Tammy hung her head. "I'll do whatever I can to help her. And I owe you an apology too, Lyla. I should never have accused you of having anything to do with those awful terrifying flyers, nor should I have threatened to leave the club."

I waved her apology away. "No, you don't. We're good." She smiled and said good-bye to Gran and Melanie.

"Guess I'm going too," Joel said, and he and Melanie gathered their things together.

"Are you working tomorrow?" I asked.

"Yep. And don't you worry. I'll be keeping my eyes wide open. I might even do some investigative work myself. Judy likes to talk."

"Just let her talk. Don't bait her. Okay?"

"Ten-four." He saluted me. "I'm nosy. She already knows that. Not that you have to be, with her."

"Okay. But be careful." I stretched again.

He chuckled. "Judy won't creep up on me. I got her number."

We all said our good-byes, and I told Mel to text me if she or Rosa needed anything. She planned to take tomorrow off and spend it with Rosa. Mel was fab like that.

I made myself a cup of coffee and said to Gran, "It could be a long night. You should change into your pj's. I can take my laptop up to bed. We can watch some Netflix while I wait."

"Oh, good idea. I've been watching *Schitt's Creek*. You ever seen that program?"

271

"Yeah, it's one of my favorite shows. I watch it when I need to unwind and have a laugh." I grabbed her overnight bag in one hand and my coffee in the other, tucked my laptop under my arm, and followed her up the stairs.

"That Eugene Levy is a real looker. I've had a crush on him since he was in the movie *Going Berserk*," Gran told me.

"I've never seen it."

"Oh, you should watch it. It came out sometime in the late eighties, I think. It's a hoot. It's got John Candy in it."

"I've never been a huge fan of John Candy movies." I yawned and set her bag on my slate-gray upholstered bench in front of the bed.

"Well, never mind that. The real star is Eugene Levy. Mmmmm. I wouldn't mind spending some time alone with him."

I laughed as she gathered her toiletries together and headed into the adjoining bathroom. I smiled. She looked so small. She was tiny but mighty, my gran. And I was so glad she'd come over. I wondered if all grandmothers had a sixth sense or if it was just mine. Gran had always known when I needed a pick-me-up since my childhood. When I would be in my room after a bad day from school, she'd show up with a treat of some kind. As a teenager, when I went through a messy breakup, she'd talk me into skipping school, and we'd go shopping and see a movie. Nothing ever came before me with Gran. To me, she was the most special person in all the world. And I counted myself blessed.

"Sugar," she called from the bathroom. "I'm going to borrow your toothbrush to clean my dentures. I forgot mine."

"I have a spare under the sink. Use that one, please." I shook my head, still smiling.

"Too late."

Chapter Forty

M y computer pinged with an instant message, and I jolted
awake. I must've just dozed off—the glow from my screen
was the only light in the room. Gran's soft snores beside me
helped me gain my bearings. I wiped my mouth and blinked,
my vision blurry from sleep. I grabbed my blue-light-blocking
glasses from the bedside table.

PuzzleGal7: *Hi. I hope I have the correct person. Is
this Mel23's friend? The Private Investigator in Sweet
Mountain, GA?*

I typed back while thinking how easy it would be to scam
someone on this platform. Mel had just made the profile tonight.

LMoody22: *Yes. I'm Lyla Moody. I work for Cousins
Investigative Services. You can contact me on the
number listed on the website if that makes you more
comfortable.*

PuzzleGal7: *No. Here is fine. Sorry, it's so late. I've
got a little one that's got her days and nights turned
around. I really would like to keep this conversation*

and my name out of the press. I don't want to draw attention to myself. That's the reason my friend went to the police. She said it would be anonymous.

I wondered if she understood how all of this worked. Her friend had spoken to our police department, and if they wanted to, they could easily track her down and subpoena her. I'd afford her the safety she needed to feel.

LMoody22: *Not a problem. Is there a reason you feel you need anonymity?*
PuzzleGal7: *Judy Galloway has moved on, and I'd like to keep it that way.*
LMoody22: *Understood. Take your time. I'm here. I'm listening.*
PuzzleGal7: *I guess I should start by saying my friend pushed me to speak with you. And I won't lie and say I'm not a little scared. It's not just me anymore. I have children. And nothing I tell you can help with the investigation in Sweet Mountain other than to give you insight into the woman you're dealing with there. I have no idea if she's involved in the crime.*
LMoody22: *I understand. And you have my word. I will keep your confidence.*
PuzzleGal7: *I'll just dive in before I lose my nerve.*

The dots floated and disappeared for a few beats. I waited. A minute or two passed, and I thought she'd had a change of heart.

PuzzleGal7: *It started after my ex and I decided to give it another try. We'd been separated for two months,* *and I found out I was pregnant with our second child. A week after he moved back in, it started. Judy showed up at a restaurant where we were having dinner one night with my parents. She made a scene. Apparently, ex connected with her on some disgusting online dating site. He went to a bar to meet her once. Said she misrepresented herself. In other words, she used some photo editor to improve her appearance. He didn't even recognize her. He told me he was three stiff drinks in when she showed up. His shitty way of explaining away why he went home with a psycho. Ex swore he never had anything else to do with her after that first date.*

LMoody22: *Did you take out a restraining order?*

That would be something I could use to verify her story, and I hope'd she had.

PuzzleGal7: *Yes. A lot of good that did. She'd enter our home when we weren't there and leave little threatening notes for me in my underwear drawer and on my bathroom mirror. We couldn't prove it was her. She seemed to show up everywhere, but she abided by the PFA and stayed one thousand feet away from us. It was terrifying nonetheless.*

That PuzzleGal7 had used the restraining order abbreviation told me she was probably on the up-and-up. I had my notepad up on my iPad and was taking notes, jotting down anything that could be useful.

LMoody22: *I can't even imagine the stress you were under. Having a young child and constantly having to*

275

look over your shoulder. *No one should have to deal with that.*

PuzzleGal7: *You're telling me. She rammed her cart into mine at the grocery store one time. Thankfully I was alone. Another time, she followed me around town while I ran errands, revving her engine and riding my bumper. I reported her that time too. She always seemed to target me and made sure ex or our child wasn't with me. I think she wanted to make him believe I was crazy or something. We constantly argued about her. Which, in hindsight, was her goal, I guess.*

LMoody22: *When did she finally move on? Nothing tragic occurred, I hope.*

PuzzleGal7: *No. She never physically harmed me. She did a number on my psyche, though. I applied for a concealed carry three days before she vanished from our lives.*

LMoody22: *She just vanished?*

PuzzleGal7: *Yes, one day, she just stopped. I don't know why. And it took weeks before I could breathe easier. Still, the months she tortured us took their toll. That and my ex is a gigantic SOB and found another woman to hook up with. And well, we didn't make it.*

I had a hard time believing that the woman PuzzleGal7 described to me, one that obsessed, would stop without force. There had to be a reason. Another person she was focusing on, perhaps.

LMoody22: *I'm terribly sorry to hear that.*

Relationships were complex enough without that sort of added stress.

> **PuzzleGal7:** *It's okay. It was probably for the best. He broke the trust.*
> **LMoody22:** *I can understand that. Do you know what dating site your ex and Judy met on?*
> **PuzzleGal7:** *Oh, yeah. It's the app Tinderly. The psycho probably belonged to every dating app out there. All those dumb idiots have no idea what they are getting into with her. Well, it's late. I should probably go.*
> **LMoody22:** *Okay. I appreciate you trusting me with your story. If you ever need anything, feel free to reach out. I'll help if I can. I'll keep your name out of our investigation. You have my word.*

There would be no need to drag her into this. But she'd undoubtedly shed some much-needed light on Judy Galloway. Again, I believed women like Judy didn't just stop that sort of destructive behavior. Usually, their behavior escalated. Was it possible she and Patricia had been after the same man?

> **PuzzleGal7:** *Thanks. I hope I won't ever require a PI but thanks just the same.*
> **LMoody22:** *I hear ya. Lol*
> **PuzzleGal7:** *My advice, for whatever it's worth, is to look for the man she's after. She'll do anything for her obsession.*

We were on the same page.

Chapter
Forty-One

The following day, after Gran's friend Sally Anne picked her up for their standing weekly hair appointments, I stood in the shower allowing the hot spray to beat against my scalp and wake me up. I'd stayed up late digging into PuzzleGal7's background. I found out that Dana Watson, formally Dana Holmes, had recently remarried. The mother of two now lived in Shreveport, Louisiana. The court record showed that Dana Watson's attorney had filed a PFA in Lafayette, Louisiana, on her behalf a little over a year ago against Judy Galloway, where she'd then resided with her ex-husband, Larry. No wonder she'd desired secrecy. She'd recently moved and rebuilt her life.

I'd joined Tinderly last night to see what the dating app was like for singles. I was sure many subscribers met very nice people on some of these services, but being in my line of work, the idea was terrifying to me. I had something tangible to explore. Judy had a record of stalking—a history of aggressive and intimidating behavior. She'd spent time in Rosa's home state. Either their paths had crossed or Judy knew someone close to Rosa. How else would she have formulated such strong opinions? But the stumbling block was that Rosa wasn't seeing anyone that Judy wanted. Unless it wasn't a love triangle this time. Threads of a plausible theory began to take shape. One I wouldn't tug on just yet. I needed proof.

The water began to run cold, and I got out and dressed. I took my time getting ready. I'd already forwarded the office calls to my cell, since I was getting in later than usual. I would be outsourcing more work today. We had only a few active cases, and two were only open because the client had yet to pay the bill. Once they did, I'd archive them. I had planned to work from home; unfortunately, my VPN connection was acting up, and I needed to access our secure search engines and databases.

The sun dominated the bright blue sky and shone through the canopy of limbs overhead as I drove up the scenic road toward historic downtown. The unseasonable storms that plagued us last week had left leaving us with breathtaking views. The gorgeous hues of the leaves—reds, golds, and burnt orange—covered the landscape. Some of the shops had decorated with similar colors. Lovely gourds and pumpkins lined walkways. You'd never know from the picturesque views that a killer lurked somewhere close by.

We were getting dangerously close to what I feared could be another murder. And the latest threat had been directly on Rosa's life. With the *trick-or-treat* reference, we surmised—after drawing up a criminal profile—that whoever was gunning for Rosa would likely make their move on Halloween. He liked to strike fear before he took action. His choice to utilize the holiday must have thrilled him. This felt like something out of a horror movie. But this wasn't a movie. And the stakes were higher than they'd ever been.

Evil. The word echoed in my mind as I unlocked the office and booted up my computer. The killer had kept their word before, following the same pattern as our club pick, *A Murder Is Announced.* We'd had a murder every time an announcement was made, including the one we'd made.

Unlike last time, there hadn't been a location given as to where the crime would take place. All we knew was that this person meant business. And I had no idea what Quinn and the state police were doing. Or if they'd take anything I found regarding Judy seriously, especially since Dana Watson's warning calls to the police department hadn't proven fruitful. I'd texted Quinn early this morning asking to meet today. I hadn't heard back.

As I stood in front of the Keurig, listening to the steady stream of my coffee brewing, I couldn't believe the situation we were in. I'd had a lot of cases in the last few years that both terrified and stumped me. But this one stretched me to a whole new level. I cast a glance over to the vacant chair at my desk. Brad would have opinions on what I'd found, and I longed to talk it over with him. I couldn't bring myself to call him. Not yet.

No. I'm capable. Think, Lyla. Think.

Who would have ever thought a good night of fun would turn our town upside down? Miss Marple, that's who. I smiled a little to myself. I couldn't help visualizing little Miss Marple roaming around my office. Getting her giant bag together and securing her hat to go out into the town and hunt for clues. What if I end up alone, like Miss Marple? An elderly spinster who spent her time sleuthing to keep her village safe?

What is wrong with me?

I laughed, shaking my head.

The door swung open, and in stomped a red-faced Courtney. "Good morning." I took a sip from my mug, a bit puzzled by her visit.

She quickly glanced around before she spotted me. Her eyes flashed with anger. "I'm only going to say this one time, so listen up! You stay away from Quinn. You don't call him. You don't text him. You don't go to his office."

I couldn't have been more surprised if she'd slapped me across the face. "What?"

"Don't give me those innocent eyes. I heard how you and Brad broke up. You couldn't stand it that Quinn chose me. That he wanted to marry me instead of choosing you all those years ago."

"What?" I drew the word out.

"Oh yeah, I got your number. You texted my man last night and again this morning. I deleted this morning's text." She took a step forward and pointed at me. "You stay away from my man!"

"Courtney, I am *not* after Quinn." I tried to control my anger that she'd deleted a critical text. "That text"—I took a breath—"was important. I'm working with him on a case. A serious case."

"Bull! You asked to meet up. You—"

I held up my hand in a stop motion, whipped out my cell phone, and dialed Quinn's number, pressing the speaker button.

"Daniels here," came over the speaker, and Courtney's eyes bulged.

"Quinn, it's Lyla. You're on speakerphone."

"Okay." Quinn sounded suspicious.

"I'm standing here in my office with Courtney, who seems to believe the text I sent you this morning regarding the Donaldson case was a booty call and deleted it."

Courtney's lips pinched together, and her face had deepened to the color of eggplant. I didn't care how upset she got. We did not have time for her jealously or nonsensical behavior.

"Courtney." Quinn's tone had an edge to it as sharp as a blade.

"I'm here, Quinn. Lyla has been trying to come between us since before the wedding. She—"

"Lyla, will you pass the phone to my wife, please."

Courtney's resolve broke, and her face crumpled. I almost felt sorry for her. Almost.

"Sure." I extended the phone to her. For a couple of seconds, she just stared at the phone in my hand. "You should talk to him, Courtney. You've got this all wrong. I swear."

Reluctantly she took the phone and pressed it to her ear. I grabbed my bag and walked outside to give them some privacy. I strolled down the street toward Nobles Coffee Company. When I came out of the shop with the largest coffee they sold and a blueberry muffin, I saw Harry standing in the pavilion area of the square. Judy stood awfully close to him and seemed to be whispering conspiratorially. She occasionally cast a glance behind her before she gave him a big hug, her hands stroking his back.

Look for the man she's after rang in my ears. I wondered if Harry had been on Tinderly recently. Getting Rosa out of the way had served him well professionally. He'd become Quinn's right hand. He'd know her buttons and how to set her up for failure and had insight and understanding of how investigations worked, and therefore how to avoid detection. But killing her would be a stretch. Unless he recruited Judy and she went off all half-cocked on her own. Maybe he'd used her and riled her up about Rosa. Maybe Judy had felt threatened by Rosa, and with

Judy's belief that Rosa had a history of being a bunny boiler, it could be a plausible theory. That didn't explain Betty, though. Could Harry have two women working with him? He didn't strike me as the Casanova type. He wasn't what you'd describe as a handsome playboy. Maybe there was more to Harry than was visible. Hmm. No, that didn't make sense. Could Patricia's murder have been unrelated, like Quinn suggested? Ahhh! I wanted to scream. The pieces were there. I just needed to put them together.

When I got back to the office, Courtney had gone, and she'd left my cell phone on the desk. By it was a sticky note with one word written. *Bitch.*

My God. I just couldn't win.

I called Piper.

"Whatcha got for me?" I heard road noise. Piper was in transit.

"I'm not sure yet. We alone?" I took a pinch off the muffin and nibbled it. God, those were good.

"Yep. Just you and me and the highway."

"Okay. How close have you gotten to Harry?" I pulled the sticky note from the pad and wadded it up, tossing it in the garbage.

"He's my new inside source at the precinct. It's easier dealing with him than with Quinn. That she-devil he married is something else."

That coaxed a laugh out of me, one I needed. "Tell me about it. Courtney just paid me a visit to ward me off Quinn."

She burst out laughing. "Better you than me."

"Thanks, pal." I snickered. "Anyway. Rosa got a flyer. One that explicitly names her as the next victim and claims to have murdered Betty Smithson by mistake."

"You're kidding." She sobered up.

"I'm afraid not. All the rumblings you've been hearing about the department clearing Rosa are accurate." I knew she'd be in the loop.

"Do we know what Betty what's-her-name was after? Good work on that, by the way."

"Thanks. Not yet. And I'm not sure how it all fits together, but I'm getting closer. I spoke to someone who gave me a tip on Judy Galloway."

"I'm listening."

I slowed my breathing. *Do I share everything?*

"Lyla. Come on. What about Judy?"

I pushed off the desk, unwound my scarf, feeling warm, and spoke to her in a language she understood. "This is off the record, and I'm not giving you any specifics. This person specifically asked to be kept out of the news and the investigation. I'm serious about protecting my source."

If I told her about the PFA, then she'd find out about Dana and her past troubles with Judy. Maybe not at first, because she didn't know where to look, but eventually. And I'd given Dana my word.

"Again. I'm listening."

"Someone warned me to watch out for her. That's all. She has a reputation for being a little unruly."

"Oh, I believe it. But I'm sensing there is more to this story than unruly."

I paced the floor. "There is. But I don't want it touched, Piper. I mean it."

"I hear you. And give me a minute to think about it."

She literally took a full minute. Or at least it felt like she had.

"Okay. Our working relationship is more important than an old scoop. You have my word. I won't go snooping, and I won't betray you, ever."

I believed her.

I gave her a summary of what I'd learned. Nothing specific. "We need to keep an eye on Judy. We need to find out who she's close to and why she's still here."

"My God! You think she's involved with the killings. You think she and Betty were in it together?"

Though I'd never found a connection between Judy and Betty, there might be one. Or perhaps she was opportunistic and was a copycat. Betty certainly seemed unique in her crimes. My thoughts raced around in circles. I needed to rest before my brain could operate optimally.

"I don't know. All I know is that Judy's eager to disparage Rosa at every opportunity and to anyone who will listen. Don't you find that suspicious? Some woman waltzes into town and shows up at a book club party right when all hell breaks loose. She doesn't belong to any clubs in the area. I checked."

Piper cleared her throat, and I could tell she hadn't. She'd taken Judy at her word. And why wouldn't she? Why would someone lie about something like that? You wouldn't suspect them if they were outspoken and eagerly sought face time in the news. Why would a killer risk exposure? Most wouldn't—especially if they'd killed before.

"From the account I got last night, the woman is volatile. She never physically assaulted this person. She did, however, stalk her and her husband. Terrorized her through her everyday life."

"But . . . why? What was she after?" Piper tried to make sense of what I was saying.

"She wanted *her husband*."

"She's credible, this woman you spoke to?"

"She is the most credible source thus far. I fact-checked her claim."

"Okay. Hmm. So you think Judy had issues with Rosa first, then moved on to your source, and then moved on to Sweet Mountain because she met someone here on a dating app?"

I sat down on the edge of the desk. That was one of the things I loved about Piper. She caught on quickly. "Maybe. And there's something else." I told her about what Dana had said about calling the police department. "And I just saw Judy hanging on Harry. Right out in the open. Which seems to be her MO. I don't know if she's using Harry or—"

"If he's involved." She finished my thought. "I'll see what I can dig up on my end."

"Thanks, and fast, Piper. We don't have much time."

Chapter
Forty-Two

That night Melanie and Rosa were at my house. We had dinner together. Rosa picked at her food, depression written all over her. Melanie came down the stairs with the throw blanket I kept on the edge of my bed, and she put it over Rosa, who stared at the TV. She cast worried glances around as I put the dishes in the dishwasher.

I needed to help Rosa regain her focus. She needed to be on guard, to be watchful and vigilant. After I washed up and dried my hands, I moved into the living room and cut off the television.

"Rosa, I know this is a nightmare. I get that you're dealing with a lot. But I need you to help me out here." I perched on the edge of the sofa. "I'm struggling to put all these pieces together."

She rolled her head to face me.

"Are you sure you've never encountered Judy Galloway before? Has anything come to you since our last conversation? Maybe you met her at a bar back home, or maybe she was a friend of a friend?"

Rosa took a deep breath and let out a long sigh before shaking her head.

"What about old boyfriends?" Maybe she'd been after Rosa's man. It made the most sense.

She moved her head slowly from side to side again before she turned away from me and clicked the TV back on.

"She's tired." Melanie moved next to her on the sofa.

"I know she's tired, Mel. Just one more question, please, Rosa."

She hit pause on the remote and turned toward me. "What?" Her voice came out weak and thready.

"I hate to bring this up. I have to ask. It's too important to tiptoe around sensitivities. Your ex-husband. Is there anything there?"

"You never told me you were married before." Melanie put her hand on Rosa's shoulder. "Why?"

Rosa closed her eyes. "I didn't tell anyone because I wanted to forget that part of my life. Close the book and never open it again. I came here to start over. And then now I'm forced to relive it all. You have no idea what it's like to live and work with such a controlling person. Someone who can push all your buttons at once and be forced to grin and bear it. That's why I never said anything. And he swore he wouldn't reveal himself to anyone in Sweet Mountain either."

"I'm sorry this is so painful. I truly am. And normally, I wouldn't bring it up. But—"

She sat up, her eyes lighting with fire. "Then don't. Don't force me to open those wounds. Don't I have enough to deal with? And quite frankly, the man's a giant pain in my backside, but he isn't the one killing people, Lyla!"

"Would you bet your life on the fact that there isn't any relevance there?" I kept my tone low, soothing. "You can be pissed at me all you want. But I'm going to step in when you are weak. I'm going to turn over every stone. Look in every dark corner. Search through all the minutiae of your life until I find out who is coming for you, because I love you. We"—I waved a hand between Mel and me—"love you. Answer a couple of questions for me. Just a couple. Okay?"

She blew out a breath and deflated against the sofa. "Fine. Why not shred what's left of my life."

I didn't go into how it could be freeing to turn the light on the boogie man—something my family and I had experienced. My mother and uncle had hidden their past from me and everyone else all my life. They'd believed it was for the best. That it would not only protect them but protect the mirage of a life they'd created. It hadn't. What they had achieved was to create distance between us. Until one day the past came after them. It's like all the good ole boys say around here: "The past has a way of coming back and biting you in the ass." Thankfully, we'd been able to grow and heal through it all. Maybe this had nothing to do with Rosa's past. Perhaps I was completely wrong. I had to know.

To be the best friend I could be to her, I had to ask. "Are there other directions I should look? What names should I be searching for? Trust me to be discreet."

She stared at me. Something odd swam in her dark gaze. Something I'd never seen in her eyes before. *Fear*. She got up and slogged her way over to the table. She scribbled a couple of names onto the notepad I had open there. I waited for her to finish, forcing myself to remain where I sat. She didn't say another word but sat back down on the sofa turned up the television.

Melanie wrapped an arm around her shoulders as tears began to make little tracks down her cheeks.

I pushed off my knees and stood. I read the scribbled names on the pad, and my pulse accelerated. I needed more information. I sat down and got to work. I wanted context regarding the names on the pad. To understand the history. Rosa wouldn't be giving me any of that just yet. I'd give her an hour or so. We didn't have a lot of time, so I ran searches on what I had. I searched in Louisiana and Georgia first and came up with more than ten thousand hits. I narrowed it down by broad date range, using Rosa's DOB as a point of reference.

The Tinderly app pinged my phone. I glanced down where I'd set it up on the kitchen table beside my computer. I had a potential match. Goody, goody. A man with gray hair and deep blue eyes smiled back at me. I was instructed to swipe left to reject and right to accept. Leaning against the backrest, I swiped left. A thought struck me. Could I search for Judy Galloway on the app? Maybe even be able to check her matches?

When I couldn't figure out how to manage it, I gave it a Google. Frequently asked questions popped up on the search engine.

You can only search for a specific person on Tinderly if you're matched with that person. To search for someone in your match list, tap the message bubble icon on the main screen > press and pull down on the screen until a search bar appears > type that person's name in the search bar.

Ugh. *Think. Lyla. Think.*

It was all right here. I glanced over at my copy of *A Murder Is Announced*. Gran had been flipping through it while she ate breakfast this morning. Where was Miss Marple when you needed her? I picked up the book and gawked at the bright yellow on a few of the pages. Gran had taken a highlighter to the book! Something I would never do or allow. For Gran, I'd make an exception. I read a few highlighted passages and shook my head.

I paused and reread the last passage, where Agatha had once again proved how incredibly wise she'd been. Her analysis of a weak person rang true. From my experience, when a vulnerable person became frightened, they became savage, like a cornered animal. Terror could evoke strange and terrifying responses from certain people.

I glanced over at my friends sitting on the sofa. The passage hadn't exactly described Rosa, but I supposed this was why I'd considered her involvement. She'd been pushed and pulled in so many directions that she'd nearly cracked. Anger fueled me all over again. I directed the energy toward this case. Something useful.

PuzzleGal7, aka Dana Watson, came to mind.

Maybe the killer has been with us all along. Maybe— lighting struck. *Oh. My. God.* Hiding in plain sight. The brilliance astounded me. How could I have missed that? How? I pulled up public records and dug even deeper. It was good to have access to so much information. People never realize how much information is floating out there. You can find out anything about anyone. You simply have to look and wait and pluck it from the air. I got a hit.

My heart began to pound against my rib cage. I had a full name and DOB. I plugged the information into the extensive search database. *There you are!*

I ran the screenshot through facial recognition software and smiled.

Hello, mastermind.

Gotcha.

Chapter
Forty-Three

Piper and her cameraman set up at the pavilion area of the square. They made sure to take their time moving from the van to the pavilion. Some of the Jane Does came to show their support of a fellow club member. I'd sent a group text out alerting everyone of this morning's events and told everyone available of their parts to play. Eleven seemed like the appropriate time. We'd draw attention from those breaking for an early lunch and those who were constantly milling around downtown. And we needed as much publicity as we could get for our unofficial press conference.

Rosa stood with her head held high, and she exuded determination and confidence. Piper glanced toward me and scratched her ear—a signal—before directing her attention forward. I slowly worked my way to the back of the crowd, weaving around and taking note of those in attendance. Folks' reactions were of the utmost interest to me.

When Rosa began, she cleared her throat and projected her voice. She sounded strong. Calm. Assertive. And I let out a breath, grateful she could manage it after all she'd been through. She kept her practiced speech short and to the point. Admitting her mistakes and thanking everyone for their support. "I've made my apologies to Mrs. Morgan personally and am willing to accept the consequences from the department. In my effort to see justice served, I became blinded to what was really taking place here in our town. And I'm ashamed to use the word, but I must. I was duped. Duped by a deranged and malicious psychopath who remains in our midst."

Gasps were audible.

I spied Gran, Sally Anne, and Melanie's grandmother with their group of friends from the senior center. Elaine wasn't with them, of course, but I did not want her to be. She'd have been the center of attention if she'd come. I'd mentioned as much to Gran when I'd called her. She'd certainly gotten the word out in her circles. However, they all appeared a little skeptical about Rosa's speech. I didn't blame them. Elaine had been gracious to accept Rosa's call earlier, still upset but kind, and that was more than we could ask of her.

Out of the corner of my eye, I spotted Harry inching around the left of the pavilion.

Joel stood off to the side with Judy, who looked like a viper ready to strike.

"They're hiding in plain sight. Someone who appears innocent and trustworthy. A pathetic person who I pity." Rosa's lip curled. "I see you, you coward. And I'm still here." Her curled lip turned into a vindictive-looking smile. She pulled off pleased and triumphant.

Harry's head jerked around like an angry peacock as he pressed his phone to his ear.

Accusations and suppositions were flying from the crowd as Rosa stepped from the stage.

A weak person can get quite savage when either frightened or cornered floated through my head.

Sirens blipped in warning as a cruiser rolled up, but it was too late. We all dispersed quickly, as planned, everyone going to their respective vehicles. Not many were carpooling, to make grouping people together for questioning difficult. We weren't breaking any laws. Rosa had every right as a civilian to speak her piece. They could charge her with attempting to hinder an investigation, though. It was a calculated risk.

I hugged my grandmother and greeted her friends briefly before making my way up the square toward the office. I'd parked behind the building today to avoid any confrontations. My idea hadn't fooled Chief Quinn Daniels. He stood leaning against the hood of my car where I'd backed it in front of the Cousins Investigative Services emergency exit, dressed in plain clothes.

"We need to talk." He kept his voice low. Anyone who knew Quinn understood it wasn't when he shouted and became loud that you needed to worry. It was when his voice was low that stirred nerves.

"Okay." I folded my arms and kept a few feet between us.

He held out his hand for my keys. "Let's go for a drive. I'm not doing this on the street."

Doing what? I wanted to ask, but didn't. I handed him my keys and got into the passenger's seat.

He was quiet as he adjusted the seat to accommodate his size. My heart was beating like that of a rabbit caught in a snare. I wasn't scared of Quinn. I was scared he'd attempt to blow my plan. The only plan I believed would work to save my friend. We had no physical evidence. Nothing more than theories. We didn't even have circumstantial evidence to work with. We needed a confession.

When he pulled onto Highway 61, I knew where he was going. I didn't say anything until he parked in the little graded dirt area utilized for parking for Red Top Mountain. "Why have you brought me here?"

He opened the door and glanced over at me. "I need to get out, and I need to talk to you. And we won't be overheard out here."

"Do I look like I'm dressed for hiking?" I motioned to my green tunic, skinny jeans, and high-heeled knee boots.

"You always keep a sweatshirt and boots in the trunk." He reached under the dash, and the little click signaled the trunk had released.

Of course he'd remember that. I did hike this time of year, with a six-pack of Gatorade and a hiking pack. After a quick mental debate, I decided I'd go with him. I needed to know what was on his mind. I could spare a few hours. And he was right. Out here, we wouldn't be overheard or seen at this time of day. And those we might pass wouldn't pay much attention. A good thing, since his new bride was so jealous and clearly disliked me. More importantly, Rosa would be with Melanie and on alert.

He dropped my workout duffel bag in front of my open passenger's side door and watched as I unzipped my boots and laced up my hikers. He slung my hiking pack onto his back and walked ahead toward the trail entrance while I changed into my hoodie and locked my purse in the trunk. I wouldn't lie to myself and say I wasn't worried that perhaps we'd pushed a little too far and the killer or killers might deviate from their plan. But, I had to trust Rosa and Melanie would be fine. I sent a quick voice message from my watch to let them know I'd be late.

Chapter
Forty-Four

"How did life turn out this way?" Quinn asked as we started up the path. "My God. Sweet Mountain has always been a town low in crime."

"Horrible people do horrible things, and it's up to people like us to stop them." I wound my hair up into a messy knot atop my head and secured it with an elastic.

"Yes, but does that have to affect every aspect of our lives?" Quinn set a punishing pace, and my thighs were already burning.

"I didn't use to think so, but apparently it does. To get involved with us means you are involved with the line of work. I guess it's rough on Courtney." From her visit earlier, it certainly seemed to have affected her mental state. And Brad thought being with someone outside law enforcement would increase his chances of peace and a break from it all. Maybe he'd find someone who could provide the distance he needed. Look at Quinn and Courtney. Ha.

Quinn pushed his pace even further, and I had to dig deep. At this rate, we'd burn out before we made the first mile. He'd chosen a moderate trail, and it was more challenging to navigate the falling debris after it had accumulated with the frequent rainfall.

Then Quinn went down hard, sliding in a mud puddle and nearly going off the steep side.

"Quinn!" I rushed toward him and went down on my knees.

"I'm fine. Dammit. Just didn't look where I put my feet." He wouldn't let me help him up. I took the pack from him even though he grumbled. He seemed more embarrassed than bruised. But I did notice the rip in his cargos and the blood that pooled on his knee.

"Burn yourself out yet?"

He sighed and ran a hand through his hair. He looked conflicted. Wow. I'd never seen him this way before.

"Let's go over to the lookout point. I'm tired." I moved on ahead of him, not waiting for a reply. We didn't talk for the ten minutes it took to reach the giant boulder nestled in the densely wooded area overlooking the lake. The roots of the trees jutted out, making steps down the cliff to the rocky beach. I unscrewed the top of a lemon-lime Gatorade and took a sip. I set one on the rock next to me for Quinn.

I watched the waves roll in. They were frequent from the boats roaring around the lake.

"I'm sorry about what happened the other day. Courtney is . . . a little much sometimes." He unscrewed the top of the bottle and settled on the rock next to me. We sat there. Shoulder to shoulder as we'd done decades before when we were kids.

"She's certainly no fan of mine." I took another sip of the bottle.

"She's not a fan of anyone she perceives as a threat. And she perceives lots of threats—people who I confide in about cases. Things I can't talk to her about. Things I don't want to talk to her about." He rubbed the perspiration from his forehead. "To your earlier point that the job flows into our personal lives."

I nodded and turned my face toward the breeze, welcoming it. "You and Brad?"

"We're done. We want different things."

He took another sip from the bottle. "He's a fool."

"Really? He wants the same thing you have. A woman who isn't in law enforcement of any kind. A separation from the job when he goes home." I shrugged.

He fought a snort. "As I said, he's a fool."

I appreciated Quinn's attempt to console me. It was a kind gesture. But I didn't like the territory we'd gone into. If Quinn was second-guessing his marriage, I didn't want to be the one he confided in.

"No. Brad's okay. He's a good guy, really. And he'll find a woman who will revel in his protection from the big bad world. It'll give him a sense that he can truly make the world a better place. He'll provide safety and security to a wife and kids. Create a little bubble for them to live in and not be tainted by the evil outside. It'll make him feel powerful, feed his need to protect and care for someone. For a family." I tucked a hair that had escaped my bun and tickled my cheek back into the knot.

"And he couldn't create that world with you because of a job." He shook his head.

"Even if I'd agreed to leave my job, I know what's out there. And I want to make a difference as well. To be a change agent in our town and world. And"—I sighed—"I'm one of those people who loves a good case. Sometimes it gets to me. Sure. The sheer evil that resides in some people. But I can handle it. It's my calling. I'm right where I need to be doing exactly what I'm supposed to be."

"You sound healthy. Like you're in a really good place about the breakup."

I turned toward him and smiled. "I am. I cared for Brad. Care for him still. I want him to be happy. To find what he's looking for, and I am fully aware that I'm not right for him. We were good for each other. Helped each other grow. It ran its course." I pulled my pack on my lap, unzipped the front pocket, and extracted my first aid kit.

"Wow."

"Wow?" I positioned myself where I could treat his knee with antiseptic. He had debris in the wound, so it took a couple of treatments.

"Wow, in a good way. I'm happy you're okay." He sucked in a breath, gritting his teeth—such a baby.

I laughed and put a Neosporin Band-Aid over his knee.

"I was a fool too." Quinn placed his hand over mine, which was still on his knee. His eyes searched mine.

"Quinn," I warned, and tried to pull my hand away.

He closed his eyes and sighed. "No. I'm not coming on to you. I just want you to know that I still love you. I will always love you, and you will always have me. I'll have your back. No matter what."

I pulled my hand away and got down from the rock. "You're *not* coming on to me? Declaring your eternal love for me?"

He scratched his head and stood. "It's not coming out the right way. I'm so good at talking to everyone else except you. What I'm trying to say is that I should have seen you. The real you. Not the fabricated version I created in my head. Not the life I imagined you living. But you. You're right. You're where you should be. Brad will see it too. Just like me. And he'll have regrets. Like I do. I am in love with Courtney. I'm going to make it work with her if it kills me. She'll adjust to what life with me looks like. And the people in it. I won't be giving up my friends. Won't." He pierced me with his cool blue gaze, and I understood what he was saying and smiled. "I love you differently. More friendly, maybe even like a sister."

I shuddered. "I'm not your sister, Quinn."

He scratched his head. "No, I know. Yeah, that sounds bad, now that I consider it. I'm not making much sense, am I?"

I smiled. "Yes, you are." Quinn wanted me to know that he'd always be my friend. That I didn't have to change a thing about myself. He loved me for the girl I'd once been and for the woman I was. It had come out all wrong. But I got it now.

"I hope I can count on the same from you?" He sounded hopeful and a little nervous.

I smiled. "Yes. I'll always be your friend. And"—I sighed— "I'll try with Courtney."

"Thank you." He leaned against the boulder and folded his arms. "You'll be honest with me? We'll work together to keep our town safe. Because we both know what lurks in the dark."

And just like that, he became the chief of police again. Intelligent, cunning, and willing to do whatever it took to ensure the safety of his town. I respected the hell out of him at this moment.

"And because we both do, sometimes we need to trust the other to do what is in the best interest of the case, correct?"

He groaned. "Now that we've settled the personal stuff, let's get to business."

"Let's." I folded my arms and faced him.

"What the hell kind of stunt was that you just pulled?" His tone held a warning.

"One that will keep my friend and town safe." So did mine.

"You know that if you interfere with the investigation, an obstruction charge is possible."

"What? Seriously, Quinn. I'm working with you, not against you. I'm helping you."

His eyes hardened. "Helping me? That's a crock of shit. And anyone else would slap you with a charge."

We were like two strong bulls gauging each other's weaknesses.

"Bring it on. You know who my family attorney is and the case I'd rain down on the Sweet Mountain Police if you pull a stunt like that. It's something that would be difficult to recover from. Don't you agree?"

He smirked. "Where's the trust?"

"That's exactly what I want to know."

"You understand that I had no choice but to suspend Sergeant Landry. That it was difficult for me, since she'd become my right hand. The case against her was overwhelming. I've called her, and she knows she'll be welcomed back on the force if at all possible. The lawsuit, as you know, and the threat to unleash another, has consequences."

Elaine would be dropping her suit. He simply didn't know it yet.

He cocked his head to one side, considering me.

"No, that's not it. You think I'm too close."

Quinn pushed off the rock. "You have a suspect in mind. Was there more at Magnolia Manor that you are keeping from me? Are you withholding?"

"I haven't any proof yet. Everything we discovered at the B and B, we disclosed. I gathered other evidence from my investigation, unrelated to what I was working on with your department. I texted you, but your wife deleted it."

He combed through his hair roughly with his fingers. "I'm listening."

"What I believe we're dealing with here is an extremely intelligent and dangerous perp. I have a plan."

"Of course you do." He blew out a breath. "Will your plan help me with my case?"

"It may close your case. May." I held up both hands. "Will you trust me to enact my plan?"

"Only if I'm in on it."

It was my turn to study him. To decide how far my trust in Quinn went. I wondered if he'd brought me out here to tell me about his belief in me and soften me up. He hadn't stretched the truth about Courtney. Not in my opinion. But I was betting he had laid it on a little thicker than he'd intended.

I certainly sounded cynical.

"Only if you can promise to remain objective. You may not like what you find out." I tossed my head back and stared up at the swaying trees—the bright blue sky peeking through the limbs. A red-tailed hawk called and circled overhead, stalking its prey. How fitting.

Chapter
Forty-Five

Halloween crept up on us. The night felt crisp, with a clear sky. It was a perfect Halloween night. The kind where kids could run around outside without their coats—trick-or-treating in full swing. Jack-o'-lanterns lit the porches on Rosa's dead-end street. The houses—their porch lights on, the front doors open—felt normal. Smiling faces stood behind storm doors with bowls of candy. Children ran around going door to door, dressed in costumes. Screams and giddy squeals, followed by laughter, filled the night. Parents with strollers stood at the end of each driveway, chatting with friends and sipping on hot cider, coffee, or tea.

We'd set a trap. We'd taken every precaution. Made every adjustment to ensure Rosa's safety. We'd all struggled with using our friend as bait. It was the only way, and we all knew it. Rosa had insisted she was up for the task, and her "press conference" had hit YouTube and made its way around the internet and onto the message board that we were aware the killer utilized.

We admired our friend. After I'd shown her my findings, she'd become energized by the same indignation I felt ten times over. Answers had invigorated her, making her determined to put an end to her torment. To remove the veil the killer had taken to hide behind. She'd been infuriated with herself for not seeing it. And even more so for wallowing. Like the rest of us, Rosa forgot she was human sometimes, that she was allowed to make mistakes and brood when needed.

I slipped inside the sliding glass door on Rosa's back deck. Melanie closed the door of the shed in Rosa's backyard, leaving a crack. She flashed her phone at me, signaling she was ready and in position, while Rosa gave out the last of her candy and shut off the porch light.

The other Jane Does were spread out inconspicuously around the street, dressed in Halloween costumes and on alert. Now that we knew who we were looking for, they wouldn't get by undetected.

I crept to the back of the house down the hall and out of sight. Rosa went through the motions of her bedtime routine. She took her time washing her face and dressing in her pajamas before fluffing her pillows and rearranging them just right. Then she shut off the lights and settled in to wait.

The sound of gunfire caused us to bolt from our hiding places. A text came through from our group message seconds before I made it to the front of the house.

Stand down. Just kids setting off firecrackers in metal garbage cans.

We moved back to our posts, thankful we hadn't given ourselves away.

The seconds ticked by gruelingly slow. Seconds turned into minutes, and minutes grew into more than an hour. And nothing. Not a peep. I sent a message in our group chat.

A visual? Anything?
Little dots lit up my screen.
Nothing came from Melanie.
All quiet, and the trick-or-treaters are winding down. Joel and I will have to get going or we'll draw attention came from Tammy.
Okay. Thanks, Tammy, and Joel. Keep your eyes peeled on the way to your cars.
Will do came from Tammy.
10-4 came from Joel.
An hour later, when still nothing had transpired, I sent a text to Melanie.
How are you holding up?
She had to be getting cold out there.
"Lyla, anything?" Rosa whispered. She hadn't taken her phone with her. She didn't want the light to give her away.
"No. All clear."
Five minutes past and nothing came from Melanie. I pushed the door open a sliver more and slid through the crack. "I'm going down to check on Mel. She's not responding to my texts."
"I'll come with you."
I heard rustling.
"No. Stay put, just in case. Maybe Mel's cell battery died. I'll be right back." I didn't believe that. I'd checked and double-checked everyone's battery life before we arrived. I slowly walked down the little narrow hallway, cringing at all the creeks the floorboards made. Old houses were impossible to sneak around in undetected.
I slid around the wall and into the kitchen. I took a chance to sneak a peek out the little window over the sink. I froze.

Someone had placed a rake between the handles of the old shed. Either Melanie was stuck inside, or . . .

My breath came in pants, and I'd started to bolt out the back door when the doorknob rattled. The pounding in my chest ratcheted up. I slunk into the dark corner of the kitchen and stayed absolutely still. The door shook once, twice, and I thought someone would burst their way inside. Suddenly, it creaked slowly open.

Blood thrummed in my ears. My hand slid to my gun holster as two figures crept into the kitchen. The plan had been to allow the intruder to come inside. To go for Rosa, and she'd be ready with me as backup. But we'd expected only one intruder. *Not two.*

One was in a glow-in-the-dark skeleton Halloween costume. I recognized the gait.

"Her bedroom is in the back of the house."

I recognized that voice. Slowly I crouched below eye level.

The shorter one in a ski mask nodded and grabbed a butcher knife from the block on the counter, not five feet from where I crouched, and started down the hallway.

Thrown by the discovery, I unclicked my holster, and the snap caused them both to go on alert.

"What was that?" A woman's voice. Judy's voice.

"I don't know." Joel pulled the mask from his head. "I can't see in this stupid thing."

His head moved around, and I could imagine that his eyes were attempting to adjust.

"Anyone there? That girl didn't get out of the shed, did she?"

I let out a little sigh. If Judy was worried about Melanie breaking free, then she was alive.

Joel glanced out the door and then closed it softly behind him. "No," he said in a stage whisper. "The rake is still in place. Get this done. We're running short on time."

What is Joel doing?

"Whose fault is that?" Judy snapped back.

When I heard the bedroom door creak open, I moved from my hiding spot. Joel stood outside the bedroom door. Loud maniacal screams shouting, "Die, whore. Die!" erupted from Rosa's bedroom.

"Oh my God! Lyla!" Joel screamed, both hands going to his mouth.

"Get the light." I charged past Joel, who obeyed my command as I pulled my gun. "Freeze!"

Stuffing from the mattress floated through the air as Judy's mouth fell agape, her eyes blazing. She raised her knife and started for Joel and me.

"Sweet Jesus! Shoot her!" Joel yelled.

The lunatic actually thought she could beat out a bullet. Suddenly, Judy screamed like a banshee, and the knife fell from her hand. Blood welled from her leg. Rosa acted quickly, rushing from beneath the bed, and in seconds had Judy on the floor and her hands cuffed behind her. A box cutter I'd not expected lay beside Judy. The box cutter Rosa had used on her ankle.

"Thank God!" Joel said from the floor.

I went to check on him, having no idea how he'd ended up there. "What were you thinking?"

He shook his head, tears streaming down his cheeks. "At the hotel, she started to wonder if Rosa's press conference was a trap. I had to do some quick thinking to get her to buy it. She thought I hated Rosa as much as she did, and when I suggested someone should take care of her, she sort of invited me along. I didn't want to say anything and ruin the plan."

"You stupid piece of s—"

Rosa silenced Judy with an accidental thump of her face against the floor while she read Judy her rights and jerked her to her feet.

Joel staggered to his feet, his eyes as round as saucers. "Melanie. She's in the shed."

"Go let her out, please, and y'all head out. We'll take it from here."

He nodded and hurried down the hallway.

"I need a doctor! I'm bleeding to death!" Judy wailed.

There was no way that the nick on her ankle would end her life.

Rosa propped Judy up against the wall and knelt in front of her. "Yeah, you might. How about I give you a chance to come clean, here and now? There was no harm done except to my mattress and a nick to your ankle. Prison wouldn't be a good place for a woman like you."

Judy shouted a couple of expletives and turned her head away from Rosa. "I'm not going anywhere. I have friends in high places. People in law enforcement that will pin this on you."

Rosa raised her brows. "Right. And pigs will fly tomorrow."

I let out an exaggerated sigh. "Judy, you've been taken advantage of, manipulated by a man who has made a habit of manipulating people and situations to get what he wants in life. Just like he used Betty. He met her on the same dating app he met you on."

"That's a lie! You're trying to get me to roll on the man I love. Rosa is jealous and wants him." She squinted at me. "Or maybe *you* want him. But he chose me! Me!"

"Wow. He really did a number on her." I turned to Rosa and made a sad face. "Promised her the same ole bull. That he'll love her forever and they'll always be together if she gets rid of one Rosa Landry. See those cameras?" I pointed to the tiny newly installed wireless cameras in the corner of the room and turned back to Judy. "They're all over the property. When this house was cased weeks ago, she didn't have the cameras. Surprise! Everything you've done. A B&E charge—breaking and entering. Attempted murder. One of our little wireless friends there captured everything. And now the footage is in the cloud waiting for us to access it and use it against you. The cops are the next street over, waiting for our call. You'll get at least twenty years, and that's with good behavior. You'll be what—in your late fifties in two decades?"

Rosa nodded next to me. "She'll be tough to look at with the fast aging that takes place inside. That is, if she survives that long."

I shook my head. "The way she makes enemies, she might not make it a year."

Judy's face paled, her eyes were wide, and terror had replaced rage. "I can't rat him out. Can't turn on the man I love."

Rosa put her hand on Judy's shoulder. "We would never dream of asking you to do such a thing."

"Nope." Headlights flashed past the windows, and the sound of tires crunching on acorns told us Judy's ride was here. I smiled down at Judy. "Time to go."

Chapter
Forty-Six

A car whizzing into the driveway at two a.m. alerted us to *his* arrival. The sound of boots running through the house echoed. "Rosa! Rosa! My God, I hope I'm not too late."

An officer blocked his path. "You can't be here."

"Lyla! I have information," he called. "Let me help."

"It's okay. Let him pass," I said from outside Rosa's bedroom, and the officer allowed him to come through.

Dean hesitated in the doorway as he took in the bed covered in blood. His eyes were wide. "What happened? Where's Rosa?"

I moved into the room, and he followed me. "We're still trying to piece everything together. Judy Galloway broke in and attacked Rosa. That we know for certain. What we don't know is why." I put my hand to my mouth and blinked back tears.

His eyes went to the spatter and tissue on the walls, and his shoulders relaxed marginally.

I swallowed and shook my head, covering my face with my hands. After two loud breaths, I allowed my hands to fall limply into my legs. "I have to get out of here." I made my way down the hall and waited. When he didn't immediately follow, I became a tad nervous.

I wondered if he'd discovered the blood on the bed wasn't human or that the tissue looked more like ground beef. I'd done my best with the blood spatter, but I didn't think it would hold up to detailed scrutiny. We were dealing with the mastermind. Which had made our trip to the butcher counter an important one.

When he filled the archway leading into the little living room, I blew out a breath. "Judy is in custody."

"My God! I'm in shock. I tried to get here in time. When she called me and told me what she planned, I . . . I didn't know what to do."

"Wait. I'm confused. Judy called you. Why?" I furrowed my brow.

"Yeah, she did." His face looked shocked, no, terrified. An excellent actor he was, or maybe he just believed every lie he told. "She told me she wanted to put an end to Rosa's antics." He raised both hands. "She never said anything about killing her." He swallowed and hung his head.

"She is crazy, after all." I sat down on the sofa and stared at the wall. All the pictures Rosa had placed there remained. "I still don't understand why she would target Rosa or call you about it."

"There's something I have to tell you." He took a seat on the sofa next to me, being careful not to edge too close. "Rosa and I were married."

I glanced up as if surprised.

"She was the love of my life. She broke me when she ended it a few years ago. She begged me to give her space and moved away. We agreed not to involve ourselves in each other's lives in any way. That's why I didn't say anything before. Why I couldn't be honest with you when we met those few times. I'd made a promise to her, and I . . . well, I couldn't break it."

"Okay. That's a lot to process." I put my hand to my head. "Wow. But why would Judy text you or want to hurt Rosa?"

He shook his head solemnly. "Judy got it into her head that we were a thing. Like you said and I warned, she's crazy."

I lifted my brows in question.

"I suppose she latched on to me because I listened to her. But I had no idea she'd go this far." He rubbed the back of his neck. "This afternoon when she called, she said she spoke to a friend who recalled Rosa and I being a thing. Told her about the messy divorce, and I guess she believed that was why I didn't want anything to do with her. Because Rosa had hurt me too bad. At first, I blew it off. But when I couldn't get it out of my head, I drove for hours to get here. I never thought she'd do something like this." He waved his hand toward the hallway.

"Yeah. I know. I didn't see her crossing those lines either."

"My Rosa. I can't believe she's gone." His chest heaved. "Despite all our differences, she was the very best of me."

"I believe that." I said, sounding a little stronger. "Judy *is* crazy. She shouted all sorts of irrational things when they arrested her."

He cleared his throat. "Like what?"

He shifted, his jacket opening a little, exposing a gun on his belt. He'd planned to find Judy in the act and take her out to protect himself. I'd have bet money on it. And now, well, he felt vulnerable.

"Craziness. She told us she did this for the man she loved. I guess she meant you. That Betty Smithson had also been involved."

His mouth tensed. "I have no idea what she's talking about. Maybe she and Betty were close too."

Close too. I buried my face in my hands. "I can't believe this. It was all right in front of me. How could I have let this happen?"

"Don't blame yourself. We have to see this for what it is. A lunatic stealing Rosa from us. It isn't something we can explain." He put a big hand on my shoulder. Those hands could choke the life out of me in minutes. "We both loved Rosa. We can help each other get through this. Why don't you come out of town with me for a while? We can go somewhere and heal. That's what Rosa would have wanted."

"You think?" I glanced up at him and put my hand on his cheek. I hoped I looked weak and feeble. A damsel in distress.

He smiled then. "Yes. Rosa sent me an email a few months ago. She said she had a safety deposit box she wanted to put my name on. She kept her inheritance in it. I think that even then she must have been harassed by crazy Judy. Maybe she worried something like this would happen. And she wanted me to have her family's property in Louisiana. It's worth quite a lot."

I smiled. "Rosa is generous like that. When she first came to Sweet Mountain, I wasn't so sure about her, you know. She could come across as harsh sometimes."

He nodded, hope blooming across his face. He thought he could manipulate me like he had every other woman he'd used.

"But when I got to know her, I understood she was just misunderstood. Dean, the last days with her weren't good. We fought. I said some cruel, horrible things to her. I told her I wished she *was* dead. That it had been her instead of Betty. What kind of a person does that make me?"

He rubbed my arm as I willed the tears to fall.

"Rosa was complicated. She could draw the meanness right out of a person when she wanted to. Don't blame yourself. She had a way of making you all enraged." His gentle strokes got a little more intense.

"Yes!" I nodded emphatically. "She does. Like when she arrested Elaine Morgan. The cruelty it took to treat that sweet old woman that way was—well, it was a heartless act. It made me believe that perhaps I didn't know her at all. It also makes me wonder if any of those things Judy said about her is true."

Dean took a deep breath. "Well, I knew her better than anyone. And as much as I loved her, she was a challenge, but my God, I didn't want to see her end up like this, even though . . ."

"Even though what?"

"She had a dark side."

"Dark side?" I wiped my face.

He nodded. "When we got divorced, she framed me. Made me look like a violent man. A cheater. Stole everything from me. The land, the one her family left her, was supposed to be for the both of us. She found a way to keep it all for herself." His hand tightened on my shoulder. His eyes didn't look kind.

Warning bells went off inside my head. "That's monstrous!" I leaped to my feet, putting a significant distance between us. I knew I'd overacted the moment the words left my lips.

He rose, his fists clenching at his side, but he gave me a sad smile. His body language conflicted with his attempt to reach me. "We should probably get out of here. If you need some time, I understand. I'll call you in a few days." He began backing toward the door.

"Okay. Oh, but wait—" I smiled. "You should probably give your statement to the police first. Not that it'll matter; they have the knife, and Judy, who last I heard was confessing. You probably want to tell your side of the story."

He glanced around, suspicious.

"She could make you look like an accessory."

He studied me and took a little step toward me. "How do you figure? I mean, you're not scared of me, are you?"

I held my ground. "No. But why would Judy do such a thing? She's a woman without a record or history of violence. Why would she do something like this?"

"She has a history." He rested his hands on his hips and cocked his head to one side, staring at Rosa's case wall filled with photographs. He moved closer. He was formidable enough to give me pause about our plan. I cast a glance at the coat closet in the corner. The door stood slightly ajar.

"Rosa suspected everyone, didn't she?" He glanced over his shoulder at me.

"Yes, she seemed to," I said, as firmly and neutrally as I could manage.

His eyes never left me. "Where exactly was the body? The bedroom? I saw the smear down the hallway."

"Yes." I'd made the blood smear down the hallway using my foot. I was losing him. I could feel it. My hands itched for my gun. I arrested my impulse, but I couldn't help going to the balls of my feet. I was ready for anything.

"You know, I think Rosa had the right idea. She didn't trust anyone." His smile went from pleasing to disconcerting before he faced the wall again—his hand dangerously close to his weapon. "I'm not so sure you and I are a good idea after all. I think—"

I gathered my resolve and acted. I moved in behind him, taking the gun from his belt in one swift movement before taking a giant step back.

"Don't move." I had my gun trained on him as I tucked his gun in the waistband of my jeans.

"Lyla. What are you doing?" He didn't raise his hands as he turned around. Didn't show any sign that he'd submit. His tone bordered on insolent, yet he worked to tamp it down. "I was only joking. You're a beautiful sexy woman, and I can't wait . . ." His tone trailed off, and the look in his eyes terrified me. I hoped in a million years I never stood this close to another person who glared at me the way he did now.

I rallied. "Save it. I know who you are, *Dean Willis*." I cocked a brow. "Not very inventive on the alias there, Michael Dean Williams. Guess you didn't believe anyone would check up on you. As they say, pride goes before the fall."

His body tensed, but he didn't move.

"And buddy, believe me when I say this, you are going down. I know what you did. Judy clued me in on how the two of you met. How you filled her head with all this bull about Rosa. I know about your military history. Your harassment and physical altercations with Rosa. How you painted her as the violent one. How you would push her buttons and watch her explode. Rosa isn't the monster. *You* are the monster."

Slowly, he bared his teeth in a smile, his hands still by his sides, showing no fear that I'd shoot him. "I have no idea what you're talking about."

Idiot. "Yes, you do. I have proof."

He laughed sardonically. "You don't. If you did, I'd be in cuffs and down at the police department."

I narrowed my eyes and put all the weight of truth in my tone that I could muster, "Oh, you will be." I smiled at him, making my glare flat. "Judy is spilling her guts about you as we speak. I just needed a minute with you. To show you that your attempt to use me failed. You are the loser."

He shook his head as if I were the pathetic one. "Like I said, you got nothing. This is just about you and me. I see that now. You want your pound of flesh about being duped. Just like stupid idiotic Judy with her need for validation. That pathetic, worthless, and clearly useless woman is going down for this, because she's guilty. You said so yourself." Michael Dean smiled smugly as if he had this whole thing figured out. "Did you know this isn't the first time she's done something like this? There's a restraining order against her."

"I've heard. When I told her that you were also after me, she flipped."

His posture became stiff. He eyed me with a disconcerting look.

I pushed. "You see, her need to prove the relationship was more important than her freedom. She told us about all the sweet *love* letters you've shared. All the nights at roadside motels. How she didn't come up with this idea on her own. Someone helped her. *You* helped her, Michael Dean. You are the mastermind."

The cords of his neck stood out. Sweat broke out on his forehead. "You can't believe a word she says. She'll say or do anything for love or adoration, or hell, just attention. Like a damn dog."

"Wow. I want to help you, Michael Dean, I really do. I can see how hard this is for you. All these women getting it over on you." I winked at him. "But there's not much I can do because, you see, Judy keeps all the correspondence with her obsessions. She never got rid of the burners." I leaned in and whispered mendaciously, "She kept everything."

Tension rolled off him in steady waves.

"No." I could almost see him vibrating. "No, I think you're pushing my buttons to manipulate me. To see if I'll incriminate myself. But you're not that clever. Just like Judy. A stupid, lackluster, over-the-hill wannabe. You think I'm stupid? You're the stupid one. I've been here all this time. Like a gator swimming the swamps, biding my time. You wanted to help your little friend, and you failed." He snorted.

"Fine." I bit out. "I may not have the evidence I need. But I won't fail her now. This is between you and me. No wires." I lifted my shirt. "I'm the judge and jury here. And I say you're guilty."

He liked that. The game. I could see it on his face.

"Tell me the truth." I made my hands shake and fired a shot over his head, deliberately missing. The closet door creaked open as Michael Dean ducked, covering his head. I gave my head a tiny shake.

Michael Dean glanced over his shoulder before dusting Sheetrock from his hair, laughing. "Wow. Someone is a sore loser."

"Tell. Me. Everything."

"What do you want to know? That I was everywhere each crime was discovered? That Betty and I were at the party together? If she'd only followed my instructions and left, everything would be fine. *She* might still be alive." He shrugged. "But who knows. I waited around outside while the guy fired the starter pistol. Waited to see Rosa bleed out. Judy missed and hit the other woman."

"Why did Patricia come back inside?"

He lifted his hands. "That I don't know. She had words with Betty, but obviously, she's no longer talking. Betty was too eager to please. A few days before, I had her driving around town in the Mustang dressed like Rosa. If Rosa looked unstable, no one would question a suicide. I planned for Rosa to take her own life, with a little help, of course. But it didn't work out. All's well that ends well. You see, Lyla. I always have a backup plan."

He took a minuscule step forward, unaware of the quagmire I'd led him into.

"Not another step," I warned the monster in front of me.

"All you women are the same. You, Betty, Judy, and Rosa. I got rid of two on that list; why not make it three? Look at you shaking like a leaf. You know, right? That I'm confessing to a dead woman?"

My finger itched to pull the trigger. Despite the tension flowing through my veins, I forced a smile as I quickly glanced up at the cameras he obviously had missed. "You get that, Chief Daniels? I'm sure this will help Judy see who this man really is. She should be more cooperative now. Not that we need it with his confession."

"What? You're bluffing!" Michael Dean's chest visibly heaved, and he sucked in air.

"No. You see, I don't bluff. I always have a backup plan too."

He glanced from me to the cameras. The closet door opened a fraction more as his face turned deep purple. Rage bubbled into a growl from his lips. I removed my finger from the trigger as he charged me and braced for impact as he bellowed, "You stupid bi—"

Rosa rushed from the coat closet and threw herself at him. I managed to get out of the way of direct impact when his big body fell against the sofa, but I'd been knocked to the floor, my gun still in my grasp. I scrambled to my feet as Michael Dean and Rosa raced for her weapon. The momentary shock he experienced when he recognized her gave her the seconds she needed to regain possession of her weapon.

"You!" he ground out. His fist reared back to punch her, and I clocked him hard in the head with the butt of my gun. He fell over like a sack of potatoes, holding his head.

Rosa was on his back and cuffing him seconds later. "Honey, I'm home!"

Michael Dean struggled beneath her, and I squatted down and pointed my gun directly at his face.

"Surprise! Oh, did I forget to mention that Rosa isn't dead? And she'll be keeping *her* property, but not to worry—you'll be enjoying your own new digs."

Sirens blared, signaling our surprise party guests had arrived.

"I just love surprises, don't you?" Rosa put her knee between his shoulder blades.

"Yes!" I smiled. "And we got two in one night."

Chapter
Forty-Seven

M y parents' entire first floor was filled with guests celebrating with Amelia and Ethan.

Six months ago, they'd come home with their new little angel. She'd undergone several treatments and her progress had astounded her doctors. All the doctor bills were paid, and they even had money set aside for anything else Sasha might need moving forward. My mother had fundraised her hind end off, and I couldn't have been prouder of her.

Now my mother and I were hosting a shower for the new parents. Sasha jumped around, squealing, with her gifts. Daddy had just given her an electronic riding pony that Amelia clearly thought she didn't need but wouldn't dare say anything for fear of sounding ungrateful.

I stood in the large family room filled with friends and neighbors, sipping on some champagne. I spotted Quinn and Courtney over in the corner of the room, looking much happier than the last time I'd seen them together, and that did my heart good.

Rosa walked past me, smiling. The last few months had been brutal on her. Turned out I'd been right about Michael Dean Williams. He'd expected to walk in on a gruesome scene. To find Rosa dead in her bed.

He'd also expected to find Judy, the stalker and intruder, who'd stabbed Williams's ex, Rosa, as she slept. He'd planned to arrive at a grisly murder that he'd pieced together through a series of rambling calls, and kill Judy, staging the scene to look as if Judy had died from a scuffle with Rosa and clearing him from any guilt.

Michael Dean's fury toward me still raged. I received death threats and hate email regularly. He believed everything would have gone just as he had planned if I and my book club had stayed out of things.

Judy, on the other hand, had rolled on him after seeing the footage from Rosa's house. She'd admitted to the police that Michael Dean had met her two months prior over the dating app. Their affair had begun shortly after. That first meeting was the start of a feverish plan. They'd plotted it out in text messages, emails, and more secret meetings. She had the texts to prove it. She wasn't as dumb or as lovestruck as Michael Dean had believed. He had actually taken her at her word that she'd deleted all correspondence between them.

Michael Dean had been truthful in some of his confession to me that awful night. He believed he'd lost everything because of Rosa. His computer proved he'd been stalking Rosa online for six months prior to coming to Sweet Mountain. He'd come upon the party's announcement on social media and decided it would be the perfect cover for the plan. More people and less chance of being caught. He'd enlisted Betty's help as well. He'd had her dress up like Rosa and show up around town. He'd wanted to disparage Rosa's character before staging her death and making it appear as a suicide.

Betty wasn't supposed to show up at the party. To prove her love for Dean, she'd decided to take Rosa out and eliminate the need for Judy. Judy had acted first, seemingly with the same plan. But she'd missed and shot Patricia instead.

After Patricia's murder, Dean had been forced to deviate. The trio had chosen to enact other announcements to make the murder victims appear linked. That was when he decided to use Betty more frequently. She must've suspected his plot against her, because she said she'd had enough and wouldn't kill anyone; Michael Dean made her his next victim. Judy saw the whole thing and even kept the knife he'd used on Betty postmortem. She gave the police directions to the location of the crime, and they found DNA all over the storage facility, along with the police cruiser Betty had used to intimidate our club members. Michael Dean had bought the car at an auction several months prior and had it repainted. The storage unit appeared lived in. Dean used it as a crash pad when he needed to be close to town but keep his presence undetected.

Michael Dean's plan to be away from Sweet Mountain during Rosa's home invasion also became problematic. The shift he'd taken at the army medical facility had been his first in years, and he'd not been exactly a model employee. A fight at the facility in which he attacked a fellow employee got him ejected. He'd made mistake after mistake.

Judy Galloway received thirty years in prison for the murder of Patricia Donaldson and attempted murder of Rosa Landry. Michael Dean Williams got thirty-five years for murder of Betty

Smithson and aiding and abetting—a longer term than Judy, the judge said, because he had orchestrated the killings. I'd been warned by several people to watch my back. In the short time Michael Dean had been in prison, he'd had several marriage proposals, and it was only a matter of time before he wrangled some other psycho to go after his enemies. If he ever did, we'd be ready.

I walked outside onto the front porch. The temperature hovered just above seventy degrees on this lovely spring day. I adored spring, even with the horrific allergies it brought.

"Lyla, there you are." Gran came out onto the porch. "We were all looking for you." I glanced back, and out came Amelia, Rosa, and Melanie. The core Jane Does.

"Hey, we wondered where you went." Melanie looped her arm through mine, and Gran wrapped her arm around my waist from the other side.

"I'm here. Just enjoying the view from this gorgeous front porch." I smiled at my friends.

"It's so lovely here," Amelia breathed. "Sasha is having the time of her life. She's got so many people loving on her she doesn't know what to do."

"You didn't think you could keep that little doll all to yourself, did ya?" Gran winked at her.

"I'm just so grateful."

Gran released me and hugged Amelia. "It's what families do, dear. You can't get rid of us. We're going to make you a true southern gal if it kills us."

Amelia laughed and hugged her back. "I'm so lucky to have found the Jane Does. Who ever thought a book club could change your life? But mine sure did."

"Speaking of our club." Melanie smiled. "Joel mentioned having a modern mystery series marathon. One series should last a few months, depending on the series we vote on. What do y'all think of that?"

"Sounds good to me." Rosa took a sip from her coffee cup and stepped up beside me.

"Sure," I agreed, staring out at the blossoming trees and the flowering shrubs being heavily pollinated by bees.

"Amelia! Someone had an accident," Ethan called, and Amelia went inside.

"I'll give you a hand." Melanie followed behind her.

"I better go help them. I raised a young'un who I thought would never be potty trained. Your father had more accidents that any kid I ever knew." Gran laughed, shaking her head as she went inside.

Rosa and I stayed on the porch. We'd been through something together. Something that connected us on a deeper level. We saw each other. The raw, desperate side that emerges when one fears for their life. We were both forever changed.

She took another sip from her cup, staring straight ahead. "Guess we're both back where we started when I arrived here last year."

"How do you mean?"

"Well, I'm back on desk duty but grateful to have a job, the town wonders about me, and not to make a big deal of a small thing"—she smiled—"we're the only two core club members who are single."

I smiled back. "It could be a time of solitary splendor. A healing time."

"Yeah." Her voice sounded vacant.

I cut my eyes her direction. "Plus, the single part doesn't really bother me anymore. I'm waiting on Mr. Right, and if he doesn't come along, then I'm good just as I am. Take Miss Marple, for example. She made it look easy."

Rosa laughed so hard she spat her coffee. "Miss Marple." More chuckles.

When we both fell silent again, her tone took on a serious note. "I'm trying to be present in every moment now. And yes, this could be a healing time. There isn't anything I'm hiding from or dreading folks will find out about. Mistakes were made, and I own them and will learn from them. It's *my* life. All mine."

I took a deep breath of pollen-filled air. When my own words eluded me, I decided to borrow some from the Queen of Mystery. "*I like living. I have sometimes been wildly, despairingly, acutely miserable, racked with sorrow; but through it all I still know quite certainly that just to be alive is a grand thing.*"

The rhythm of life in Sweet Mountain would go back to normal. Amazing, if you asked me. Pride filled me at the resilience of our little town, and I wouldn't want to be anywhere else.

Acknowledgments

I want to thank all those who had a hand in bringing this book to publication. I'm incredibly grateful to my agent, Dawn Dowdle, for helping me find a home for this series at Crooked Lane Books.

Thanks to the people who work diligently to bring it all together. To the team at Crooked Lane Books, who make the book shine, the illustrator, Mary Ann Lasher, for the gorgeous cover, and the promotions and marketing team for all their hard work.

Much love and thanks to my sweet husband, children, and family. They are always cheering me on. And last but certainly not least, to my readers, this novel wouldn't have been possible without you. Thank you for reading.